BANISHING THE BOGWITCH

William Stafford

ISBN-13: 9798572646115
ISBN-10: 1477123456

Cover design by: Art Painter
Library of Congress Control Number: 2018675309
Printed in the United States of America

For Spanish Jackie

BANISHING THE BOGWITCH

BANISHING THE BOGWITCH

"You can take it back to wherever it came from." Jenna's sixteen-year-old face scrunched into an unbecoming scowl. "She's not doing it."

The man at her grandmother's back door blinked and smiled a smile as thin as his patience. "Young lady, that is not for you to decide." He looked hopefully past the teenager's shoulder. "If I could speak with Mrs Spenser in person..."

"Not possible," Jenna folded her arms. "She's out."

Technically, this was the truth. Despite the cottage being equipped with all the conveniences of the modern age, including hot and cold running water and an eco-friendly flushing toilet, Jenna's grandmother insisted on using the ramshackle privy at the bottom of the garden. "Ain't sanitary," she would often remark, "Doing your business indoors, where you do your eating and your sleeping." Jenna had given up arguing about it. In fact, she was rather pleased not to have to share the indoor facilities with the old woman, whose personal habits were questionable at the best of times. And the worst of times too, come to think of it.

"Then perhaps I can leave it here and be on my way." The man took an audacious step over the threshold, but Jenna stood her ground. "It is rather heavy, you know."

Jenna eyed the bulky object in question. It was one of those carrying cases businessmen would put their suits in. Just like Dad used to –

This one was grey and bulging in all the wrong places. Whatever it contained, it was certainly no business suit. The man had his eye on the kitchen table with a view to laying the bag down on it.

"Like I said," Jenna set her jaw, "She's not doing it. Find some other old bag."

The man's eyebrows shot up his forehead but before he could speak, the squawking tones of Iphigenia Spenser addressed him from behind.

"Who's she calling an old bag now?" she clucked, all frizzy white hair and enough raggedy shawls to fill a jumble sale. "Obadiah Smedley! Is that you darkening my doorstep? Ah, you've brought the old bag, I see! Splendid! Marvellous! Jenna Jones, shake your woolly noggin and get the kettle on for Councillor Smedley. The poor man must be parched, lugging that heavy thing all the way from town."

She bustled into the kitchen, brooking no interruption from either of them. Filling the blackened kettle at the tap and setting it on the hob, she regaled the room with a litany of her ailments, whether her granddaughter or her visitor wanted to hear about them or not.

"A good dose of syrup of figs should sort that out," she concluded with the satisfied expression of someone who had completed The Times crossword. "Now, come on, Jenna, look sharp. Clear your books away, so Councillor Smedley can set the bag on the table."

Jenna pouted. She gathered up her textbooks and notepads – summer reading before college began in September – with a show of annoyance that went completely ignored. Councillor Smedley and Mrs Spenser exchanged nods and, with more reverence than perhaps was due, he placed the bulky bag on the kitchen table as though he were putting a favourite infant to bed. He stepped back as if to admire his handiwork. Jenna's grandmother clapped her hands with glee.

"Ain't it exciting!" she eyed the bag with wonder. "And such an honour! Ain't you proud of your old granny, Jen? Of all the folks they could have picked, the Council chose me." She jabbed her own breastbone with her index finger. Jenna succumbed to the impulse to roll her eyes.

"I don't think you're up to it, Gran. You've just reeled off a long list of what's wrong with you. Let the 'honour' go to someone else."

"I've still got breath in my body and bones in my leg, young lady. Besides, they carries me about in a chair, don't they, Councillor Smedley?"

"That is correct," Smedley beamed smarmily. "From your door, if you like. You'll be treated like royalty."

"I like the sound of that," Iphigenia beamed, showing teeth like subsidence in a cemetery. "About time I was treated with a bit of respect. Heaven knows I don't get it in my own home." She cast a pained look in her granddaughter's direction but all she got for her histrionics was another roll of Jenna's eyes.

"But it's not only that, is it?" Jenna pointed at the bag. "You have to wear that ridiculous get-up for a start. You'll catch your death."

Smedley held up a finger to interject. "Ah, well, now, you see, the get-up as you call it, has been updated. All the holes have been patched up so there's no chance of any draughts going where they shouldn't. And there's a wetsuit provided to keep the wearer snug and dry."

"You see!" Iphigenia exclaimed in triumph.

"You!" scoffed Jenna. "You in a wetsuit! This gets dafter by the minute. You do know where they take you in your wetsuit and fancy chair?"

"Around the square and down to the pond," Iphigenia looked to the councillor for confirmation.

"Exactly!" Jenna slapped the table. "And then what happens at the pond? They chuck you in. That's what happens. You'll be down A and E in Praxton within the hour."

Iphigenia pouted and in that instant the teenage girl she had herself been many moons ago was apparent. "No, I shan't!"

"Treat you like royalty? In a pig's eye! The royals had a better time of it during the French Revolution."

"It's purely symbolic," Smedley wheedled. "The Banishing of the Bogwitch is an important ritual for this community."

"Important, my left bum cheek!" Jenna railed. "I've told you my gran is too old and too fragile for you to toss her about on a chair, never mind chucking her in some cold and filthy water. Now, do us a favour and sling your hook, mate, before I get my hands on something sharp."

"Jenna!" Iphigenia clutched the brooch that pinned her shawls together. "You apologise to Councillor Smedley at once!"

Jenna turned her head. Smedley straightened, as though someone had flicked a switch inside him.

"Did you say 'Jenna'?"

"So what if I did?" Iphigenia was suddenly on the defensive.

"Jenna as in 'your granddaughter Jenna' as in 'your granddaughter Jenna who lost her parents in a tragic road traffic accident'? *That* Jenna?"

"Shut up!" Jenna roared. She ran from the room. Smedley pulled a face.

"Then I suppose we must make allowances. Must be terribly disturbing to lose one's mum and dad at such a young age."

Iphigenia scoured the kitchen for something to throw at the patronising prat. "My Jenna's a good girl. She's been through the mill."

"I'm sure," Smedley smiled greasily. He stepped back from the kitchen table, markedly leaving the costume where it lay. "The boys will be here for you at ten to eleven, so be ready. And nothing heavy for breakfast, eh? We don't want them to put their backs out."

He ducked out of the back door. Iphigenia muttered an aspersion about his parentage. She looked at the costume bag, lying like a shrouded corpse on her kitchen table.

Such an honour!

***

The settlement of Little Fladgett boasted three public houses. Perhaps 'boasted' is too strong a word. Two of them you wouldn't mention in despatches but the third might merit a word or two or three on an online reviews site, those words being along the lines of 'not entirely unpleasant'. One thing the Fox and Grapes had going for it was it had rooms to rent. The facilities had garnered the pub as many as two stars on Trip Advisor. It was quite a feather in the little town's cap. There being no other option, the Fox accommodated all overnight business under its roof. Not that there was much of that, because very few ventured to Little Fladgett by choice.

One such reluctant visitor was Wendy Rabbitt, journalist, and the brightest star in the local television firmament, in town to cover the weird and wonderful ritual the locals staged every year without fail. Her report would form part of an off-and-on series of similar stories. Wendy had already covered the practically suicidal cheese-rolling in the county's hilly western side, and the pea-pushing race through the county town's cobbled streets. Now she was in Little Fladgett. Big whoop. The place was accessible only by one route, a Roman road across the wetlands that surrounded it. Why anyone would want to settle in the middle of a bloody swamp was beyond Wendy's understanding. But a thousand years or more ago, settle they had. The twats.

Because of the remoteness, Wendy had come up a day early and was ensconced in her room above the public bar. Her plan to fill the evening by researching the area was foiled by the location's frustrating lack of Wi-Fi. Which was dandy.

"All right, all right," she answered the rumble of her stomach. She snatched up her room keys – she had valuable camera equipment stashed under the bed – and headed down to the bar. Perhaps there would be toasted sandwiches on offer, or a packet of crisps at the very least.

She found the bar, with its dark wood furniture and faded crimson upholstery, sparsely populated. An elderly man was slumped over the racing pages of a newspaper. Two others were engaged in what looked like an overly complicated game of cards, although neither of them seemed to be moving much, and a couple of old men in cloth caps sat separately at the L-shaped counter, behind which a sullen, middle-aged woman cleaned pint glasses with a linen towel. The bedraggled nature of her hair and the puckered lines around her pillar-box-red lips gave her the overall appearance of the backside of a poodle that had been left out in the rain. She barely acknowledged Wendy's arrival with the slightest nod. Her earrings jangled like distant sleigh bells.

Wendy smiled professionally and asked for a menu. The lines around the barmaid's mouth deepened as she considered the foreign-sounding word.

"Kitchen's closed," she announced with a sniff. "Shirley's preparing for tomorrow," she added as if that explained everything.

"Big day tomorrow," one of the men in cloth caps piped up, without lifting his gaze from his pint of bitter.

"Well, she knows that, don't she?" laughed the barmaid. "That's why her's here, ain't it? Filming it for the telly. Ain't that right, love?"

Wendy became acutely aware that every eye in the place was upon her. She prepared herself for the inevitable... It didn't come. "Yes, that's right," she grinned, hands up in mock surrender. "It's really me! I'll do selfies and what-not later. Just let me grab something to eat first. That's right: even people off the telly have to eat."

Nonplussed, the patrons of the Fox and Grapes returned their gazes to whatever it was they had been gazing at before, which was, in most cases, nothing in particular. Wendy's lips twisted into a shrug.

"I've had better receptions," she admitted. She hoisted her backside onto a vacant stool beside the bar.

"Oh, we don't get no reception round here," said the barmaid. It was then Wendy noticed the old-fashioned, rather bulbous television set bracketed above the counter. The screen was thick with dust and the dried spit-up of long-dead flies and, most decidedly, it was off.

"That explains it, then," Wendy cheered up. "You don't get the local news channel."

"If it ain't on Netflix..." said the barmaid.

"Coming tomorrow, are they?" said the man in the cloth cap who had spoken before.

"Who are?" Wendy frowned, while maintaining her professional smile.

The man's rheumy eyes looked her up and down. "Camera

crew. And all that gubbins."

"What? Oh! Oh, no! Just me, I'm afraid. Tight budget and all that. I do it all. The camera, the sound recording, the presenting, the lot! Mind you, the equipment – the gubbins, if you like – is a lot smaller than it used to be, makes it more portable, you see –"

But the man had already lost interest.

"Oh, don't you pay no mind to old Herbert," the barmaid patted Wendy's hand with a palm like cracked sandpaper. "What can I get you? Drinks-wise?"

"Um..." Wendy shook her head as she scanned the shelves and optics behind the bar. "Gin!" she decided with a slap of the counter. "Gin and tonic, if you please."

The barmaid arched a pencilled eyebrow. "Slimline?" she asked significantly. "Or normal?"

"Surprise me," Wendy said.

***

Several gins later, things had loosened up considerably in the bar at the Fox and Grapes. Someone was bashing out 'Daisy, Daisy' on the upright (but only just) piano, and the patrons sloshed their drinks all over themselves as they swayed about in time with the music. Wendy was leading the chorus, exhorting the men to sing louder, and plying them with drink after drink. She was running up a bar tab her expenses wouldn't cover but it was worth it. Already she had learned a great deal about the local legend and the significance of the annual ritual.

To wit: the original bog witch was some old wise woman living on the fringes of society. The inhabitants of Little Fladgett would seek her help with ailments of the body and the spirit, but when little children had started disappearing, the finger of suspicion fell on the outsider. She must be using the blood (and who knows what else) of those innocent victims to strengthen her dark magic. It was rumoured that she feasted on their flesh. A mob routed the woman from her hovel, subjected her to a travesty of a trial no kangaroo would endorse, before reaching the inevitable guilty verdict. The woman was dragged through the streets of Little Fladgett and pelted with filth and stones, before being strapped to a stool and ducked in the pond until she drowned. Now, every year, when there is nothing going on between bank holidays, the townsfolk re-enact the bog witch's final moments. Well, it was something to do and a bit of a laugh, and a boost to the tourism trade.

"Yeah," Wendy slid a foaming pint of ale along the counter to an old man in a cloth cap, "But there's no such thing as bog witches. Is there?"

The man lifted his head long enough to give her a baleful stare. "Course there ain't," he sniffed. "As long as we does the ceremony, that is."

"Too right," chimed in another, holding up a glass that was almost empty. Wendy signalled the barmaid to give him a refill. "It's the ceremony that keeps the bog witch at bay."

Wendy yelped out an incredulous laugh. The men's faces darkened.

"It's true!" said one.

"Aye!" agreed the other. "There ain't been no kiddies going missing for nigh on five hundred years."

"Because every year you gang up on an old woman and chuck her in the pond?" The gin-and-its were sitting sourly in Wendy's stomach. "Sounds like plain old-fashioned misogyny to me." *I have stumbled upon a right nest of nutters*, she wailed inwardly. *And somehow, I have to turn this load of old bollocks into a fluff piece of local colour that only half a dozen people will see anyway.*

She had always held it a mistake to schedule the local news against the Australian soap on the other side.

"Zigactly," the old men slurred in sloppy unison.

"Woe betide Little Fladgett if ever we are remiss in our duty."

Wendy gave the barmaid a 'can you believe this twaddle?' look, but the barmaid proved no ally.

"Must be something in it," she pouted. "Or else what's the bloody point?"

Ignoring the men's pleas for one more round, Wendy slid off her barstool and took herself to bed. As far as she was concerned, this assignment could not be over and done with too bloody soon.

***

Jenna could hear Gran bashing about in the kitchen, doing something percussive with a cast-iron frying pan. Jenna groaned and pulled a pillow over her head. The noise she could do without but in a couple of minutes, the aroma of food would nudge at her nostrils and prove impossible to resist. She had always been partial to a slice or two of fried bread. Perhaps if she lay in bed long enough, Gran would bring her breakfast on a tray with a sardonic, "Here you are, Lady Muck."

But then Jenna remembered. This was not the morning to be lounging in bed in the vague hope of room service. This was the morning for springing out of bed and putting a stop to nonsense before some daft old bat not a million miles away did herself a mischief.

Jenna threw back the covers and swung her feet to the floor, slotting them into her carpet slippers in one smooth move. Her pyjamas had hot air balloons on them and were altogether too bright and cheerful for this time in the morning, so she shrouded them in the dowdy, shapeless and threadbare dressing gown that had erstwhile been her grandfather's. Cinching the belt at her waist, she plodded down the stairs.

Gran was serving up as Jenna entered the kitchen, scooping delicious fried bread onto a plate. "Morning, Jenna, love. Going to need to line our stomachs. Got a big day ahead."

Jenna pulled out a chair and plonked herself on it. "You're not going through with it? I was hoping a good night's sleep would bring you to your senses."

"Oh, I couldn't sleep," Gran poured a mug of coffee. "All the excitement! It's an historical day."

"You mean 'historic' and no, it isn't. Not really. It's just a load of silly beggars indulging in sadism against an old woman."

Gran was aghast. "Less of the old, thank you! Now, eat up; I want you to help me get into that wet thingy. I do hope I've got enough talcum powder for my crevices."

The fried bread turned to ashes in Jenna's mouth. She pushed the plate away.

"But first," Gran announced, "I need to make myself a bit lighter for the lads."

She unlocked the back door and hurried out. Jenna didn't need to ask where. The daft old bat was really going through with it – and she wants me to help her! Well, not if I can help it!

Jenna eyed the bulging costume bag hanging on the kitchen door. She could hide it. Say Gran must have stashed it somewhere and it wasn't Jenna's fault if Gran couldn't remember where she'd put it.

No. That wasn't fair. No one would believe that for a second. Especially not Gran. She may be a bit eccentric but old Iphigenia Spenser still had every single one of her marbles. It's just that a few of them were cracked and chipped these days.

So, not the costume then...

Jenna cast around the kitchen for inspiration. Come on, come on, she tapped her foot. The old girl will be back from the privy any minute –

That was it! The privy!

Jenna yanked open the back door. There it stood, at the far end of the crazy paving, leaning menacingly like something out of a German Expressionist film.

No, I couldn't. Could I?

I must!

Jenna stole along the path, snatching the line prop as she passed. Taking care to make as little sound as possible, she wedged the wooden pole across the privy door. Gran was caught! She'd never be able to push the door open from the inside and there wasn't the room to have a run-up and give it a good shouldering.

Jenna chewed at her lower lip as guilty feelings gnawed at her conscience.

It would only be for an hour or so... Just until it was too late for the stupid ceremony.

A voice came from beyond the door. "Are you there, Jenna love?"

Jenna froze. Perhaps the time had come to perform a bird impression.

"I could do with some paper bringing out," Gran called hopefully.

Jenna backed away, slowly and silently, imagining herself a ninja on rewind. She got to the kitchen. Eventually, Gran would give up shouting, wouldn't she?

She put the radio on. Sorry, Gran, didn't hear you, with the local news report wittering on.

She returned to her seat at the table. The fried bread had congealed already, and the coffee seemed to have acquired a greasy meniscus. Jenna closed her eyes. Sorry, Gran; so, so sorry...

It's just for a little while longer.

Hearty knocking at the front door startled Jenna's eyes open. She leapt several inches in the air. Who could that be? Surely Gran hadn't tunnelled out and made her way to the front of the cottage... It didn't make sense.

The knocking continued. The flap on the letterbox rattled and lifted.

"Coo-ee, Mrs Spenser! Are you ready for us? We've come to take you away from all this!"

Laughter. Raucous, male laughter and the faint tinkling of little bells.

Shit!

Shit, shit!

It was the troupe of Morris men whose task it was to convey the Bogwitch around the streets.

"Your carriage awaits!"

More laughter.

Jenna panicked. "J – just a minute, please!" she called out, her voice cracking with nerves.

"Right you are," said the Morris man. "But get a move on. We don't want to waste valuable quaffing time."

What to do, what to do, what to do?

Jenna's gaze returned to the costume bag.

No.

No, no.

But what else am I going to do?

Steeling herself, she unzipped the bag.

For Gran, she resolved.

***

Wendy Rabbitt dry-swallowed another couple of paracetamols and checked herself in the mirror on the wardrobe door. She hadn't slept – hadn't been to bed. She had worked through the night, writing up the background for her report, the historical significance of the ceremony she was about to film. It was a load of old bollocks, to be sure, like all superstition, but her evening of boozing it up with the locals had shed light on some of the dafter aspects of proceedings. They pelt the Bog-witch with wet cabbage leaves and this is because – what was it again? – something about warding off evil plant spirits with the good, because everyone knows cabbage is good for you. Wendy shrugged. They might as well be propounding the benefits of a Vegan diet for all she cared. And, she would be willing to bet, the local greengrocer was laughing all the way to the building society.

The barmaid – whose name turned out to be Brenda – was at her station behind the counter. One might think she had not moved, but the change of leopard-print blouse to a floral one, as well as a different pair of opulent earrings, suggested she had at least had a pitstop at some point. An arched eyebrow and a tilt of the head indicated the breakfast menu on a small chalkboard. Wendy smiled a brief, 'Not for me, thanks' and breezed out of the bar, toting a shoulder-bag of camera equipment as if it were nothing.

She found the streets – all four of them – festooned with green bunting. Closer inspection revealed the decorations to be hundreds of cabbage leaves strung up like traitors as a warning to other vegetables.

"Pretty," she murmured.

"Morning, love," an approaching man tapped a finger on the peak of his cloth cap. "You'll get the best view in the square."

"Thanks," Wendy said, jaws tight. She didn't like being told how to do her job. "Think I'll get an establishing shot of the procession coming into town. It will come this way, no?"

"No," said the man. "This year it'll come from the other side on account of it being Old Ma Spenser who's been chosen to be the guest of honour. Like I say, square's your best bet."

"Thanks," Wendy offered a thin smile. "Well, don't let me keep you. I'm sure you want to get a good spot."

The man did not move. He looked Wendy up and down. Where was the bonhomie, the camaraderie, and other French words, of the night before? Now the woman was all cold and curt and other words beginning with c. It was as though last night – only a few short hours ago – she had only been plying him with drink to milk him for information.

She *used* me, the man realised, his cheeks reddening with shame.

"Off you toddle," Wendy made a shooing gesture. She unshouldered the bag, set it on the pavement and slid back the zipper. "I need to check my levels."

The man in the cloth cap sloped away, grinding his teeth. The stuck-up bitch needed taking down a peg or two.

He'd show her.

***

At the centre of the town square stood a concrete rostrum, euphemistically referred to as 'the bandstand' although no one could remember a time when any band had ever stood on it. It was to this relatively high point that Wendy Rabbitt headed.

From there she would be able to capture the action and spin her tripod 360 degrees as the procession made its way around the square.

She checked the white balance and clipped a lapel mic to the collar of the peasant blouse she had chosen to wear for the occasion. Stretch jeans and a pair of Chelsea boots completed her outfit. Wendy liked to think it gave her a friendly, accessible air. She could go in for tight close-ups when she needed to come across as more authoritative. All that remained now was to wait.

The square was filling up as locals and visitors picked out their vantage points along the temporary railings. Wendy marvelled at how many people there were. Did people really go in for this folklore nonsense? Or was it only a bit of a laugh and an excuse for a booze-up? It was searing questions of this nature she hoped to pose in her report, and prove once and for all she was capable of much more than fluff pieces that more often than not got bumped if there was a chemical spill on the motorway.

There was a buzz of conversation, an air of expectancy – They're really looking forward to this, Wendy was amazed to note. Oh, the simple pleasures of country life! Give me Harvey Nichols any day of the week!

The clock on the town hall chimed the eleventh hour. A hush fell over the quadrilateral crowd. All heads turned to the High Street at the end of the square. It was along this thoroughfare that the procession would come.

And then –

Accordion music, a blaring fanfare followed by a jig, heralding the arrival of a troupe of Morris dancers. They skipped and hopped with green kerchiefs in their hands, clearing the way for the guest of honour. Four Morris men, their faces painted green, bore a high chair on their shoulders. The chair was covered with polythene sheets and on it, clinging to the arm rests for dear life, sat the guest of honour, this year's lucky Bogwitch.

Jenna was panting, her heart racing at every jar and jolt of the chair. She was sweating beneath the hook-nosed rubber mask, glad she had foregone the rubber wetsuit.

"Hurrah!" cried the crowd as the parade came to a halt. The spectators took full advantage of the pause; they pelted the Bogwitch with cabbage leaves, fresh and rotten. Jenna found that if she raised a hand to protect herself, her position on the precarious polythene became more hazardous, so she had to cling on to the arms and take the missiles on her rubber, warty chin.

All around the square, the chair was carried to ensure that everyone got a good shot at the Bogwitch. Parents held up small children so they could hurl their leaves, but Jenna had nothing to fear from their weak-wristed efforts. It was the teenagers that threw the hardest and with the most accuracy. Sometimes the whole fucking cabbage, Jenna found out rather painfully.

At least, Gran was spared this ordeal. Jenna hoped the old girl was all right, shut in that privy...

The accordion player ended with a flourish and a crackly P.A. system bore the voice of Councillor Smedley through the air.

"Friends," he announced. "When is it time?"

"The time is now!" the crowd answered cheerfully.

"The time for what?" Smedley cupped his ear.

"To banish the Bogwitch!" replied the crowd, enjoying the litany.

"The what?" Smedley feigned ignorance.

"The Witch of the Bog!" laughed the crowd.

Smedley pretended to cotton on. "Boggy," he said.

"Oy!" said the crowd, punching the air.

"Boggy!"

"Oy!"

"Boggy, boggy, boggy!"

"Oy! Oy! Oy!"

Oh, fuck me, thought Jenna. They're all deranged. I'll tell you what time it is. Time for me to make my exit.

But before she could clamber down, the chair set off again. Jenna slipped and had to cling on.

"Steady now," Smedley said. "Don't drop her. Not just yet anyway."

Laughter.

"Friends, if you please, follow the Bogwitch down to Potlar's Pond."

The crowd let out its biggest cheer so far. Good as gold, they filed out of the square, traipsing after now sombre Morris men. Now there was no jolly accordion music, just the steady, solemn beating of a drum.

Help, thought Jenna. I'm a non-entity; get me out of here.

***

The participants in the procession did a reasonable job of maintaining an air of solemnity as they followed the high chair. They knew as soon as the Bogwitch hit the water a carnival atmosphere would erupt. The pubs would open their doors wide, selling the special edition Bogwater Brew that could jeopardise your eyesight and clean your oven a treat. There was a mini funfair for the kiddiewinks – the local authority turned a blind eye to school attendance on Bogwitch Day. Indeed, many clerks and council officers were taking part as Morris dancers, stewards and parking attendants. Musicians would commandeer the parks for a makeshift festival of folk and traditional music. Ice cream vendors would dispense lime-green 'sauce' on their cornets to mark the occasion. For some, it was better than Hallowe'en, better than Christmas. Traders and punters alike rejoiced on Bogwitch Day. There was nothing better on the calendar that proved such a boon for the local economy.

Clinging to her lofty perch, Jenna found vague memories from her childhood rising to the surface of her mind like bubbles of swamp gas in the bog: Mum and Dad bringing her to visit Gran on Bogwitch Day. Trying valiantly, but in vain, to get her five-year-old arms to fling a cabbage leaf at the scary old lady on the chair.

Now, I'm the scary lady, Jenna mused. But there's no way in

Hell I'm going in that fucking pond.

The drumming, and the parade along with it, came to a halt. Even though the eyeholes of her mask were skewwhiff, Jenna could see they had arrived at their destination. Her chair was level with the top of a chute, something akin to a ski slope. The Bogwitch would be tipped from her seat to career down the slide and arc through the air to land kerplop in the centre of the placid pond. The chute was a recent addition, insisted upon by the Council to appease the gods of Health and Safety – although from Jenna's viewpoint it looked neither healthy nor safe. Previous generations had been content – had taken delight in – hurling the living effigy into the water via the old leg-and-a-wing method still popular with playground bullies today. Jenna longed for a return to the methods of yore; at least that way she would be able to wriggle and writhe and hope to kick a couple of heads.

Every eye was trained upon her as the drummer commenced a roll to eke out the suspense. Everyone knew what was going to happen; it was merely a question of when.

There seemed to be no escape. Jenna braced herself, hoping she could keep her gob shut when the pondwater closed over her head.

But the drumbeat faltered and stopped short of its climax. People were shouting in protest, chief among whom was the drummer. Jenna peered down to glean the nature of the kerfuffle.

A large woman in a bright yellow mac and sou'wester was striding around in wading boots, drenching everyone within range of her super-soaker water gun.

"How do you like it, eh?" she repeated. "It's only a bit of water, direct from the pond this morning. Where's the harm, eh?"

Children, screaming and crying, were dragged out of reach by angry parents. Stewards attempted to approach the woman, but she squirted them squarely in the face, knocking them onto their arses. Most of the crowd beat a retreat. Those who stood their ground got wet.

"She'll run out of ammo soon enough," advised one man in a hi-vis tabard. The woman took him out with a shot to his mouth, sending his dentures flying into the pond.

A shrill whistle heralded the tardy arrival of the police. The remnants of the crowd parted to let Constable Dimwoodie through. He addressed the woman through a megaphone.

"This is the police," he bellowed, accompanied by crackles and whistles. "Lay down your weapons!"

"Weapons!" laughed the woman. "They're toys!"

"Put your toys down then."

"Make me!"

Constable Dimwoodie was aghast. This wasn't how things went on the telly. "Don't make me call for back-up," he tried to sound ominous.

"Ooh.." mocked the woman.

The constable found himself nudged roughly aside and the megaphone yanked from his grasp. Councillor Smedley was taking charge.

"Now, look here" he barked. "You've had your fun but you're spoiling it for everyone else. Some of these people have come a long way."

"For what?" the woman sneered. She didn't seem to have need of amplification. "To see a woman abused? Bunch of sickos, if you ask me."

"Now, that's ridiculous. This is a time-honoured tradition and it's all good-natured fun."

"You get in the chair then," said the woman, adopting a challenging stance.

"Well – I – er –" Councillor Smedley floundered. "But it's traditionally a lady."

"In the mask, who's going to know?"

"Well – I – er –" Councillor Smedley was tongue-tied and infuriated.

"Go on, get your arse up there," the woman pointed aloft. "Typical man. Happy to let a woman take the fall."

"But we already have a Bogwitch," Smedley asserted.

"No, you don't," said the woman. Everyone followed her pointing finger. The high chair was empty. The Bogwitch had scarpered.

Smedley was incandescent. "Do you realise what this means, you stupid cow? You have doomed us all."

"Bollocks," said the woman. "You're just worried about tourist income."

"But –" The enormity of what had happened was sinking in. Smedley's knees buckled and he dropped the megaphone.

"Oi," complained the constable, stooping to retrieve his property.

"The legend..." Smedley's mouth gaped and closed like a bewildered goldfish.

"That's bollocks and all," said the woman. "And I should know."

"And why's that, Miss?" said the constable.

"Because," the woman blew on the nozzle of her water gun, "I'm a bog witch."

***

This is fucking gold! Wendy Rabbitt could not believe her luck. Disruption at the ducking! Riot at the routing! Skirmish at the soaking! Drenching deferred! The headlines boiled in her mind faster than she could grasp them. All of a sudden, her frothy fluff piece about quaint traditions had taken an edgier, more political turn. She had to get an interview with the instigator, the remarkable woman in the silly sou'wester.

Wendy elbowed her way through the stragglers, microphone thrust before her like an Olympic torch, hardly bothering to utter so much as an 'excuse me' or a 'thank you'. By the time she reached the woman in yellow, the constable was dithering about whether to arrest the interloper or not to bother. Councillor Smedley was entertaining no such doubts.

"Take her down!" he urged. "Throw the key away!"

Dimwoodie's eyes rolled. Smedley's eyes followed their

path: his gaze came to rest on the twin evils of the lens of a video camera and the pop shield of a microphone.

"Care to make a statement, Councillor?" That rotten reporter was grinning at him like the Cheshire Cat with a rictus. Wish she would bloody disappear!

Councillor Smedley had received precisely zilch in the way of media training, but even he could see it would look bad, having the nutcase arrested on television. People had come to Little Fladgett for a fun day out and, much as it might assuage Smedley's rampant ire to see the silly cow carted off, sometimes one had to be magnanimous. He turned on his best public-relations smile.

"We were trying something a little different this year," he extemporised, "But there were a few teething problems, a bit of miscommunication." He edged closer to the lens in a bid to fill the frame and command the reporter's attention. "And, unfortunately, it was members of the crowd who received the soaking and not the Bogwitch as intended. But we are not going to let this put a – heh – *dampener* on proceedings. The festivities will resume and there's still plenty of fun to be had for all the family, with the pin-the-wart-on-the-Bogwitch stand, and plenty of refreshments to be found. I myself can't wait to sample a pint of Bogwater Brew, which has –"

He became aware that the lens was drifting away from him in a slow pan to the left. The self-proclaimed bog witch seized her moment to come forward. She nudged the councillor aside with excessive force and beamed at the camera.

"For too long," she boomed, making Wendy Rabbit flinch in her headphones, "we bog witches have been woefully and willfully misrepresented by the media, and this kind of nonsense has got to stop. Our once highly prized skills are mocked and denigrated. Our esteemed status as healers has been much and often maligned. Time was, having a bog witch in the community was a boon, a privilege, but the public consciousness has been turned against us. I'm taking a stand to put the record straight."

"Bloody feminists," Smedley could be heard muttering not far away. "They have to make everything about *them*, don't they?"

The woman in yellow rounded on him. "Oh, but it is! The patriarchy of this town, manifest in the Chamber of Commerce above all, has exploited the wrongful stereotyping and wilful mistreatment of women for profit all in the name of questionable entertainment."

Wendy Rabbitt found she had to stifle a yawn. Why couldn't somebody just hit somebody? Television is a visual medium, after all. She tuned out of the asinine debate that was brewing and scoured around for another angle. Something pale and pink caught her peripheral vision. She squinted... Oh, God, it was, wasn't it? Some arsehole was showing his – well, his arsehole, mooning directly at the camera. For f–

Wendy's blood ran cold. It was the old grouch in the cloth cap, wasn't it? She cut the recording and scanned the footage, the crowd, the procession, the water gun... There he was, in practically every shot. She could use none of it. What a bloody waste. What a bloody waste of time.

She began to pack up. The woman in yellow cut herself off mid tirade.

"Is there a problem, Ms Rabbitt?"

Gratified though she was to be recognised, Wendy Rabbitt could only snarl out a response. "I'm done here," she snapped. And perhaps everywhere else too, she couldn't help thinking.

"But you haven't interviewed me yet," the woman pouted. "I am a bona fide bog witch."

"You can bog off," Wendy growled.

Councillor Smedley let out a snort of derision.

***

For the rest of the day, Iphigenia Spenser gave her granddaughter the silent treatment, a process that involved lots of heartfelt sighs, narrowed eyes, and petulant pouting. And the conducting of domestic tasks at a higher volume than was usual or necessary. She had yet to forgive Jenna for locking her in the lavatory and thereby robbing her of fifteen minutes of waterlogged fame. Jenna apologised repeatedly, with increasing displays of abject contrition, even going as far as making her gran a nice cup of tea – well, she put the kettle on, which was almost the same thing.

Now, as Iphigenia rattled around the objects in a kitchen drawer, emulating the racket produced by a Wagnerian percussion section, rooting around for the tea strainer, it was Jenna's turn to emit a sigh.

"I keep telling you, Gran, you don't need to sieve the tea. It comes in little bags these days."

She was hoping it would provoke Gran's customary response about not trusting new-fangled nonsense (which, as far as Jenna could tell, was an umbrella term for everything invented since the Dark Ages – including umbrellas too, no doubt), but Gran remained resolutely tight-lipped on this and every other subject. The afternoon wore on, eroding Jenna's patience and adding to her exasperation.

A dismal viewing of *Countdown*, fraught with additional tension as Gran forced herself to refrain from calling out the answers and disparaging the dress sense of the competitors, was interrupted by knocking at the front door. Jenna looked to her grandmother, who resolutely crossed her arms and kept her eyes on a maths problem.

"I'll get that then, shall I?" Jenna stood. "Although both you and I know it's never for me."

On the doorstep was Constable Dimwoodie. He took off his helmet, tucked it under his arm, more as an aid to getting through the low-slung doorway than as a show of respect.

"Hello, Miss – ah – can I come in?"

"What?" Jenna said, her mind racing. She hadn't done anything illegal, had she? Well, not recently. Certain her cheeks were turning a traitorous red, she asked what it was about.

"Bogwitch," Dimwoodie said, in all seriousness.

"Oh," Jenna said. "You better come in, then."

Moments later, the constable was ensconced at the kitchen table with Jenna sitting opposite and Iphigenia fussing around making a fresh pot of tea and topping up the biscuit barrel. The presence of a third party presented a welcome opportunity for a respite from her self-imposed vow of silence.

"Now," Iphigenia said, placing a steaming mug before him, "get yourself on the outside of that. What's all this about a bog witch?"

"One showed up at the pond," it was Jenna who answered. "I've told you this. Disrupted the whole shebang with a massive water pistol. Is that what this is about?"

Dimwoodie nodded, hands around his mug. "A woman has been questioned. And released. But this is not about her."

"What, then?" Iphigenia pushed a plate of fondant fancies forward. "If I'm in hot water for not getting chucked in cold water, you can thank a certain young lady not a million miles away."

"Eh?" the constable frowned. Jenna translated.

"She thinks she's in trouble for not doing the parade. You're not in trouble, Gran. Is she in trouble?"

"I don't know anything about that," Dimwoodie shrugged. "I'm here to ask if you've seen anything *untoward* this afternoon."

"What like?" Jenna said.

"Um – like a – um – bog witch."

"I have!" Gran thrust her hand in the air like a prize pupil. "I did. I seen one! Not long since. There I was, shut up in the privy, thinking my number was up and I was going to finish up like Elvis, when the door is pulled open, and there, gawping at me, is only the bloody Bogwitch herself!"

"You what?" Dimwoodie perked up and flipped open his notebook.

"Ignore her," Jenna advised, as Gran continued to rant.

"Only it wasn't the Bogwitch herself, was it? How could it be? Because this year I was meant to be the bloody Bogwitch. Me! Wasn't I? So, this bloody Bogwitch was an imposter, wasn't she? And a guilty one. Guilty of impersonating a bog witch and wrongful imprisonment of a senior citizen too, I shouldn't wonder."

Dimwoodie's eyes sent an appeal for help to the younger woman. Jenna, safe in the knowledge that Gran would not address her directly, pulled a face that showed how much she regretted the decline of her sainted grandmother's mental faculties.

"I'm going door-to-door," the constable expanded. "There's been sightings, you see. In these very parts. Folk are twitchy, see, after this morning didn't go to plan."

Iphigenia's expression darkened. "You mean the ritual was buggered up so the Bogwitch is back to taunt us? Bloody fast work, if you asks me."

Jenna scoffed. "It was me, wasn't it? I'm your bog witch. I ran home to let my gran out of the outside lavvy, didn't I?"

Dimwoodie was none the wiser.

"It was me!" Jenna continued. "I was the one in the costume. I was the one carried around on the chair. I took my gran's place, didn't I? To save her from the indignity and a broken hip too, I shouldn't wonder. And when it all kicked off, I saw my chance to slip away, and I pelted it all the way home. Not an easy feat in that costume, I can tell you. I bet you there's not a single toxin left in my body. Talk about sweaty!"

Iphigenia's face expressed her disgust at the mention of the word. Constable Dimwoodie jotted it all down.

"So," he looked up from his pad and met Jenna's gaze. "Where is he, then?"

"Where's who?" Jenna said.

"The kiddie."

"What kiddie?" Jenna said and her gran in perfect unison, as identical chills ran through their bones.

***

Tommy Thornbush was as inquisitive as any four-year-old. His mother described him as 'into everything', while his nursery nurse styled him as 'a bit of a handful'. He had been excited to see the procession and to fling his cabbage leaf at the nasty old Bogwitch, just like everyone else. When the water-squirting had started, he had squealed in delight, clapping his hands like he was enjoying a pantomime. His mother, mindful of her make-up, had taken a dimmer view of the disruption and had pulled her little boy farther back into the crowd and out of the line of fire (well, water!). As people turned and fled, she had lost hold of his hot little hand and then had lost sight of him in the melee. When space cleared, Tommy Thornbush was nowhere to be seen and, his mother noted with horror, like a boot to the belly, there was the Bogwitch, who only seconds earlier, had been atop a high chair.

"That's ridiculous," Iphigenia said. "Coming around here and accusing my Jenna of – whatever is going through that nasty mind of yours, Daniel Dimwoodie." She patted her granddaughter's hand in a show of solidarity, and Jenna knew then she was forgiven.

"I'm sure he'll turn up," Jenna tried to convince herself as much as the constable. "Have they checked the ice cream stalls?"

"We have checked everywhere," the constable was dour, all of a sudden. "I'm short-handed. I've had to deputise blokes from the security firm that was brought in for crowd control."

"Bah," Iphigenia said. "They did a bang-up job keeping that woman with the water gun away."

Dimwoodie ignored this observation. "We're speaking to everyone. There's to be a search of the area before sundown. Perhaps you'd care to join in?"

"Not with my hips," Gran said.

"Yes, of course," Jenna said. "But isn't this all a bit, you know, rushed? He can't have been gone for much more than an hour."

Dimwoodie shook his head. "Can't be too careful when it's kiddies. Especially round here. Especially – well, you know the legend. People are anxious."

Jenna let out a bitter laugh. "Are you seriously telling me

people think that the Bogwitch, who may or may not have existed hundreds of years ago, is back and has already claimed her first victim?"

The policeman paled. "I'm sure if it was your little lad, you'd want everybody to do everything they could."

Jenna couldn't argue with that. "Let me put my wellies on and I'll be right out."

Gran wagged a finger. "And tell everybody in the search party there's a cup of tea here for anybody as wants one."

The constable got to his feet and pocketed his notebook. "Thank you. You are both very kind."

He went out. Jenna slipped her arms into the sleeves of her anorak.

"People don't really believe all that, do they, Gran? This is the twenty-first century."

The old woman smiled sadly. "People have always been arseholes," she said. "Now, you go out and find that boy. And mind what you're treading in. I don't want half of Potlar's Bog traipsed into my Axminister."

***

A decent number had turned out for the search party but nowhere near as many as those who had thronged the square. Those with children of their own had taken their offspring home to safety behind locked doors and drawn curtains. Everyone was hoping it was a case of a kiddie wandering off somewhere, heedless of the concern and consternation he caused. No one wanted to entertain the idea that was bubbling at the back of every brain, that the Very Worst had happened and the Bogwitch was back!

Jenna scanned the line of searchers that was fanning out at the edge of Potlar's Bog. She had never seen so many green cagoules in one place. Lots of people had sticks, traditional crook-handled walking sticks, telescopic metal ones decorated with floral prints, and there even some of those ski-pole-looking things, favoured by pretentious wankers. Jenna scoured the assembly for a familiar face, which was not easy, given that everyone was focussed on the ground just in front of their toecaps. She thought she could see Tim, teenage son of the newsagent. Nice lad. Or would be, when his spots cleared up. Perhaps she could amble over and insinuate herself beside him...

She scolded herself for thinking of Boys at a time like this. Honestly!

Under the direction of Constable Dimwoodie, the line was becoming a V. At the end of the left arm was a figure in bright yellow, positively glowing amid all the green and camouflage gear. It was the woman from before! She had forsaken her super-soaker (or had had it confiscated by the coppers) and was instead holding a forked branch in front of her and seemed to be paying it more attention than where her wading boots were treading. Jenna gave Tim one last look and shrugged. She plodded over to join the weird woman.

"All right?" she said, falling in beside her.

"Ssh!" hissed the woman. "I think I'm getting a twitch." She paused to make a tentative sweep of her forked stick. "False alarm," she sighed. Only then did she look at the girl beside her. "Oh, it's you, is it?"

Her voice had a Welsh lilt Jenna hadn't noticed earlier when she'd been haranguing and drenching the crowd.

"What is?" Jenna said.

"It's you. The girl from the chair. You were the Bogwitch."

The people nearest bristled at the name. The woman ignored them.

"Well, yes, I am," Jenna admitted. "How did you – I mean, I had a mask on and a wig and everything."

The woman winked. "Takes one to know one, love."

"Takes one what to know what?" Jenna didn't know whether to feel insulted.

"Birds of a feather," the woman grinned. "I too am a bog witch. Out and proud!"

"I think you said something about that before," Jenna nodded. "Before I made a sharp exit. Thanks for the distraction, by the way. I was wondering how I was going to bugger off with my dignity intact."

"My pleasure, sweetheart. But if you don't mind me saying, aren't you a little bit on the young side? Don't they usually pick an old biddy for their demeaning nonsense?"

"Well, yes, they do, and they did. My gran. But I sort of took her place at the last minute. She'd catch her death or break a hip or something."

The woman shook her head in disbelief. "Those bastards and their stupid traditions. Do you have a name, love?"

"Yes." Jenna frowned; it seemed like a daft question.

"And?"

"Oh!" The penny dropped. "It's Jenna. Jenna Jones."

"Pleased to meet you," the woman held out a pudgy hand that was cold and damp to the touch. "I'm Cassandra. As in, Cassandra Clune."

She seemed to be waiting for something, watching Jenna's face for a response. Recognition, perhaps. She could divine from Jenna's blank expression, she wasn't going to get it. "Never mind. I'm glad you got away."

"So am I. Glad *you* got away, I mean. I would have thought you'd be banged up in the slammer."

Cassandra laughed. "I got lucky there. That councillor Smedley, is it? He didn't want any argy-bargy on the town's special day. So, I got off with a caution. They confiscated my guns though," she added with a sigh. "Hold up!"

She came to an abrupt halt. "Do you see that?"

"What?"

"My stick! See the end bobbing up and down?"

Jenna peered closely. She couldn't see – and then the tip of the stick pointed at the ground and then at the sky and then at the ground again.

"That's you, that is!" she cried with scorn. "You're doing that with your wrists."

"I can assure you I am not!" Cassandra was aghast. "Here!" she thrust the stick at Jenna. "You bloody well have a go."

Jenna took the forked stick in both hands. Feeling foolish, she waited for something to happen.

"You're gripping it too tightly. Blimey, have you never had a boyfriend? Loosely, love, but not so loose that you drop it. There! Now, clear your mind – that was quick! – and let the rod take over and –"

The divining rod jerked in Jenna's grasp. Jenna let out a startled cry and dropped it.

"Oops," she said.

"Never mind," Cassandra smiled, "Well now, what have we here?"

She parted a clump of long grass, revealing something shiny in their midst. Jenna stooped to retrieve it. It was a badge, a metal circle showing a picture of a bog witch with a red line running diagonally through it. Jenna held it up and called to the constable.

Blowing his whistle, Dimwoodie came running. Jenna handed him the badge.

"Is it…"

Dimwoodie pulled a face, turning the find over in his hand. "Could be… All the kids were wearing these. I'll check with Tommy's mum. This could be the first lead we've had. Proof that Tommy came – or was brought – this way. Well done, Jen."

"Actually, it was…" Jenna jerked a thumb in Cassandra's direction.

"Yes, well," Dimwoodie said, warily. He strode away.

"Huh." Cassandra picked up her stick and cleaned the pointed end. "Wouldn't be surprised if he thinks I planted that badge there. We bog witches are forever plagued with suspicion."

Jenna wrinkled her nose.. "Are you really a bog witch?"

"I bloody well am!" Cassandra looked affronted. "Bring me back to yours for a cup of tea and I'll tell you all about it."

***

"Now I'm telling you," Wendy Rabbitt paced the floor of her room at the inn, which amounted to little more than rotating on the spot with her smartphone pressed against her ear, "I'm onto something here. I'm going to stick around and follow the story. Things have taken an unexpected turn with that little boy going missing. Yes, I think somebody's got him. No, I don't think it's the bastard Bogwitch. But there are plenty of folk in this shithole who do. And that's my angle: fear and superstition alive and kicking in twenty-first century Britain. And at the heart of it, a sweet little chap who never did any harm – No, I haven't met him, but that's the kind of thing you say, isn't it? For all I know, he could be a sick little fucker who likes pulling the legs off frogs and setting fire to kittens, I don't know. No, I'm not saying that at all – Well, I don't want to speak ill of the... missing, do I? No, I can't use anything from this morning. Can't have some old git's saggy arse on a teatime bulletin, can we? But I've been back to the square. It's deserted now. Little bit sad, little bit eerie, with that cabbage-leaf bunting flapping about. Got a shot of a balloon bobbing along the road. Very arty. Especially if we slow it down a bit, drop out the colour so it's a ball of green in an otherwise grey world – No, I know we don't have the time or money for special effects or I'd get that saggy arse pixelated out, wouldn't I? But to establish the mood of the place, a party in tatters kind of vibe. And then I'll interview the main players. The woman herself if I can get her. Calls herself a present-day bog witch. I know! The place is crawling with nutters – literally! They're out on their hands and knees practically, looking for little lost Whojimmyflop. I got some shots of them setting off. Community pulling together. Lots of grim faces. Couldn't see the mother, though. Might track her down for a heartfelt appeal to the abductor. Few tears, bit of snot, always goes down well. Going to need a helpline number. I know most of our viewers have never heard of Little Fladgett, let alone been there, but it makes us look proactive. Like we care, you know? Of course we care. I care. That's why I want to stay here until the bitter end. Or happy end, of course, of course. That's what everyone wants, isn't it? Little boy back in the bosom. Of course. That's what we all want. That's what I want. It is."

***

When it became too dark to see a hand or anything else in front of one's face, the search for Tommy Thornbush was suspended. Constable Dimwoodie assured everyone they could resume at dawn's crack, and he had taped off the tuffet where Tommy's Bogwitch badge had been found. Some people thanked and congratulated Cassandra on her find but Jenna heard mutterings from others who wouldn't be surprised if the crazy cow had planted the badge there herself to make herself seem innocent. Which she clearly wasn't, in their point of view, and that dim-witted copper ought to take her in and chuck the key in Potlar's Bog. As far as they were concerned.

Perhaps it was the murmured gossip that emboldened Jenna to invite the curious woman back to the cottage for a cuppa. She liked to think of herself as a champion of the underdog – huh, she reflected bitterly, the only way I'm likely to be champion of anything.

"I would love to!" Cassandra Clune beamed like a child's drawing of the sun.

"I can't promise biscuits, mind," Jenna felt obliged to make a disclaimer.

"I should hope not," Cassandra tittered. "I wouldn't want to risk this gorgeous figure!"

The laughter drew scowls from the search party stragglers. Oops, thought Jenna, hardly appropriate. That poor kiddie. His poor mother.

"We've done all we can for today," Cassandra placed a reassuring hand on the sleeve of Jenna's cagoule. Jenna was startled; it was as though the weird woman had read her thoughts.

"Are you really a..." Jenna ventured.

"A what?"

"A witch?"

"We prefer 'wiccan'."

"Wicked!"

"No, wiccan."

"No, I mean, that's wicked. As in, that's pretty cool."

"Is it?" Cassandra looked pleased.

"Well, I think so. But I don't think my gran will be impressed. So perhaps we ought to keep it on the downlow."

"If you don't think I'll be welcome…"

"Oh, no, you'll be treated like royalty. She'll fill your gob with cake and your earholes with stories of how everything was so much better in the old days."

"I like her already!" Cassandra enthused. "This way?"

She headed up a path of crazy paving. Jenna followed.

"Yes… How did you… Have you got your dousing stick out again?"

"You don't need divination to read the name on a mailbox," Cassandra chuckled. For a large woman, she had rather a dainty tread, as though permanently on tiptoe. You could swap her wading boots for ballet shoes, Jenna mused, and her gait would be exactly the same. She found she had to hurry to keep up.

It did not occur to her until later, many hours deep into the night, that she had not by that point disclosed her grandmother's name.

***

The welcome was exactly as Jenna had predicted. Her grandmother served up fruit cake and ginger snaps, and cup after cup of piping hot tea. What Jenna had underestimated was Gran's interest in their guest's professed profession. Gran was, in fact, endlessly fascinated and wanted to know all the, what she called, ins and outs.

"So, tell me," she pushed a plate of sponge fingers toward Cassandra. "It's not all hanging about in swamps and feasting on human flesh."

Cassandra chuckled. "Well, there's a bit of the former and precious little of the latter. None, in fact." She held up a sponge finger. "This is as close as I come to devouring anything resembling human anatomy." She bit off the end and rolled her eyes in epicurean delight.

Iphigenia cackled. "I reckon they look less like fingers and more like a bloke's whatsit."

"Gran!" Jenna was appalled.

The two older women laughed, like chickens falling down a drain. Jenna tried to yank the conversation back to less questionable matters.

"And you make a living out of – doing what you do?"

"Jenna!" It was Iphigenia's turn to be appalled. "Don't be so rude!"

"No, it's all right," Cassandra smiled. "Well, I'm no Whojimmyflop, Richard Branflake, but I get by. Most of my clients are online. People from all over, wanting consultations, ordering remedies. You might not think to look at me but I am a global concern."

She and Gran set off laughing again.

"Oh, don't look so disapproving," Cassandra shot Jenna a smile. "I can joke at my own expense, can't I? But my work I take very seriously. I tailor each remedy, each reading, to the individual customer. Not like some websites where the stuff is mass-produced, and the readings generated by a whadyacallit – a bot."

"Bot!" Iphigenia tittered. "Bot-bot!"

Jenna frowned at the teapot and wondered what was in it.

"Do me!" Iphigenia pushed her cup and saucer (the best china had been unearthed from the dresser) across the table. "Read my leaves."

Cassandra grimaced. Iphigenia flinched. "Is it that bad?"

"She can't read your leaves, can she, Gran?" Jenna was exasperated. "We use teabags."

Iphigenia thumped the table in vindication. "I told you those new-fangled things were no good."

"I don't really do tea leaves anyway," Cassandra said. "I look at the whole person. Then I concoct a remedy from bog water and assorted herbs and what-have-you."

Jenna's nose wrinkled. Again, it was as though Cassandra was reading her thoughts.

"You must get beyond the negative connotations of 'bog'," she smiled. "I know it's a word synonymous with 'toilet'. Let me assure you, I don't go around scooping water out of toilets."

"Even so," Jenna reddened. "A swamp."

"You'd be surprised," Cassandra said. "The high peat content of your average bog has many medicinal properties. It's all very scientific, actually. Been around for centuries. What those women were doing by intuition and time-honoured practice, back in the day, I do today with pipettes and test-tubes and so on."

Iphigenia pulled a skeptical face, but Jenna was intrigued. "And this is how you make your money?"

Cassandra laughed. "I'm hardly starving, am I, love? I have clients on every continent. They can purchase my treatments – all tailored to their requirements – or they can enrol in my correspondence course and learn the skills of the trade for themselves."

"Coo..." Jenna said. Her eyes slid to the textbooks stacked on the dresser. Perhaps there were alternatives to A Levels after all...

Iphigenia didn't like the way her granddaughter was looking at their colourful visitor. There was admiration – perhaps adulation – in the young woman's eyes and, as for the guest, she was basking in the attention, lapping it up like a cat locked in a creamery. Slapping the table, Iphigenia got to her feet. She made a pantomime of yawning and stretching, and of looking at the clock, and being astounded by how late it was getting. Taking the hint, Cassandra stood up too and thrust her arms into the sleeves of her bright yellow mackintosh.

"Time I was hitting the road," she sighed, amused by the distraught pout the announcement elicited from her latest admirer.

"You could stay here!" Jenna cried, jumping up. "You can have my room and I'll have the sofa."

Iphigenia looked to the ceiling for inner fortitude.

"You're very sweet," Cassandra patted Jenna's arm, "Both of you have been so very kind. But I'm all right with my camper van parked behind the pub. The Fox and Grapes – do you know it? Charging me an arm and a leg to use their facilities. To be quite honest with you, I think I'd be better off in the bog."

She laughed, like an operatic soprano warming up.

"Why don't you come and visit me tomorrow?" she offered. "See what being a modern-day bog witch is really like."

"Ooh, yes!" Jenna enthused.

"I'm busy," Iphigenia said, with a sour and surly scowl.

"About ten?" Cassandra suggested, plonking her floppy sou'wester on her head.

"Great!" Jenna said.

"I'll show you out," Iphigenia said. She took two steps back and opened the door.

"Well, goodnight, then," Cassandra waved a pink and pudgy hand.

"Goodnight!" Jenna waved back.

At last she was gone, and Old Ma Spenser rammed the bolts home and turned a key in the lock – neither of which was her customary practice. Usually both the front and back doors were left unlocked overnight, in case of an emergency dash to the privy.

"Will she be all right, Gran?" Jenna chewed her lower lip as she helped to clear the table. "Walking back to town in the dark."

"I should think so," Iphigenia's shawls rose and fell in a shrug. "She is a bog witch, after all."

**

Wendy Rabbitt could not believe her good fortune. The disappearance of Tommy Thornbush had earned her a spot on breakfast television. *National* breakfast television, no less! The producers instructed her to stand in the town square and answer the presenters' questions, which would be along the lines of 'What is the mood in the town?' and 'What are the police doing?'.

Wendy downed her second espresso. The sun was coming up over Little Fladgett. She tried to come up with an opening salvo for her piece. What was that old line about 'a glooming peace this morning with it brings'? Or 'The sun for sorrow will not show its head.' Even though the sun was brightly, palpably, irrefutably, shining. No one was going to argue with a bit of Shakespeare, were they?

All she had been able to garner from Constable Dimwit was that the search would resume – had probably already resumed by now – and there had been what he called 'a significant find' in the closing moments of last night's efforts.

"Do you mean a body?" Wendy had pressed him.

"What? Oh! No! Eww!" the constable had shuddered. "Just a clue, that's all."

"Meaning?"

"Meaning just let us get on with our job."

"I will if you will."

"And what does that mean?"

"It means," Wendy had thrust her microphone under Dimwoodie's chin, "I'm just trying to do my job. Would you care to give a statement on air?"

The constable was puzzled. "Well, we all need to breathe, don't we? Unless you're a fish – or – or a bog witch!"

He seemed startled by his own train of thought.

Give me strength, Wendy appealed to the brightening skies. "I mean a statement live, on the air. You know, on the telly."

But the constable wasn't listening. He strode off, chuntering to himself.

"Live in five, four, three," a voice counted down in Wendy's earpiece. She heard the familiar, famous intonations of the TV presenter, smooth as ironed treacle, announce, "We now go live to Little Fladgett, where our correspondent Wendy Fladgett is at the scene of the disappearance. Good morning, Wendy."

"Actually, it's Rabbitt."

"What is?"

"The name."

"Little Rabbitt."

"No, the town is Little Fladgett. I'm the Rabbitt. You called me Wendy Fladgett?"

"Did I?"

The director intervened with a harsh whisper. "Stick to the fucking point, love. We cut to Weather in two."

Wendy panicked. She coughed. "A glooming sorrow this morning, over the shocked and early morning community here in Little Rabbitt – Fladgett! "

Back in the studio, the presenter pouted solemnly, as if what Wendy had said had made any sense. "And what is the general mood in the town?"

"Well, it's as you'd suspect – expect! People are shocked and upset but there's something about a tragedy like this, isn't there? Brings out the best in people. Everyone's taking part in the search. There's real community spirit here."

"And the police? What can you tell us about their investigation?"

"Well, obviously it's ongoing so it's – still going on. But my sources tell me that before the search was suspended at sunset last night, a *significant find* was made."

"A body?"

"No. A significant find."

"Like what?"

"The police are understandably remaining very tight-lipped on this one. They don't want to tip off any potential suspect that they have a lead."

"Suspects? So, they're treating this as an abduction."

"Well. They're not ruling it out."

"Wendy Rabbitt at Little Fladgett, thank you. Now here's Melinda with the weather. Any chance I can get my shorts out this weekend?"

Wendy yanked out her earpiece. Shit. Shit shit shit.

Her national television debut had not been the glittering moment she had hoped. They would be coming back to her in an hour. She needed something more concrete, more newsworthy to tell them or – even better: show them.

But what the hell might that be?

In the meantime, she had to go back to The Fox and charge her battery pack. The last thing she needed was her own personal news blackout.

As she crossed the car park, her attention was caught by the lime-green camper van stationed there. Just coming out of it, in that bright yellow mackintosh was the stupid woman who had fucked up the ceremony. Perhaps she could be persuaded – no, confronted! Live on air! How does she feel knowing that her shenanigans had resulted in the disappearance, possibly kidnapping, possibly murder even, of a sweet little boy?

Wendy smirked in anticipation. She would probably get a news Bafta for this one.

***

"Excuse me," Wendy approached the woman in the mackintosh. "Could I have a word?"

Cassandra Clune looked the interloper up and down. "You can have two if you want. And I don't mean 'Merry Christmas'."

She locked her camper van and, depositing the keys in a bumbag at her hip, strode away. Wendy found she had to scurry to keep up with her quarry; for a large lady, she reflected, Cassandra Clune couldn't half shift.

"I'd like a minute of your time."

"What for?" Cassandra didn't deign to turn around.

"Some people are saying it's your fault."

"Oh, yeah? What is?"

"The little boy. Going missing. They say you're to blame."

There. That stopped her in her tracks.

Cassandra drew herself up to her full, intimidating height. Wendy began to wonder if this was how the moon felt during an eclipse.

"Who are you?" Cassandra boomed. "Why are you harassing me?"

A little crestfallen at not being recognised yet again, Wendy shook her head. "I'm not harassing you. I only want to ask you a few questions. Is that OK?" She whipped out a digital video camera, seemingly from nowhere. "Is this OK?"

Cassandra's button mushroom nose wrinkled in a sneer. "A reporter," she diagnosed, as though identifying a smell.

"It's a chance to put forward your side of the story."

But Cassandra was walking away.

"There is no side," she huffed. "The only person to blame for that boy's disappearance is whichever sicko who took him."

"So you think he was taken, then?" Wendy resumed pursuit.

"I don't know, do I?"

"You don't think he was taken by the Bog Witch?"

"No!" Cassandra laughed. Was it Wendy's imagination or was the big woman slowing down? Encouraged, she continued.

"You don't think you had any part in this? When it was you who disrupted the ceremony? Don't you think it might be back? The Bog Witch that has kept this community in fear for centuries?"

There. That stopped her in her tracks a second time.

Cassandra jabbed a pudgy finger at the lens. "Listen to me," she growled. "Once and for all. People have to put aside their prejudices against bog witches. They are not supernatural beings. They – we! – are ordinary women who are trying to use our knowledge and skills to help people."

Wendy let out a scornful laugh. "What are you saying? You're a bog witch?"

"I am indeed." Cassandra adopted a haughty stance. "Out and proud!"

Wendy was finding it difficult to hold her camera steady. "Shouldn't you be a bit more..."

"What?"

"I don't know... Mossy?"

With an exhalation of disgust, Cassandra turned away. Wendy, of course, gave chase. Without turning, Cassandra bellowed. "I'm off to join the search for that little boy. If you had any decency, you'd put down your camera and do the same. Or at least put out an appeal. But no, you'd rather harass innocent people, wouldn't you?"

She picked up the pace, leaving Wendy in the street, already dismissing the big woman's parting words. A voice in her earpiece made her jump.

"We're live in five," the director said, hundreds of miles away.

Wendy groaned.

***

The search yielded nothing. Constable Dimwoodie had called in reinforcements from Greater Fladgett and even though the volunteers had doubled in number and redoubled their efforts, no further clues to little Tommy Thornbush's whereabouts had come to light. Councillor Smedley was growing increasingly antsy and irritable. Even though the Little Fladgett Chamber of Commerce assured him that finding the little lad was the priority, he couldn't help worrying how the local economy would be affected.

The best-case scenario would be if the kiddie turned up, unscathed and happy, having wandered off across the bog. No harm done. You know what kids are like, heh-heh. Gave us all quite a scare but it just goes to show how a community can pull together in a time of crisis.

The worst? Well. Smedley didn't like to dwell on the worst. Because it involved the lad turning up dead, and not from any accident.

Oh, they'd flock to the town then! The ghouls. Little Fladgett would be on the map at last but for all the wrong reasons.

Perhaps there was a middle ground. The laddie is found but

he's a bit ill from exposure or what-have-you. Nothing that a couple of days in bed won't sort out. Perhaps some glucose from a drip. That would be preferable, wouldn't it? There would still be a positive spin to the outcome.

Outcome! It was what everyone craved. Tommy's poor mother, at her wits' end, because of the not-knowing. With an outcome of any sort, you can deal with it and move on, terrible though it may be.

But what if there was no outcome? What if Tommy Thornbush never turns up? What then? How long does hope live on?

And what happens to the tourist trade then?

***

During the days that followed, both hope and the search dwindled. With a heart like a cold ball of lead, Constable Dimwoodie officially called off the hunt. The reinforcements went back to Greater Fladgett and the local volunteers resumed their daily lives. There was a pall of sorrow over Little Fladgett and the streets, so recently festooned with greenery, were now tatty with deteriorating posters bearing the smiling, innocent face of little Tommy Thornbush.

Wendy Rabbitt had run out of people to interview. She had also worn out her welcome at the Fox and Grapes. Brenda the barmaid took great pleasure in handing the reporter an itemised invoice, which Wendy tried to hand back at once. Brenda folded her arms in refusal.

"But I've booked until the end of the week," Wendy protested.

"Calendar malfunction," Brenda sniffed. "Whole place is going to be chocka on account of the beer festival this weekend. Always is this time of year. I'm pre-booked."

"Then perhaps I could cover the festival for you? Make this pub the heart of it? Community hub and all that. Folk getting on with their lives after this recent, ah, upset."

Brenda sneered at the word. "It was tragic what happened

to that kiddie." She slammed the electronic card reader on the counter. "Just insert your PIN and bugger off. No need for a tip."

Wendy paid, insisting on a receipt. The station would stump up to reimburse her. What an unholy waste of time the whole palaver had turned out to be. She headed for the stairs.

"Er – where are you going?" Brenda called out in surprise.

"My room," Wendy smiled sweetly. "I've paid for the day and checkout time is not until three."

She didn't allow her face to fall until she had closed the door to her room behind her.

Shit.

Shit, shit!

She began to throw clothes into her suitcase. The sound of an engine revving and rumbling drew her to the window. Down in the car park, that plus-size lunatic's lurid green camper van was farting black smoke as if to conceal itself from predators.

What a racket! Wendy returned to her packing. Then she froze.

Maybe the fat nutter had the right idea – well, *one* right idea at least. Perhaps I should hire a van like that... That way I'd be able to come and go as I please and not have to resort to shit-holes like this.

She shook a woodlouse from the bra she had snatched from a drawer.

A right shithole.

She put her packing on hold and hung out of the window in order to get sufficient reception to google nearby van rental places. The lime green monstrosity was just pulling away.

Where are you off to, Fatzilla? Wendy wondered. And should I be following?

***

Cassandra rang the doorbell and stepped back, steeling herself. Perhaps I should have left the engine running, she wondered. In case I have to make a quick getaway...

A moment or two passed. Cassandra grimaced. Ought I to ring again? Would that seem like impatience? Like harassment? Heaven knows the poor woman had enough tribulations on her plate.

No. I'll wait. Give it another couple of minutes. Then I'll pop my business card through the letterbox so she'll know I've been. Like I said I would.

When the call had come from little Tommy Thornbush's mother, Cassandra could not have been more surprised if she'd heard from His Holiness the Pope. All the woman had said, in a flat monotone that indicated she was drained of emotion, was that she had found the phone number online and she wanted to meet. She had given the address and rang off before Cassandra could ask to what the meeting might pertain.

She probably wants to tear a strip off me, Cassandra reckoned. People often did, lashing out in their ignorance and pain. But, like she always told the girl at the parlour where she got her legs waxed, the quicker the strip got torn off the better. Sometimes all people needed was an outlet, a chance to vent, and someone like Cassandra, the eternal outsider, the weirdo with outlandish ideas, fitted the bill. People would keep it together for their nearest and dearest, shielding them from the full extent of the trauma, but a stranger made a perfect outlet.

A shadow moved and grew in the glass panel of Tina Thornbush's front door, which then opened a little – enough for Cassandra to see a sharp nose and a bloodshot eye over the length of brass chain. The eye moved up and down. The door closed long enough for the chain to be unhooked and then opened wide, revealing a hunch-shouldered figure, dowdy from days of self-neglect.

"Miss Clune," she said, in a rasping voice, rendered harsh from sobbing.

Cassandra twitched. "Actually, it's Mx."

"I'm sorry?" Confusion clouded the distraught face.

"Mx!"

"Have you got something in your throat? Would you like a

glass of water?"

"Call me Cassandra," Mx Clune smiled diplomatically.

"Please," Tina stepped back. "Come in."

She's not going to harangue me on the doorstep, Cassandra realised as she stepped over the threshold. Was that a good sign? Or a bad?

She waited while the door was closed and the chain re-attached, then followed the woman's plodding footsteps into a living room, dark with closed curtains.

"Please." Tina gave a quick stab of her finger in the direction of the sofa. Cassandra smiled her thanks and lowered herself onto the upholstery. Although there was a brace of armchairs, Tina Thornbush opted for a more austere, hard-backed chair that was part of her dining room set.

She's punishing herself, Cassandra diagnosed. Thinks she's to blame for her son's disappearance.

Perhaps she is.

Tina Thornbush worked her fingertips as though counting them over and over. Cassandra waited, smiling patiently and sympathetically. Even though the small woman appeared thoroughly drained and exhausted, Cassandra knew people could often summon up the energy and vitriol from somewhere in order to let rip with a good old cathartic rant.

Eventually, Cassandra's hostess lifted her head and spoke.

"I found your number online."

"Yes," Cassandra continued to smile, even though her cheeks were starting to ache a little.

"I knew you were in town," Tina continued. "The parade. The television."

"Ah. Well. I shall be out of your hair soon, don't you worry."

"Oh, no!" Tina cried out in alarm. "You mustn't!"

Cassandra was puzzled. "You don't want me to leave?"

"No!"

"You don't think –"

"What? I don't think you're to blame for what happened to – Tommy. I don't think that at all."

Cassandra was more baffled than ever. "Then what..."

"Why did I invite you here?" Tina sat up straight and fixed Cassandra with a red-rimmed stare. "Ms Clune. Mx. Cassandra. You are a witch, aren't you?"

"Well, yes. Sort of."

"And you deal with – things us ordinary folk don't."

"Up to my knees in it, usually." Cassandra had no idea where this interview was heading.

"Then perhaps you can help me."

"If I can, I will."

"Good. I want you to use your witchery, or whatever you call it, and contact the Other Side – or whatever it is, and ask them, whoever they are, what has happened to my little boy."

More than a little stunned, Cassandra blinked rapidly. "I'm not sure –"

Tina Thornbush lost what composure she had. "The police have come up with nothing!" she wept. "The search has been called off. I don't know where else I can turn. Oh, please, say you'll help me! I don't know what else I can do."

Her narrow shoulders heaved as, wracked with dry sobs, the distraught and frightened mother crumpled into her own lap. Cassandra extended a comforting hand to gently pat the woman's back.

"There, there," she cooed. "I'll give it a go, eh?"

***

She had to clear the passenger seat of biscuit wrappers and recyclable coffee cups before she could guide Tina Thornbush into the camper van. The smaller woman was practically somnambulating. Cassandra found she had to strap her seatbelt on for her. Tina stared blankly ahead, her face grey in the afternoon sun. Cassandra had explained, although she was not sure how much (if any) of it had filtered through the catatonia to Tina's brain. As soon as Cassandra had agreed to conduct a séance, the poor woman had shut down, turning in on herself like an introverted snail.

Cassandra knew she would need more boots on the ground – well, hands on the table, if she was going to make a good fist of leading a séance. She had never done one before and a couple of quick peeks at YouTube only reinforced the idea that she was hopelessly out of her depth. But, she was willing to put aside her own feelings of inadequacy, not to mention her skepticism, for the sake of the wreck of a woman to her left.

As to who should make up the quorum, Cassandra had few acquaintances in the vicinity who would be likely candidates. She turned the ignition key. The engine shuddered to life, the entire chassis vibrating with potential.

Cassandra took a road leading out of the town centre, retracing the route of the ill-fated procession. A little while later, the lime green camper van pulled up outside the cottage of Iphigenia Spenser and her granddaughter Jenna.

"Here we are!" Cassandra announced with a bright smile and a sharp yank of the handbrake.

Tina Thornbush blinked. Slowly.

That's something, I suppose, thought Cassandra.

***

Jenna and her grandmother required little persuasion. They agreed to participate in Cassandra's séance at once – although Iphigenia insisted on pronouncing the word to rhyme with Beyoncé, giving rise to much eye-rolling from Jenna.

"It's a good excuse to use up the scented candles you always give me for Christmas." Iphigenia rooted around in a kitchen cupboard. "And I've got that nice tablecloth with the lace. I was saving it for best – well, who better than a visitor from Beyond The Veil?"

Jenna was excited. It was like the films. You know the ones, where a bunch of reckless teenagers dabble with things they shouldn't (including each other) and then they get bumped off in increasingly horrible and gratuitously violent ways... These thoughts gave Jenna pause. Ah, but, she reassured herself, we're not a bunch of reckless teenagers. In fact, I'm the only teenager – she gulped. Did that make her the prime target of any vengeful spirit?

She had to remind herself that she was not living in a work of fiction, was not starring in her own biopic. Cassandra was a professional, wasn't she? She knew what she was doing, didn't she? They weren't in any danger at all. Were they?

It was all a bit of a laugh, wasn't it?

No.

It was to help that poor woman. Try to give her some peace of mind.

Jenna couldn't imagine what Tina Thornbush must be going through. To have a child go missing! Awful. She supposed putting your phone down and momentarily losing track of it probably didn't go halfway to match the panic, the cold and clammy hand of fear that grips your heart and gives it a squeeze...

Cassandra commandeered the front room and was issuing orders and requests. Draw the curtains! Turn the lights off! Wait! Turn the lights on again, then light the candles, then turn the lights off.

Iphigenia grumbled, having barked her shin on a chair that had been moved from its customary position.

While Iphigenia and Jenna busied themselves, Tina Thornbush sat in silence with the blank expression of a doll. Cassandra made several surreptitious consultations of her phone. Google had provided hundreds of sites with instructions on how to hold a séance. There were some contradictions, but Cassandra thought they couldn't go far wrong if they kept things simple and stuck to the basics. One thing on which all the websites agreed was there should be no distractions, which included and necessitated the switching off of all electronic devices. Once things go under way, Cassandra would be on her own with no helpful search engine to advise her.

"Aww," Jenna complained when she heard this instruction. "I was going to do a story for my Instagram."

Cassandra was firm on the matter. "We must not annoy the

spirits," she warned, although it was with an equal measure of reluctance that she too switched off her phone. From there on in, she was flying solo.

She gestured grandly at the round table that had been given pride of place in the centre of the room. Candles flickered on every available surface, their fragrances competing for dominance.

"It smells like a whores' beauty pageant," Iphigenia observed, taking a seat at Cassandra's right. Jenna slipped onto the chair at Cassandra's left and Tina Thornbush surprised everyone by moving of her own volition to the empty seat opposite the medium. Jenna reminded herself why they were doing this and resolved to keep her giggles to a minimum.

Cassandra looked at each participant in turn and smiled warmly. She was doing a fine job of projecting a calm and assured exterior, while on the inside, her heart was attempting a jail break by hurling itself repeatedly at the bars of her rib cage.

"Now," she began, her voice slightly lower in her professional register, "The first thing to say is that we must have no expectations. The spirits may prove incommunicative. On the other hand, there might be so many of them wishing to get through, their messages might be garbled and unclear."

Tina Thornbush nodded, as though already resigned to failure.

"Are you sure you wish to continue?" Cassandra asked.

"Yes, yes!" Tina met her gaze with desperate eyes. "Anything you can do. I know I'm probably being silly and, like you said, I shouldn't expect anything, but please! If there is anything. Anything at all."

"We can but try," Cassandra reached across the table to squeeze the poor woman's hand. "But let's have no more of this talk of being silly, shall we? Positive thoughts and positive energy only. Now, this is how we do it."

She took a stick of chalk and wrote YES and NO in two squares on the table. Iphigenia bit back a pained outburst. Her best tablecloth!

Cassandra placed an upturned wine glass in the gap between the squares. "We shall each place a fingertip lightly on the glass. No pushing, if you please! Relax and let the spirits guide us. I shall be the medium, the conduit for this sitting."

Iphigenia chuckled. Jenna knew she was dying to crack the old joke: Medium? Extra large more like! She sent her grandmother a warning look and wondered if it would count as positive energy to kick an old woman's shin under the table. Iphigenia composed herself, her eyes twinkling with candle flames.

As one, the women reached for the glass and placed the tips of their index fingers on its base.

"Good," Cassandra said. "Now, for the sake of clarity, we can only ask questions that have a Yes or No answer. Is that understood?"

"Like that game, Jen," Iphigenia interrupted. "That game your dad used to play with you. And every time you said Yes or No, he pinched one of your Jelly Tots. Do you remember?"

"Yes," Jenna said, prickling at the memory.

"Good job we're not playing now," Iphigenia cackled. "You would have lost again."

"Gran..." Jenna pleaded.

"Oops," Iphigenia said, remembering what they were trying to achieve.

Cassandra made a big deal of clearing her throat. She tilted her head from side to side, stretching her unseen neck. With a final cough, she closed her eyes and asked the first question.

"Is there anyone here who has information for us?"

Her words hung in the air. After a few seconds of silence, Cassandra opened one eye. Mrs Spenser was smiling encouragingly. The granddaughter was looking intently at the upturned glass, and Tina Thornbush – Cassandra's open eye widened when it was struck by the full intensity of the mother's glare. A little unsettled, Cassandra closed her eye and shifted her buttocks on the inadequate dining-room chair. She repeated the question and again it was met with silence and inactivity. She tried another tack.

"Is there anyone who wishes to speak to us? Anyone at all? Come through, o spirit; pass through the veil."

Jenna was thrilled to hear vocabulary from some of the films she had seen. Her gran was also impressed, but Tina Thornbush continued to glare.

"Spirit?" Cassandra ventured, hopefully.

The glass juddered. Jenna let out a yelp and sprang back.

"Ooh," said her grandmother, "You better stick your finger back on it, chicken. I think we've had a breakthrough."

Jenna was uncertain. "It wasn't you, giving it a push? I know what you're like."

"On my honour," Iphigenia grinned. Jenna looked to Cassandra, who nodded. Jenna cautiously replaced her finger on the glass.

"Remember," Cassandra said, softly, "Positive thoughts, positive energy. Now," she upped her volume, "Are you there, o spirit?"

At first, there was nothing, but then, slowly, almost imperceptibly to begin with, the glass edged away from the centre of the table, heading for the square marked YES. Jenna had the sensation of her finger being dragged along with the glass. A shudder shimmied through her.

"Yes!" Iphigenia announced. "Well, he wasn't going to say No, was he? Is it a he? What's his name? Ask him his name."

"Gran!" Jenna snapped. "She can't do that, can she?"

"Why not?"

"Unless his name is Yes or No, it's not going to work, is it?"

Iphigenia thought about it. "I suppose not, no."

Cassandra's face was a mask of patience. "May we continue?" she smiled – not without effort. "Have you something to tell us, o spirit?"

They watched and waited.

Nothing happened.

"Does that mean Yes?" Iphigenia asked. "It's still on the Yes."

A sigh escaped Cassandra. "Oh, yes, we have to reset the glass after every question."

She moved the glass back to the centre. They all put their fingers on it and waited.

"Ask it again," Iphigenia prompted. "Go on."

Cassandra closed her eyes and took a deep breath. Perhaps this was a mistake. The old woman wouldn't shut up, the girl was too skittish, and the – ah! Cassandra remembered why she was putting herself through this ordeal, why she was risking her professional reputation. For Tina.

Pushing down a surge of negative thoughts, she asked again if the spirit had something to tell. The glass moved again, returning to the same square as before.

YES.

"Is it animal, vegetable, or mineral?" Iphigenia addressed the glass. Everyone did their best to ignore her. Cassandra reset the glass.

"Do you have something to tell us about Tommy Thornbush?"

The glass vibrated under their fingertips, as though considering its response. Then it set off across to the YES square.

Around the table, three sighs of relief. But Tina Thornbush was frowning, staring intently at the glass as though she was trying to shatter it with her thoughts.

"Is he alive?" Cassandra asked quietly.

Again, the glass juddered on the spot before, at last, approaching the YES option.

Jenna gasped. Cassandra fanned her own face with her free hand. Iphigenia was watching the boy's mother, who was breathing heavily and glaring like a bull about to charge.

Cassandra put the glass back and posed the next question. "Has the – has the Bog Witch got him?"

There was an almighty roar. It came from Tina Thornbush, who sprang to her feet and flipped the table in a surprising show of supernatural strength. Eyes wild, teeth bared, she tore from the cottage, panting like a wild animal.

The three remaining women blinked at each other in shock.

"Well, shit," Iphigenia mourned. "That was one of my best

glasses."

***

At the window, peering through a crack in the curtains and witnessing the entire ritual, had been local TV reporter, Wendy Rabbitt. 'Had been' because when the enraged woman burst from the cottage, she collided with the reporter and flung her into a hedge. Somewhat stunned, Wendy sat in the privet, considering her next course of action. Either she could enter the cottage and demand to know what the fuck was going on, or she could pursue the fleeing woman, who seemed rather upset about something. It was a tough one.

Pulling herself from the foliage, Wendy limped off after the Thornbush woman. The cottage could wait; it wasn't going anywhere.

She jogged along the lane, using her smartphone as a torch. There were no streetlamps this far out of town, of course. The council tax wouldn't run to it, she supposed.

She could hear rather than see the distraught mother lumbering ahead, her breath loud and low like a massive dog's. Wendy too was beginning to puff and pant, unaccustomed to prolonged outbursts of physical activity. After a few minutes she had to stop for a breather, by which time further pursuit was futile. She had lost track. Oh well, she could always head back to the cottage and grill those three idiots.

She turned back. The glare of her flashlight app illuminated the figure of Tina Thornbush directly in front of her, her features contorted into a demonic sneer. Her eyes were hooded, aflame with malevolence, and there was something mannish about her stance, something... evil. Understandably, Wendy Rabbitt let out a scream. She dropped her phone as she turned to run, plunging into the darkness, not daring to look over her shoulder to see if the transformed figure of Tina Thornbush was giving chase. Certain she could feel the *thing's* breath on her neck, Wendy stumbled blindly, twisting her ankle in a rut, crashing through a perimeter hedge, and falling onto her hands and knees into wet and boggy mud. Whimpering, she clawed and crawled along, clambering over stones, splashing through puddles, until the swampy ground tugged at her feet, sucking at her shoes until she was forced to a standstill.

Making noises a frightened puppy would be ashamed of, Wendy tried to see all around her, having completely lost her bearings. The night was as dark as God's nostril. An owl hooted a cliché somewhere in the distance. Wendy jumped.

I am in the bog, she realised with a wail of terror.

Where better for a bog witch to come and claim me?

***

Cassandra got no sleep. She trundled around the country lanes all night – in her camper van, of course – looking for Tina Thornbush. The poor woman had rushed off in such an agitated state, Cassandra feared she might have done herself a mischief. The beams of her headlights threw every bump in the rutted roads into stark relief, casting distorted shadows. Each one, to Cassandra's nervous eyes, looked like a dead body. But none of them was. Around the metal sanctuary of her van, the bog sprawled as though lying in wait, a sleeping beast, a behemoth waiting for prey. Silly moo, Cassandra scolded herself. You're only scaring yourself.

As dawn broke and the dimmer switch in the sky turned slowly to ON, Cassandra turned the van around and headed back to the cottage in case there was any news there. Jenna had said she would text if there was but way out in the wilds, phone reception was as scarce a commodity as peace of mind.

Neither Jenna nor her grandmother had been to bed, opting to stay up in case the Thornbush woman came back.

"She's left her cardigan for one thing," Iphigenia observed. "She won't want to be without that. It's from Marks."

They heard the camper van pull up and went to the doorstep.

"Any word?" Cassandra asked as she got out.

Jenna shook her head sadly.

"No," Iphigenia said. "You?"

"Gran! She wouldn't have asked us if she'd found her, would she?"

Iphigenia scowled. "Suppose not."

"I've been all over," Cassandra said. "But, not knowing the area very well, I might have missed the odd turn-off or two. Perhaps when it gets light proper, I'll go out again."

"I'll come with you," Jenna offered.

Cassandra looked doubtful. "I don't know if it's a good idea, dear."

"Why not? I'll bring a flask."

"It's just that –" she cast a precautionary glance over her shoulder and then ushered the others indoors, "It's just that – well, if what I think happened last night happened last night, it might not be safe. Finding her."

Jenna was puzzled.

"What do you think happened last night?" Iphigenia prompted.

"Well..." Cassandra looked askance in her reluctance.

"Out with it!" Iphigenia snapped. Then she cackled. "I haven't said that since my wedding night."

"Gran!" Jenna turned strawberry red.

Cassandra bustled through the front room and into the kitchen, pointedly averting her gaze from the table. Jenna and her gran had restored the furniture to order but Cassandra was strangely quiet until she had installed herself at the kitchen table and the others had joined her.

"Now," Iphigenia said. "What's going on?"

Cassandra looked at her pink little hands, which were writhing together like randy octopuses. Then she looked dead ahead.

"We made contact last night." Her voice was small, as though her throat was constricted.

"What?" Jenna said. "You mean all that moving-the-glass stuff was actually really real?"

"I thought it was you," Iphigenia said. "Pushing that glass

around to make that poor woman feel better."

Cassandra squirmed. "Well… it was. A bit. There was an element of – Let's just say I had some influence on the responses – but that's not what I'm talking about."

She pressed her lips together. Jenna and her gran leaned in.

"You're not talking about it at all," Iphigenia pointed out. Jenna, exasperated, shook her head. She gave Cassandra's wrist a squeeze.

"You saw how she got," Cassandra's lips worked as though she was in a poorly dubbed film. "Tina. How she changed. Little thing like her, how did she get the strength to flip the table over? I'm not sure I could do that. Did you see her eyes, her face? Like they were no longer hers."

"What are you saying?" A vague sensation of dread was tickling Jenna's backbone.

"I'm saying," Cassandra swallowed a lump of air, "We made contact with a spirit all right. And that spirit got into the weakest of us – mentally speaking, I mean."

Jenna sat back, stunned.

"Who?" Iphigenia urged. "Who got into Tina Thornbush and flipped my table and smashed one of my best glasses? Who?"

Cassandra was at a loss. "I don't know. But I have an inkling, a terrible feeling in the pit of my stomach, that we have aroused something very dark, very evil."

"Like what?" Jenna asked in a voice that was little more than a squeak.

Cassandra shook her head. She did not want to give voice to her suspicions.

"Spit it out!" Iphigenia slapped the table. Then she chuckled, "I haven't heard that since my wedding night."

"I think," Cassandra summoned the strength to speak, "I think we may have summoned the actual Bog Witch."

***

There had used to be a public library in Little Fladgett, a small yet somehow imposing structure that had housed a decaying collection of dusty, musty and fusty volumes that no one ever consulted. The councillors in their wisdom had closed it down years ago and allowed a carpet warehouse to take over the lease. Nowadays, the locals had to make do with an ad hoc stack of books left in an old phone box, which was all right if you wanted to take pot luck on a bit of random fiction to entertain you, but no good at all if you needed to research local history.

And so, early in the morning after their attempt at a séance, Jenna and Cassandra rode in the camper van to Greater Fladgett, their bags bulging with packed lunches provided by Jenna's gran. "Brain food, that is," the old woman had beamed proudly as she waved them off from the doorstep, leading Jenna to think of zombie films for some reason.

Cassandra had to manoeuvre awkwardly around a car that someone had left or parked or abandoned at the cottage gate. She swore under her breath as she strained behind the steering wheel. Whose the hell was it? No consideration, some people.

A quick call to Tina Thornbush's landline had yielded nothing more than a 'What do you want?' and a 'Leave me alone!', so at least they knew she had got home safe if not exactly sound.

"I'll check in on her later," Cassandra announced. "Give her a chance to calm down a bit after last night."

Jenna merely nodded. She had been frightened when Tina Thornbush had flipped both the table and her lid. The demonic expression on her face had kept Jenna awake for most of the night. Cassandra was no longer pushing the idea that Tina Thornbush had been possessed by the Bogwitch; instead, she made offhand remarks about documented cases of mothers gaining superhuman strength at times of great stress. Jenna chose not to press the point. This explanation was much more palatable.

Nevertheless, they were off to arm themselves with information 'just in case'.

They drove across the bog, which even in the morning sunshine managed to appear desolate and foreboding. All the colour seemed to have been leached out of the moss and the wildflowers. Like a black and white film, thought Jenna. Extra creepy.

They had to pass through Little Fladgett to get to the B-road that would take them to its larger neighbour. On the High Street, the handful of shops were opening up. Shopkeepers setting out their wares and their A-boards, paused to give the passing camper van a cold appraisal, as though there was something offensive about its lime-green hue. Jenna shrank in her seat, nervous under their blank scrutiny. An eerie silence pervaded the air, seeping into the van, hanging heavy around Jenna's ears until Cassandra's pudgy thumb stabbed at the radio, startling Jenna with a burst of music.

"That's better." Cassandra tapped along on the rim of the steering wheel. "Can't go wrong with *Funky Cold Medina*. The oldies are the besties."

Jenna was not so sure, but they had reached the end of the High Street and therefore the town, so she sat up straight. And almost jumped from her skin as the wind slapped a poster of little Tommy Thornbush on the windscreen. The boy stared at Jenna in both plea and accusation until the wind peeled the paper away again and set it dancing in the air.

"As if we needed a reminder," Cassandra tutted. "What we're doing all this for."

Jenna gave a hum of agreement. According to last night's activities, the little boy was still alive – unless it had all been a load of bollocks, stage-managed by Cassandra in a bid to make the poor mother feel better.

The song gave way to blaring, urgent jingles, heralding a news bulletin.

"Fear and suspicion continue to stalk the streets of Little Fladgett. The quiet, bogside town was rocked to its foundations two weeks ago when three-year-old Tommy Thornbush went missing, believed snatched, during the annual bog witch festivities. While some point the finger of blame at outsiders who disrupted proceedings, thereby providing a distraction for the kidnapper. A painstaking search of the immediate area yielded nothing, and police say they have interviewed a potential suspect who was subsequently released without charge."

"That'll be me!" Cassandra beamed with pride. "They're talking about me on the radio!"

"I don't think it's anything to boast about," Jenna grumbled.

"No such thing as bad publicity," Cassandra grinned.

"They didn't mention your name," Jenna pointed out.

"Nit-picker!" Cassandra snapped.

They both laughed.

The voice emanating from the speakers gave way to that of Councillor Obadiah Smedley. "It is the council's view that people have nothing to fear," he droned. "The kidnapping was an opportunistic crime – if indeed it was a kidnapping. We still don't know if the little boy didn't wander off of his own accord. But, rest assured, the Banishing of the Bogwitch will be back next year. Bigger than ever. There's even talk of fireworks."

The councillor was cut off mid-promo.

"We now speak to local law enforcement officer, Constable Daniel Dimwoodie, who is on the line now. Good morning."

"Morning," Dimwoodie's voice crackled.

"How are things in Little Fladgett?"

"In some ways, life goes on like before," Dimwoodie sounded sad. "Well, it does, doesn't it? It has to."

"Constable Dimwoodie, would you say that you are overwhelmed by the enormity of what's going on in your town?"

"Sorry, I have to go."

There was a click, followed by the dialling tone.

The newsreader sounded triumphant. "We'll bring you more on this story as it happens."

A trombone parped the jingle for some haemorrhoid cream. Cassandra switched the radio off.

They drove on in grim silence.

***

Tommy Thornbush woke up. Sort of. Still groggy from the 'medicine' he had been given, he rubbed his eyelids. The Man had said the medicine would make him feel better, although he didn't remember feeling poorly. The room was dark. Shadowy figures loomed and even though Tommy knew they were only boxes, he didn't like them in the dark. He wanted his mummy.

There were sweeties in bowls and Tommy had gorged on them until he'd made himself sick and the Man had been angry, but he didn't shout and he didn't make Tommy cry, but Tommy had cried anyway, so the Man had given him more medicine to make him feel better. As far as Tommy could tell, 'feeling better' meant the same as going to sleep.

He wanted his mummy.

***

Cassandra pulled up outside the library in Greater Fladgett but kept the motor idling.

"Out you pop," she smiled at Jenna, who frowned in return.

"Aren't you coming with?"

Cassandra shook her head. "Divide and conquer. You go and put your shit-hot study skills to good use in the archives."

"And what will you be doing?"

"Oh, putting my own special skill set to work. You know, the personal touch."

Jenna did not know, but she let herself out of the van. "But you'll pick me up later, yeah?"

"Of course!" Cassandra beamed. "Bang on closing time. Ta-ta!"

She waved and Jenna shut the passenger door. The younger woman watched the almost luminous camper van pull into traffic, eliciting a few angry honks and beeps from other vehicles. When Cassandra was out of sight, Jenna's shoulders slumped. A whole day rooting around in the library. Not her first choice for a day out. She was supposed to be on holiday, damn it.

Then she remembered the poster of little Tommy Thornbush that had startled her and felt a blush of shame as she was reminded why she was there.

If we have raised *the* Bogwitch, Cassandra had said, we need to know exactly who – or what – we're dealing with. It's a bit like fire extinguishers if you think about it. Different ones are for different fires. They're all colour coded. Your electrical fire. Your chemical fire. You can't just use any bog-standard extinguisher – why are you laughing? Oh, right, 'bog standard'! See, I'm hilarious without even trying. But you take my meaning. We need to find the right way to extinguish the Bogwitch. Knowledge is power, so I want you to fill your notebook and your brain with all the pertinent information you can dig up.

Jenna trudged through the main entrance and consulted a Perspex sign that listed all the sections of the library.

"Archives, third floor," she murmured. She went in search of a lift. And found one, but it was out of order, so she had to haul herself up six flights of stairs.

The double doors with ARCHIVES stencilled on their glass panels were locked. "Opening Times 10:00 til 4:00" a sign informed her.

Great start, Jenna scowled, checking the time on her smartphone. Forty minutes to kill...

She went all the way down to the library's coffee shop in the basement and ordered a skinny white.

It was going to be a long day.

***

Cassandra doubled back, circumventing Little Fladgett and edging around the far side of Potlar's Bog toward more cultivated land. A long, high wall ran alongside the road, the perimeter of the grounds of Fladgett Hall, her urgent destination. She drove through the gates and along the drive until a man in a high-vis tabard ushered her to a side car park labelled 'Coaches'.

Charming, Cassandra muttered, but she was not disposed to

arguing. Not just yet at any rate. She locked the van, slung her capacious bag over her shoulder and strode to the front of the building with a determined look in her eye.

Originally Elizabethan, Fladgett Hall had been added to and 'improved' by every incumbent squire throughout its history, and now it was a striking if clumsy agglomeration of architectural features. Wattle-and-daub elevations cringed behind neoclassical pilasters. A Romanesque portico sported mock-gothic gargoyles whose reptilian hands shielded their eyes from the Frank Lloyd-Wright extension to the eastern wing. The building had never enjoyed listed status, and the succession of squires had taken full advantage of this to stamp their indelible mark on the estate. It was, in short, a mess. A sprawling, expensive mess, as though Victor Frankenstein had taken up architecture while off his tits on laudanum. To assist with the upkeep of the monstrosity of wood, brick, thatch, glass, and stone, guided tours were on offer. For an extortionate fee (compared to the price of a cinema ticket) members of the public and hordes of schoolchildren were shepherded around the house and drip-fed nuggets of the building's history. There was a tour due to start at ten o'clock. Hence the urgency of Cassandra Clune.

A wooden sign on a pole instructed tour parties to queue at the foot of the steps that led to the main entrance. Cassandra obeyed. There was no other bugger in evidence, she realised, glancing around. Good! She would have the guide all to herself. All the better to give them a grilling.

At ten o'clock precisely, a woman in a pencil skirt emerged from the main entrance, the brass buttons on her crimson blazer glinting in the morning sunshine. She approached the 'Q Here' sign with caution.

"Morning," Cassandra said cheerily.

The guide tried to peer around her.

"Oh, dear. You're not the Cardinal Wolsey School, are you?"

"Only at weekends," quipped Cassandra.

The woman ignored her. Instead, she addressed some remarks to a walkie-talkie.

"No. No sign of them, no. Perhaps they're stuck on the motorway."

The response crackled and popped so much Cassandra imagined a dolphin on the other end pouring milk into a bowl of cereal. She watched the guide's face fall.

"Ah."

She pocketed the walkie-talkie and turned a professionally blank expression to Cassandra. "I am sorry but the ten o'clock tour is cancelled."

"Eh?" Cassandra was baffled.

"Due to lack of interest."

"But I'm here! I'm interested. Like you wouldn't believe."

The guide flinched. "I was expecting a school trip. Only now I find out they're not coming. Parents terrified the Bogwitch is going to make off with their little angels. Honestly."

"Ah." Cassandra pursed her lips in sympathy. "Then, perhaps the little chat we're going to have will prove mutually beneficial. Coffee shop this way, is it?"

**

"Newspapers don't go back that far," said the archives assistant with the slightest of sneers. "Back then it wasn't like it is nowadays."

"No, I suppose not," Jenna mumbled. It would be too easy if it was. "But you must have something from back then."

The archives assistant pursed her thin lips. "Not exactly from back then..."

"Oh," Jenna was downcast.

"...but something *about* back then, if I remember rightly. Wait there."

Before Jenna could respond, the archives assistant disappeared into a back room with a glint in her eye. Nonplussed, Jenna gazed around. There were posters for an exhibition about the local peat-cutting industry. Scintillating! There were advertisements for websites where you could look up your family tree. Above all, there was the all-pervading aroma of musty paper that no amount of plug-in air fresheners could hide. There was also something inescapably gloomy about the place with all those old volumes lining the shelves, that no amount of fluorescent strip lighting could dispel.

Creepy, thought Jenna. She wondered how long the woman would be. There had already been three texts from Cassandra, asking how Jenna was getting on, that Jenna had yet to answer. So far, the morning had been a complete waste of time, unless you counted the increase in caffeination as a plus.

Beaming with the pride of a challenge completed, the archives assistant re-emerged bearing a box with a hinged lid and a faded, handwritten label.

"I knew I'd seen something somewhere," she grinned, setting the box on the desk. Jenna's fingers itched to open it but the woman thrust a proforma at Jenna's face. "I need you to sign here. I'm afraid one may not take materials out of this room, but there are study carrels available over there."

"Um," Jenna said. "What about photocopying? May one do that?"

The assistant's face hardened as though stricken by a sudden frost. "I am afraid not. This book is too delicate and fragile. One is, of course, free to take notes."

Whoopee, thought Jenna. When your back is turned, Mrs, I'm going to take pictures with my phone.

She let herself be ushered to a cluster of desks separated by short partitions and furnished with green-shaded lamps. It's like something out of a film, Jenna enthused. And I'm going to discover a long-lost secret or a curse or something...

When the assistant had returned to her station, Jenna opened the box. She took out a small, hidebound volume that was bloated from some long-ago water damage. The cover was bare, apart from a few stains, and Jenna had to hold the spine under the lamp to make out the title imprinted there.

"Being a True Account of the Historye of Potlars Bogge in the Borough of Fladgett."

Jenna smiled.

This'll do for starters, she thought.

***

"Top up?" Cassandra pointed at the tour guide's empty coffee cup.

"I'd better not," the woman looked regretful. "I've got a party due at two and if I have any more caffeine, I'll zoom around the house like a greyhound on a rocket."

"You've been very helpful," Cassandra smiled. She took out her purse. "Let me give you something."

The tour guide looked offended. "Oh, I couldn't possibly –"

Cassandra held out a business card. "It's just a free consultation. Any time you like."

The tour guide looked disappointed. Cassandra got to her feet. Her chair legs squawked and the table juddered with a tremor. She gave the tour guide's hand a tight little squeeze and bade her farewell.

"Er – um," the tour guide stalled. "None of this came from me. If His Lordship – I mean, I like this job and I'd like to keep it."

Cassandra tapped the side of her nose. "Mum's the word." Her face twisted into a conspiratorial wink.

She walked in quick, short steps back to the van, eager to tell Jenna what she had discovered. Emitting a triumphant laugh, she speed-dialled Jenna, almost dropping her phone in excitement. There was no answer. How frustrating! Although, Cassandra supposed, phones probably weren't permitted in the library.

Yeah.

That must be it.

***

Jenna's hand was cramped from all the notes she had taken. She flexed her fingers and rubbed her knuckles. Cassandra had better appreciate all my hard work, she thought darkly. After all, I'm from a generation that hardly writes anything down. I mean, why bother, when you can dash off a meme or a string of emojis?

She looked at the clock. Where did the time go? She took out her phone. She had missed several calls from Cassandra and one from Gran, but Jenna didn't dare play any messages while the baleful eye of the archives assistant was upon her. She packed up her things and returned the book, safely snuggled in its protective box, to the front desk. The archives assistant made her wait until a thorough check of the item had been performed. Jenna smiled. The archives assistant made a tick on a list and dismissed Jenna with a gesture.

Charming. Jenna hurried down the stairs and out into the stark sunlight of the afternoon and the welcoming briskness of the fresh air.

Seconds later, the lime-green camper van drew up to the kerb.

"How did you know?" Jenna climbed in.

"Woooh!" Cassandra said, spookily. "Nah, in all honesty, I've been going around the block for the past forty minutes. Strap yourself in; I've got a story to tell you."

"Words out of my mouth!" Jenna stretched the seat belt across her chest. "You should take it up professionally."

***

They held their tongues all the way back to Old Ma Spenser's cottage, although they were both bursting to share what they had learned. Instead, with an anguish that was almost delectable, they waited at the kitchen table while Iphigenia fussed around, sorting out tea and biscuits. When, at long last, all three were settled with steaming cups before them and sugary temptation within easy reach, no one spoke. Then they all spoke. Then they all shut up again.

"Bugger me," Jenna's gran broke the impasse. "Jenna, why don't you go first, chicken? Or we'll be sat sitting here all night and our tea will get cold."

Jenna, clearly thrilled, took out the notebook she had bought new for college. It was bulging with notes, bookmarks, and post-its.

"Blimey," Iphigenia said. She took a slurp of tea. "Proceed."

Jenna looked to Cassandra, who nodded. Jenna cleared her throat and began to read.

***

The tradition of 'banishing' the bog witch dates back to the eighteenth century. A spate of child murders kept the settlement of Little Fladgett in terror throughout the summer of 1720. A deputation of locals went to consult the squire, one Hugo de Fladgette, seeking his permission to rout their prime (and indeed only) suspect from her home, chasing her across de Fladgette land. Hugo, an ardent hunter, announced he would take charge of the 'affair', as he called it,. Assembling a team of cronies and assorted servants, the date of the rout was set for April the 30th.

At sunset, Hugo and his men circled the humble hovel of Old Mother Kipper, a ramshackle hut at the heart of Potlar's Bog. Hugo called for the old woman to step out and surrender herself to God's holy justice.

Answer came there none.

"Show yourself, witch!" Hugo roared, brandishing his flaming torch.

Again, there came no answer.

Hugo signalled to his men. Moving as one, they tightened the circle around the dwelling and, following their leader's signal, they tossed their torches onto the patchy thatch. The roof went up in a flash, flaring brightly before collapsing in on itself. With a screech, a bedraggled figure burst from the door as the building tumbled behind her. Eyes flashing, the figure pushed one of the men aside and tore across the bog and into the gathering darkness.

Hugo laughed. "The game's afoot! After her!"

The men gave chase but they were not familiar with the lie of the land. While their quarry hopped nimbly from stone to stone, as sure-

footed as a goat on a mountain, the pursuers were prone to twisted ankles, lost boots, stumbling and falling, and not getting very far at all. Hugo took off his hat and swatted at the nearest man in exasperation.

"I shall catch her for myself," he declared, giving the next man a swift kick as he tried to stand up again. "Fools! And so is she, for she forgets I was born and bred on this land, and I know this godforsaken bog at least as well as she!"

He plunged into the shadows, unheeding the slipperiness of the stones and the suction of the marshy ground. On and on he went until he found her, a silhouette at the edge of Potlar's Pond. He drew his flintlock and trained it on the wretched woman.

"I have you, witch," he snarled. "Come one step closer and I'll blast you to eternal damnation."

The figure did not move or give any indication of hearing a word Hugo had said.

"Now," Hugo's face, illuminated by the flickering flames of his torch, took on a demonic aspect, "You are going to turn around and walk out into the middle of the pond. And I am going to wait here to ensure you never walk out again. A fitting end for a witch. Why, if you drown, it will be a sign of your innocence, will it not? Let that be a comfort to you and may God have mercy on your soul."

The figure turned slowly and stepped into the water, her skirts billowing and filling, growing heavy as they drank. She kept on walking until the water covered her head. Three bubbles rose and burst on the surface, and then there was nothing. But Hugo de Fladgette did not look away, could not look away.

His men found him at first light, standing at the water's edge, staring across the pond, his mind completely gone.

They took him back to Fladgett Hall and it was many months before he would respond with anything approaching awareness or intelligence. Hugo de Fladgette was never quite the same but at least the child murders ceased.

Every year since then, the locals have re-enacted the drowning of the old woman. At first it was to keep the bog witch at bay, to remind her of the treatment she would suffer were she to take another child.

As time passed, the ritual has taken on a more elaborate and celebra-
tory air, and the locals hold it an honour to be chosen to play the old
woman cast into the pond.

"See!" Jenna's grandmother crossed her arms indignantly.
"An honour! And you denied me my chance!"

"Oh, Gran. I thought you'd got over that."

Iphigenia bobbed out her tongue. "Perhaps if certain parties hadn't meddled, the town wouldn't now be short of a little
boy."

"Gran!" Jenna was appalled.

"No, no," Cassandra smiled sadly. "There might be something in Iphigenia's words. I mean, this is why we're doing all
this, isn't it? For that kiddie."

Jenna nodded. She closed her notebook.

"Your turn."

Cassandra took out her smartphone. She opened the Voice
Memo app and pressed PLAY.

***

CASSANDRA: I appreciate your talking to me, ah –

TOUR GUIDE: No names, please!

CASSANDRA: But it's right there on your badge clear as day.

TOUR GUIDE: Is this a video?

CASSANDRA: No.

TOUR GUIDE: Well then. Where would you like me to start?

CASSANDRA: The beginning?

TOUR GUIDE: A bit of background first.

CASSANDRA: OK...

TOUR GUIDE: I've been working at the Hall on and off for about
ten years. As a guide, selling tea towels in the gift shop, even
serving up cream teas in the summer gazebo. But it's all been

on a casual basis. As and when. To suit them. And, most of the time, to suit me as well. But, as I say, it's been ten years and there's no sign of them taking me on on a permanent footing. Which would mean sick pay and paid annual leave and all the rest of it.

CASSANDRA: I don't see –

TOUR GUIDE: I'm a woman with a grudge, is what I'm saying. This is why I'm telling you what I'm telling you. Might as well because it turns out loyalty and honesty don't get you anywhere.

CASSANDRA: I'm afraid I'm not in a position to pay you. Perhaps another coffee?

TOUR GUIDE: (Indistinct noise). Just you make sure that thing's recording because I'm only going to say this once. And if any of it comes back to bite me on the backside, I shall deny all knowledge. We never met. Right?

CASSANDRA: Right!

TOUR GUIDE: Right. Here we go. When I first started as a tour guide, I was given a guided tour myself of the house and grounds and a fat sheaf of papers containing stories and facts to learn. Then I was let loose on the place so I could get my bearings and find my own way around – useful if I was to guide others, as you might imagine.

Inevitably perhaps, I got lost. I must have deviated from the prescribed route through the house and ended up near His Lordship's private apartment, where access is strictly verboten. He's hardly ever there, spends most of his time down in London, but it was just my luck, wouldn't you know it, for him to catch me trying to open a service door. You know the sort of thing, painted to look like part of the wall, so as not to ruin the line of the dado, or whatever.

"What the blue blazes do you think you're doing, woman?" he blustered through his walrus moustache. "Who the devil are you?"

Well, I stammered and showed him my name badge. I was wearing the uniform and everything so you would think that would have been a clue. "I thought this might lead me back to the foyer."

"Oh, you did, did you?" His breath reeked of old tobacco and Scotch. He manoeuvred himself so he was between me and the service door. "Well, it doesn't. So off you pop. Back on your merry way. Retrace your steps along the red corridor and take a left at the bust of Aphrodite."

"Um, thanks," I said. I didn't know whether to curtsey.

"And don't let me catch you in this wing again."

"No, sir, my lord, sir." I scurried away as quick as I could. There was a glint in his eye that led me to think he was going to pat me on the backside at any second, so I made sure to get out of his reach.

I asked other members of staff if they knew anything about the mysterious door but all I got was blank looks and shrugs. I imagined it was because I was new, an unknown quantity, and not yet to be trusted. Whenever I brought it up, they quickly changed the subject. Or perhaps I was imagining things.

And then there came the floods. Do you remember, a few years back, when it seemed like it would never stop raining? Potlar's Pond broke its banks. Every field was a swamp and as for the bog itself, it was like peat soup. Impassable. Even more treacherous than usual. Here at Fladgett Hall, we had problems. The cellars were filling up like sinking ships and the estate manager, Mr Philby, had to get in some industrial-strength pumps. The place was in uproar. All hands on deck, kind of thing. We had to close to the public – but not until after I'd turned up for my shift, oh no. And Mr Philby running around like a headless whatsit, recruiting anybody and everybody he could find to help him protect the Hall. Sandbags stacked behind the doors, that kind of thing. Taking all the paintings off the walls and carrying them upstairs. Rolling up carpets. We practically cleared the ground floor; we worked through the night. His

Lordship was away, in London or Monaco or somewhere, so at least we didn't have him to contend with. And then it stopped. All of a sudden, like someone had turned off a tap. And we all breathed a sigh of relief. The weather had done its worst but Fladgett Hall was unscathed – well, apart from a few loose tiles off the roof.

And so as the water receded, we set to putting the house in order. And I found myself helping to roll out the carpet in the corridor that led to His Lordship's private apartment. And there was the door, the mysterious door. I'd all but forgotten about it, and it was ajar! My chance had come!

I dismissed the others, sending them to fetch Louis XIV chairs or vases or something, and I approached the door, sneaking up on it, you might say, holding my breath. It was a big moment for me, and I reached up to push it open and all of a sudden the door was snatched back, and a man came staggering out, gasping and gulping the air. He pulled the door shut behind him and with trembling hands, he locked it. He sank to the floor, gibbering and raving, his eyes wild and staring. It took me a while to recognise him, but it was Mr Philby, the estate manager, and his hair had turned completely white.

WAITRESS: Is everything OK with your scones?

Cassandra switched off the recording.

"So?" Iphigenia Spenser shrugged. "I don't get it. What was in that room?"

Cassandra pulled a face. "I don't know. I don't think she knows. Or perhaps she does and wouldn't tell me."

"We need to ask him," Jenna said with a grim look. "The estate manager."

"Phillips," Iphigenia said.

"Philby," Cassandra corrected. "I thought that, too. If we can get any sense out of him."

"I still don't get it," Iphigenia scowled at the phone on the table. "What's all this got to do with the price of fish?"

"I'm not sure," Cassandra admitted. "But whatever's behind

that door was horrible enough to turn a grown man's hair white. Why would something horrible be hidden in Fladgett Hall?"

Jenna's eyes darted while the cogs behind them turned. "You think it might have something to do with the missing children?"

"Could be," Cassandra said. "And how convenient it would all be to blame it all on the local legend of the Bogwitch!"

Jenna was scandalised.

"I hate men," Iphigenia grumbled.

***

Cassandra declined the invitation to bunk up on the settee. Iphigenia was relieved. She doubted the elderly piece of furniture could have withstood the assault.

"I have a perfectly good camper van parked right outside," Cassandra reminded them. "But I will take you up on breakfast."

She bade them goodnight and left. Iphigenia looked pointedly at the table and then at her granddaughter. Jenna got the message. She tidied plates, cups and wine glasses away – well, she moved them nearer to the kitchen sink, which in her view was the same thing.

"Night, Gran," she pecked the old woman on the cheek.

"Night, love," said the old woman.

Jenna traipsed up to her room. Iphigenia moistened a dishcloth under the tap and wiped the tabletop, deep in thought.

So far she had put up with all this malarkey. More than tolerate it, she had encouraged it. It was good for Jenna to have a project, something to get her out of the house. Good for the girl to have a friend – and that Clune woman was an interesting character and no mistake. They both wanted to do something about that missing kiddie, that was understandable, only natural.

But what if they get too close, too close to something that ought to be left untouched?

Iphigenia resolved to burn that bridge if they ever got to it. There was no point getting worried about it just yet. That little boy might turn up yet.

She dropped the dishcloth into the sink, turned off the light and shuffled to bed.

***

Jenna assumed she would be unable to sleep. Her head was buzzing with the day's findings yet within minutes of pulling the duvet up to her chin and turning off the bedside lamp, she zonked out. Exhausting work, investigating.

At some time around three a.m. Jenna's eyeballs moved behind their lids, scanning an unseen vista, tracking the progress of a low-hanging mist across the lumpy landscape of Potlar's Bog. The mist gathered at the edge of the swampy ground and coalesced into an eldritch figure, ragged and bedraggled, a thing of moss and swamp grass and fog. The thing's head twitched as though listening out for something or tracing the direction of a smell. Then it began to move in gangling strides, its gait rendered ungainly by its long and reedy skirts.

It's heading right for us! Dream Jenna realised. *It's coming to the cottage!*

With a gasp, she sat bolt upright in bed. It was only a dream, she told herself repeatedly, her eyes wide, searching for reassurance in the dark. Panting, she reached for the bedside lamp. Cold fingers curled around her wrist. Before Jenna could scream, a clammy, mildewed hand clamped over her mouth.

Ssh! hissed the Bogwitch.

***

Jenna was frozen in terror, to be sure, but there was also the chill of the Bogwitch's touch seeping through her skin, rendering Jenna cold to the marrow. She was aware of the hideous presence beside her on the bed, although the mattress did not sink to accommodate the added weight – hang on a minute, do evil spirits have weight and mass and so on in this world?

Evil spirit! I like that, I must say! The Bogwitch spoke in a burbling hush, her words like something moving through water. *A fine way to refer to your guest!*

Jenna squirmed. The Bogwitch tightened her grip.

Oh, stop wriggling, poppet! I ain't here to hurt you.

For some reason, Jenna chose to disbelieve this assertion and she wriggled all the more, with extra work from her elbows for good measure. She kicked over the bedside table, making an almighty, lamp-destroying crash.

Honestly! The Bogwitch hissed in exasperation. *If I had wanted to hurt you, I would have done it by now, don't you worry about that.*

Jenna stopped struggling, more from fatigue than anything else. The Bogwitch regarded this as an encouraging sign.

Good. Now, sit still and listen.

The door burst open and Iphigenia's hand slapped the light switch. Jenna felt a rush of air as though a huge bubble had burst. She screwed up her face against the sudden onslaught of light.

"Jenna Jones!" her grandmother tutted. "Another bad dream! You need to get your bumps felt, my girl."

"No – I – it..." Jenna was suddenly aware of empty space beside her, save for a damp patch on the duvet and a few spots of moss and reeds shed on the bedside rug.

"Look at this mess!" Iphigenia wailed, stooping to right the toppled table. Jenna sprang to her feet, grimacing as something slimy squelched between her toes.

"I'll sort it, Gran. Go back to bed. I'll buy a new lamp, I promise."

"You better," the old woman scowled. Then her expression softened, and she patted her granddaughter's cheek. "Get back into bed, chicken. See if you can get back to sleep. You know where I am if you want me."

"Yes, yes," Jenna nodded. "Goodnight."

Iphigenia shuffled out. Jenna waited with bated breath until she heard Gran's door close before tiptoeing across the room and turning off the light. She sped back to the bed, launching herself at the duvet and pulling it up to her chin. She listened.

She waited.

"Are you there?" she whispered.

Hold your horses, was the hushed response. *This manifestation lark is a bit involved, you know.*

There was just enough light through a chink in the curtains for Jenna to witness the Bogwitch reappear. The rushes and clumps of moss rose from the rug, swirling and gathering until the shape of a figure materialised. It was like watching the wind get dressed, Jenna thought. Or a bubble donning a disguise.

Oof said the Bogwitch. *Do you mind?*

Without waiting for permission, the Bogwitch grasped a wooden chair from the corner, tipping Jenna's childhood collection of plush unicorns to the floor. The Bogwitch set the chair near to the bed and sat on it. Jenna was reminded of a similar scene from years ago, when a smiley policewoman had visited her, to see how she was getting on, living with her granny... Is that what's going on, she wondered? Some kind of twisted emotional flashback to help me process my parents' –

First off, the Bogwitch butted into Jenna's thoughts, *I should point out that this is not a dream. I really am here – sort of. I have to use matter from the bog to give myself presence. It's a skill that only seems to work in darkness. As you have just witnessed, the instant light shines on me, POP! I am gone. Or rather, I'm still there but not in any form. But I can see from the look on your face, you're not taking this in. You will get used to it.*

Jenna baulked. "I don't want to get used to it! Just tell me what you want and then – off you pop."

Oh! Very good! I see you are a clever girl. Exactly the kind of clever girl I need to help me.

"Help you? With what?"

Putting right an ancient wrong. How's that for size?

"What did you do?"

The Bogwitch grunted. *Because I am a bog witch, you immediately think I am to blame.*

Jenna's face flushed red and she was glad of the heat in her cheeks. "No, no, I didn't mean – You should meet my friend, Cassandra. I think you'd get on."

Oh, no, my dear. I am afraid you are the only one who can see or hear me. I don't make the rules. But you will help me, won't you? When you have heard my story, helping me will be your dearest wish, I am sure.

"Er –" Jenna didn't sound at all sure. "I'm not promising anything, but go on then, tell me your story and I'll do my best not to fall asleep."

Charming!

***

I have roamed the bog for many years. You may say 'haunted' but it is I who is haunted. By what happened. By what was done. I have lost count of the years. Sometimes, I am more present, more here. *Sometimes I am a whisper on the wind, a bubble in the bog water. This time, I am stronger than I have been for ages! I think it's because I am more in people's minds, on people's lips. I fade or grow depending on people's belief. Speak of the devil and he shall appear!*

Well. Here I am.

And I am tired. Tired of roaming. Tired of coming back. But with all this talk of children, I shall get no rest at all. Belief in me grows with every passing hour.

And so I need you to help me. You who can have an effect in the physical world. You who can talk to people. You who can discover the truth of it all.

I want you to clear my name.

***

Jenna's face scrunched up like a discard crisp bag. "You want me to what?"

Oh, I think you heard me.

"No, I heard you. It's just that I thought you were going to ask me to find that little boy."

I didn't say, Don't find the little boy! By all means, find the little boy – and if in so doing you are able to clear me of all suspicions, all accusations, -- you seem unsure.

"Damn right I'm unsure. I'm still not sure this is happening. Me talking to you, I mean."

You can hear me, can't you?

"Yes."

You can see me?

The Bogwitch waved a hand, gloved in moss and stringy grasses, in front of Jenna's nose.

"Yes."

Well, then. If you do this, Jenna Jones, if you'll help me, I shall award you your heart's desire.

Jenna scoffed. "Now you're sounding like a storybook."

The Bogwitch gurgled a laugh, like a plug hole draining. *I do a bit! But seriously, my dear, I will reward you. There must be something...*

Jenna thought about it. Her gaze moved to her dresser, to the photograph of her parents.

Of course! the Bogwitch cried. *It shall be done!*

Jenna gaped. Impossible! But, if the Bogwitch can read my thoughts, who is to say what else might happen?

"I'll do it!" Jenna resolved. "I'll help you."

But she was addressing an empty room. The first streak of sunlight was stretching through a crack in the curtains. Jenna felt foolish. It was only a dream, she castigated herself. I have not – repeat not – been talking to an apparition and agreeing to help it because it promised to let me see my mum and dad again.

I haven't.

***

"You're quiet this morning," Cassandra observed between nibbles on a slice of toast. She had joined Mrs Spenser and Jenna for breakfast in their kitchen. Across the table, Jenna was staring absently at the side of the cereal box.

"Don't rock the boat!" Iphigenia urged with a cackle. "Although she's never been one for running around and screaming and tearing her hair out has our Jen."

"I should hope not! Now, listen," Cassandra placed a crust on her plate, a sure sign she meant business, "I was up half the night, trying to track down our man Philby."

Jenna's eyes flickered. She had been up half the night too. Or had she? She was not certain either way.

"All I've done is narrowed it down to a list of psychiatric hospitals in the area, of which there are not many, thank goodness. That's assuming Philby was treated locally. He could have gone farther afield."

"That's what I'd have done," Iphigenia nodded, upending the teapot over her visitor's cup. "Got as far away from Fladgett Hall as I could."

"Ah." Cassandra stirred another sugar lump into her cuppa. "But, he wasn't thinking rationally at the time, was he? According to the tour guide, Philby was a gibbering wreck."

Iphigenia was shaking her head. "But of course he could have moved away since then. After he got better. I know I would." She shuffled around to offer Jenna a refill but the girl shook her head.

"You say you were up half the night?" she asked Cassandra.

"Couldn't sleep so I thought I'd make good use of the time. But don't worry: your grandmother's tea has perked me right up."

Jenna struggled with her next question. "Did you – did you – have you – did you see anything?"

Cassandra pouted while she considered her response. "Well, I did get distracted by cat videos once or twice."

"No, I mean outside your van."

"What like?"

"I don't know..." Then Jenna steeled herself and blurted out, "Like the Bogwitch!"

There followed a brief silence, during which Iphigenia lowered herself onto a chair, deep in thought, and Cassandra peered at Jenna, waiting for the girl to say more.

Eventually, Cassandra said, "No, I can't say there was anything like that. I think – I hope I would have noticed something like that."

She sipped her tea.

"What about you, Gran?" Jenna turned to Iphigenia, who was pointedly keeping her gaze averted. "Did you see or hear anything? And did you bolt the front door last night?"

Iphigenia didn't answer.

"She must have done," Cassandra chimed in. "I distinctly heard her unbolt it when she let me in for this delicious breakfast. What's all this about, Jenna? Have you – has something happened?"

Jenna bit her lower lip. "I – I'm not sure."

"Bad dream!" Iphigenia announced, startling them both. "That's all it was. A bad dream. I went into Jenna's room to find her smashing the place up."

"Hardly!" Jenna protested. She clarified for Cassandra. "Bedside table got knocked over, that was all."

"I see…" Cassandra peered at the teenager in a manner that suggested she could see more than she was being told. Clearly, nothing more was going to be said so she got to her feet to break up the meeting. "Right, then. I've drawn up an itinerary, plotted the most efficient route to get around all the psychiatric units. Jenna, are you coming with?"

"Um…no," Jenna averted her gaze. "I've got something else to do."

"Oh?"

"I'll tell you later."

"Oh. Right then. But don't hesitate to call me if you need to. Meet back here at teatime? If that's not presumptuous, Mrs Spenser?"

"Um…" It was Jenna's gran's turn to appear distracted.

"Right then," Cassandra stopped at the door to give Jenna another chance. "Are you sure you don't want to come with?"

"No," Jenna said. "I mean, yes, I'm sure, and no, I don't want to go."

"OK." Cassandra seemed a little piqued. She went out. A moment later, her camper van started up and she was off.

Jenna set to clearing the breakfast things. Her grandmother's hand caught her wrist – but these fingers were warm and dry.

"Are you all right, chicken?" Iphigenia's eyes searched her granddaughter's face.

"Because I'm tidying up? I can't win, can I?"

"No. Because of – last night."

Jenna broke free of her grandmother's grasp and carried plates and cups to the sink. "Like you said, it was only a bad dream."

She turned on the tap. The water gurgling down the plug hole sounded like a voice.

***

Jenna walked into town, taking a path across the bog, although she soon questioned her thinking in choosing this route. With every step she grew more anxious, more convinced that at any second, the creature that had visited her during the night would jump out of nowhere and be upon her. To Jenna's nervous eyes, every clump of grass was a hand, stretching out of the ground, every gust of breeze a swish of the Bogwitch's reedy garments, every squelch of her shoes, a sinister chuckle. Jenna had never been happier to see the B-road hove into view, with its cracked and faded asphalt, leading into the heart of Little Fladgett.

She stepped from the silty path onto *terra firma* – firmer than the bog, for sure. She steeled herself, redoubling her hope that what she was about to do would be enough. She didn't want another nocturnal visitation, thank you very much.

Back straight and head held high, she strode toward the town centre.

***

The receptionist answered Cassandra with a sneer. "We ain't permitted to disclose information of that nature. On account of the GDPR Protection of Datas and all that."

Cassandra had guessed this was coming. She pouted in an expression that suggested she was crestfallen but understood and accepted the reply. She turned to leave, rotating slowly like a statue on a turntable. It worked.

"Sorry!" the receptionist called after her.

Got her!

Cassandra whipped around, a blur of floral print and billowing kaftan. "It's not your fault," she reassured the receptionist. "It's policy. Wouldn't want you getting into trouble. But I've come such a long way. Maybe I could trouble you for a glass of water?"

"Of course!" The receptionist sprang into action. "Have a seat over there." She pointed to a corner lined with upholstered benches. Cassandra blinked a slow benediction and went to sit down. A moment later, the receptionist emerged from a side door with a glass of water. She handed it to Cassandra, who accepted it with meek gratitude. The receptionist stood over her while she sipped, as if she didn't trust her not to steal the tumbler.

"Thank you," Cassandra said between sips. "You are very kind."

She took her time.

"Your uncle, you said?" the receptionist prompted.

"Who?"

"You were looking for your uncle."

"Yes. I am. But I keep coming up against dead walls and brick ends." She laughed. "Oh, you know what I mean!"

The receptionist chuckled. Cassandra finished the water and handed back the glass, surprising the receptionist when she didn't let go. Her expression clouded.

"Oh," she said.

"What's the matter?" The receptionist was alarmed. "What's wrong?"

Cassandra turned the glass and the receptionist's hand with it, peering through the former at the latter.

"What is it? What are you doing?" The receptionist tried to pull away. Cassandra's eyes flicked up, fixing her quarry with a stare.

"It's probably nothing," she gave a tight smile. "But here's my card. You know, just in case."

She produced a business card seemingly from nowhere in a dexterous sleight of hand. She pressed it into the receptionist's empty palm.

"Thanks for the water. Most refreshing. Most kind. But I had better hit the road."

She walked unhurriedly toward the exit while the receptionist studied the card. Cassandra's hand was flat on the push plate when the receptionist called out.

"Um, Miss Clune?"

Cassandra grinned.

***

The sun was bright. It gleamed off the shop fronts. Good, thought Jenna. Give me as much light as possible to keep the Bogwitch at bay.

Not that I truly believe that last night was anything more than a bad dream. No!

But it won't hurt to have light. It's supposed to be good for you, isn't it, sunlight? Vitamin D and so on. Yeah.

She took a deep breath and approached the front door of Tina Thornbush's house. Perhaps she won't be in. Perhaps she has nipped out to the shops... No.

When your little boy has been abducted, you don't nip out to the shops.

The police station, then? She might be there.

Jenna changed her mind about reaching for the doorbell. She clenched her fists. Stop trying to talk yourself out of this, Jenna Jones. The last thing you want is another – dream like last night.

Before she could contradict herself again, she stabbed at the doorbell with her index finger, six short buzzes. She stood back, wondering if there was still enough time to leg it. The more time that passed, the less likely it became that she'd be able to make a clean getaway. Also, the more time that passed, the more likely it became that the door would not be opened.

What if she's hurt? Jenna's mind began to gallop across a landscape of dark and panicked thoughts. What if she can't get to the door? What if she's in there, injured in some way? What if she's done something stupid? People do, you know. When they're having a horrible time of it. And having your little boy taken definitely counts as a horrible time. Oh, God. She's in there, full of pills and bleeding to death and the gas is on and –

Jenna supposed one more push of the doorbell wouldn't hurt. Before she could put her finger on the button, the door was snatched open from inside and Jenna found herself under the scrutiny of a pair of red-rimmed eyes, set in a pallid face.

"Oh," Tina Thornbush said. "It's you."

She stepped back and opened the door wider, an invitation to come inside. All around the weary woman hung gloom and shadows. Every curtain in the house was drawn, every light switched off.

Damn, thought Jenna, glancing along the street in both directions. I never thought she'd actually ask me in. Forcing herself to smile, she stepped over the threshold and wiped her bog-encrusted boots on the welcome mat.

"Hi!" she said, louder than she'd intended. "How are you?"

The hallway became darker as the front door was closed behind her. Jenna could hear Tina Thornbush breathing heavily and was sure if she were to turn around, those red-rimmed eyes would be glowing in the dark...

Instead, Jenna breezed through to the kitchen, where the daylight was only dimmed a little by the blinds.

"I thought I'd pop in," she tried to maintain a casual, cheery tone. "See how you are. If you need anything. After - you know. The séance."

She had reached the sink. She turned around. Tina Thornbush was in the doorway. Not a red-eyed monster but a slouching slump of a woman with all the spirit drained from her.

"There's no news, I suppose..." Jenna trailed off. Then she was suddenly inspired to put the kettle on. "You have a seat. I'll make us a nice cuppa."

In the end, she had to steer Tina Thornbush to the kitchen table and lower her onto a chair. This conversation is going to be a bit one-sided then, Jenna predicted. Good. I'll just say what I need to say and then get the hell out of here.

The rumbling of the kettle slowly built to a roar. Jenna used the noise as an excuse to avoid small talk. Besides, what do you say to a woman whose little boy has been snatched? She's not interested in what the weather's doing. She won't have watched the baking competition on the telly last night.

She busied herself with cups and teaspoons, keeping her smile plastered on. I must look about as reassuring as a ventriloquist's dummy, she reckoned. Hurry up, kettle! I want to get this over and done with.

***

The receptionist led Cassandra to the rear of the building where members of staff were permitted to smoke out of sight of the patients. "As long as we don't set the kitchen bins on fire, we'll be fine."

Cassandra simpered and declined the proffered cigarette. Instead, she winkled an extra strong mint from its wrapper and popped it into her mouth, while the receptionist took a long drag that seemed to have a restorative rather than a detrimental effect on her wellbeing.

"You were saying..." Cassandra prompted, the sweet a bulge in her ruddy cheek. The receptionist took another suck, briefer this time.

"Philby..." she said, giving the name resonance. "Philip fucking Philby."

Cassandra's eyebrows sprang upwards. Even without the swearword, it was a stupid bloody name. "Go on."

"When he was first admitted, I had just started here so I didn't really know what was, you know, *normal* in a place like this. He was – whatdyoucallit – catatonic for weeks. Didn't say boo. The nurses had to feed him, do everything. He just sat there. The doctors said he could snap out of it at any time, or he could be like that for the rest of his life. Well..."

"He snapped out of it."

"Not half! One minute he's sitting there, staring at nothing, and they wheel him down to the physiotherapy unit. There's a pool there. Best to keep them active. You know, stop the muscles from, you know. Well, they sit him on the edge of the pool, dangling his feet in, while the therapist is getting ready, and all of a sudden and quick as a flash, he jumps up – Philby, I mean – and grabs his nurse by the throat and pulls her over his shoulder and into the water. Then he launches himself on top of her and holds her under. He's strangulating her under the water and the physio is trying to pull him away, but Philby is lashing out and he elbows the physio in the face, breaking his nose. There's blood spreading in the water and Philby is screaming and splashing like he doesn't want to get any of the blood on him, and he clambers out of the pool and runs out. Well, the physio is looking after the nurse and helping her out of the pool, so it's a minute or two before he raises the alarm. Only by then it's too late. Philby has legged it. We're not a high-security unit – I mean, we've tightened up since then but, well, stable door and all that. Philby was gone."

"And was he ever found?"

The receptionist shook her head. The cigarette was a column of ash between her fingers. She tapped it away and then flicked the butt into a nearby bin.

"No, it was all hushed up, of course. The Trust made sure of it. Paid off the nurse and the physio. Kept it out of the papers."

Cassandra crunched what was left of the mint between her molars. "And how come you know so much about it?"

The receptionist coughed. "It was my job to wipe the CCTV. But these things have a way of coming to light, don't they? Especially, if the price is right. That website ripped me off, if you ask me."

Cassandra nodded, masking her distaste for this mercenary woman. "And would it be possible for me to speak to them? The physio, the nurse?"

"Doubt it. They moved away. That's what I heard. Canada, maybe."

"Ah."

"Anyway, I thought we'd come out here to do a reading." The receptionist wiped her palm on her skirt and held it under Cassandra's nose.

"Yes. Of course."

Cassandra took the hand by the fingertips and peered at it as though it contained the secrets of the universe.

***

Jenna cradled her cup of tea in her hands. The one she had made for Tommy's mother sat ignored on the kitchen table. I know how it feels, Jenna mused bitterly. No, that wasn't fair. The poor woman was bound to be a bit distracted. You couldn't expect her to be the life and soul. Tina Thornbush hadn't moved from the kitchen doorway and was looking at her visitor with an absence in her eyes that was somehow malicious. Jenna braced herself. The sooner she said what she was there to say, the faster she could piss off out of there.

"Um..." she ventured, her throat dry despite the tea. "I have something to tell you. A message, kind of. I—"

There was movement in the hallway behind Tommy's mother, something stirring in the shadows. Jenna's blood turned colder than the tea. The Bogwitch!

"I know things are difficult – impossible for you," Jenna forced herself to continue, to look away from the green glint of the Bogwitch's eyes. "But I have to let you know – perhaps it will put your mind at rest a little bit, I don't know. I'm hoping it will help, but I'm just going to come out and say it."

In the hallway, the silhouette shifted, as though the Bogwitch might step into the kitchen at any second.

"It wasn't the Bogwitch!" Jenna blurted. "The Bogwitch didn't do it. The Bogwitch didn't take your little boy!"

Breathless, Jenna got to her feet and backed away from the table. Tina Thornbush barely blinked. Did she even hear me, Jenna wondered?

The shadow of the Bogwitch loomed large in the door frame. Jenna's hand groped for something behind her back.

"That's got to be some comfort, no?" she babbled on. "Knowing it wasn't some – kind of..."

The Bogwitch took a step forward, a moss-encrusted foot on the chequered linoleum.

"Monster!" Jenna cried in triumph. One tug on the cord sent the blind rolling swiftly up the window, flooding the kitchen with daylight. "Aha!" Jenna laughed like a maniac. The Bogwitch was gone. Panting, Jenna leant against the kitchen sink. Tina Thornbush's eyes swivelled to her and there was something mechanical or puppet-like about the movement. Tina Thornbush lurched forward, her eyes boring into Jenna's. Was she always this tall, Jenna wondered? Was she always so broad-shouldered?

Tina Thornbush flipped the kitchen table effortlessly. Her lip curled in a snarl and her features seemed to swim before Jenna's eyes as though the face was a veil fluttering over a horrifying mask beneath.

"You dare!" a low voice rumbled. "You dare to invoke that creature!"

Jenna gasped out a squeak. Her hands scrambled for something to throw – the kettle, a saucepan, a loaf of bread, all bounced ineffectually off the advancing horror's head and chest. The thing that had been Tommy's mother kept coming. Jenna leaned back even farther, her backside lifting onto the rim of the sink. She gave Tommy's mother a sharp kick in the crotch but it only gave rise to a rictus of diabolical amusement on that malevolent face. Jenna's bum was in the sink now. Wetness seeped through the seat of her jeans. She seized upon a bottle of washing-up liquid and squirted it into the demonic eyes.

Jenna! The blind! urged a voice from the hallway. Jenna was confused. She gave the plastic bottle another squeeze but it was empty. She bounced it off her assailant's forehead.

The blind! the Bogwitch insisted. Jenna scrambled to her feet, standing in the sink, ankle deep in dirty water. Green eyes glinted in the doorway. Jenna dodged the grasping hands of Tommy's mother and tugged the cord for all she was worth. The blind only increased the darkness a little but it was enough. The Bogwitch launched herself across the threshold and onto Tommy's mother's back. Tina Thornbush let out a roar, spinning on the spot in an attempt to shake off her passenger.

Go! The Bogwitch yelled. *I can't hold him for long.*

Tina Thornbush crashed against the fridge, dislodging Tommy's finger paintings from the magnets that held them in place. A potted plant plummeted to the floor. Tina Thornbush flailed around, banging into cupboards, knocking crockery from shelves.

Go! The Bogwitch yelled again.

In the sink, Jenna dithered. The Bogwitch clamped her hands over Tina Thornbush's eyes.

I can't hold on for much longer!

Tina Thornbush continued to buck like an unbroken horse. Jenna leapt from the sink, releasing the blind at the last possible second. The Bogwitch instantly disappeared, and Tina Thornbush found, as she came to her senses, that peculiar girl from the cottage had vanished too. She trudged through the hall to close the front door Jenna had left wide open.

Some people have no manners, she concluded, drowsily. Look at the mess she has made.

It didn't seem to matter.

***

As Cassandra drove back from the psychiatric unit, she went

over and over what the receptionist had told her. In exchange for a bog standard (ha!) palm reading about tall, dark strangers and letting go of the past, the woman had spilled her guts, or rather the guts of what had become of Philip Philby. Could it be that he was the child abductor? Living rough and preying on the vulnerable? And what was it that had sent him around the bloody twist in the first place? Perhaps a return visit to Fladgett Hall was necessary, Cassandra reckoned. Try to see what was in that room for myself...

It was only luck that brought Cassandra out of her thoughts enough to swerve and avoid hitting the figure in the road. The brakes screamed in protest. but they obediently brought the camper van to an emergency stop, jack-knifed across the lane. Cassandra swore and took stock. Apart from a little surprised, she was OK and she believed the van to be unscathed. As for the person in the road, they were jiggling the handle on the passenger door. They were trying to get in!

Cassandra prepared to donate a piece of her mind when she realised who it was. She unlocked the door and Jenna clambered in.

"Cheers!" The girl stretched the seatbelt across her chest. "For a minute there I thought you didn't see me."

"Me? Didn't your grandmother ever tell you about the dangers of sauntering down the middle of the road?"

"What are you talking about? I was standing at the side, saw you coming and stuck my thumb out."

"What?"

"What?"

"Perhaps I imagined it. Perhaps it was somebody else..."

"Or *something...*" Jenna added.

"It's been a long day," Cassandra righted the van. "My head is full of all sorts."

"Yeah," Jenna agreed, grimly. In the rear-view mirror, she caught a glimpse of the Bogwitch sitting pretty (well, not exactly) in the back of the van. She met Jenna's gaze and raised a twiggy finger to her mossy lips.

"Me too," Jenna said.

***

Before Jenna was picked up by Cassandra, she had tried to head for home by avoiding any and all shadows, wary that the Bogwitch could appear in the dark spaces between buildings, the mouth of an alley, or even lurking under the produce-laden tables outside the greengrocer's. The sun cast half the pavement into shade so Jenna had to stick to the sunny side of the street where possible, feeling childishly superstitious. The old rhyme about stepping on a crack resulting in a catastrophic spinal injury for your mother came to mind. Huh, Jenna scoffed, I must have stepped on a bloody big crack back in the day.

It was while Jenna was waiting to cross the town's only busy thoroughfare that the Bogwitch secured her attention.

Hoi! came the burbling voice. Jenna's eyes darted in all directions. Yes, the sun was coyly veiled behind a cloud at that moment but surely there was too much light for that awful apparition to, um, apparate? Was that even a word? Why not go with 'appear' and keep things simple? But no semantic ramblings could block out the Bogwitch for long.

I'm talking to you! the voice persisted. There was the glint of green eyes, like bubbles in algae, in the slit of a nearby pillar box. *Over here!*

A finger, pale as an etiolated stalk of cress Jenna had learned about in primary school, beckoned from the letterbox. Jenna glanced around to see if there were any witnesses before taking a tentative step toward the post box. She pretended to study the list of collection times on its little door.

"What do you want?" Jenna whispered. "I tried to tell her it wasn't you who took her little boy, but you saw how that went down."

You're welcome, by the way, the Bogwitch sounded snitty.

"Am I?"

I saved your backside back there, Mistress. You are fortunate I was present.

"What?" Jenna was confused. "I know the poor woman's distraught – who wouldn't be in her position? But I don't think she'd really hurt me. Not really."

Not she. He.

"What?"

Come, let us adjourn to somewhere more accommodating. The cellar of yonder tavern, for example, might prove more conducive to conversation.

"Oh, no," Jenna backed away. "I'm not falling for that one. Get me somewhere dark so you can attack me. You can piss off."

Attack you? Mistress mine, have I not, only moments ago, saved your sorry hide?

"Saving it so you could have it! You probably want to wear it so you can appear more normal instead of all those reeds and rushes you're made of." Jenna's jaw dropped. "Then you can move about in daylight and prey on all the little kids you want! You monster!"

She gave the pillar box a swift kick and instantly regretted it.

How many more times? the Bogwitch grumbled. *I have not taken any children. I never have!*

"Well, of course you'd say that, wouldn't you?"

"Aye, aye, what's all this?" A man's voice surprised a tiny scream out of Jenna. The burly frame of the town's only postman towered over her, a barrel-chested fully grown adult who sported short trousers all year round. "Can't have you kicking government property."

"I wasn't," Jenna said. "Besides, I thought you'd all been privatised."

The postman shooed her aside and twisted a key in the lock. "Same shit, different paymaster."

Jenna gasped as he pulled the little door open. Sunlight poured into the pillar box's interior as the postman's meaty hands pulled out piles of letters in a blunt act of evisceration. He stuffed the envelopes unceremoniously into his high-vis shoulder-bag. There was no Bogwitch to be seen. Of course there wasn't. Not in broad daylight, you silly girl.

At that, the clouds thickened and the sky darkened. Raindrops the size of two-pound coins began to fall.

"Don't let me catch you tampering with the mail again!" the postman called after the fleeing young woman, who was scurrying across the road, turning up her collar against the wet weather, too caught up in her thoughts to turn and award him a two-fingered salute.

Listen, the Bogwitch continued, *you know I ain't going to harm you. I have just saved your skin, haven't I? I want you to help me. So let me help you help me, if you get my meaning. To the cellar beneath the tavern. The entrance is around the back. Let us meet there in a trice.*

"I just want you to leave me alone," Jenna wailed. "Just...bog off, why don't you?"

Because I cannot! the Bogwitch wailed back. *The cellar!*

Jenna blinked. The greengrocer was in his doorway, giving her a wary look.

"I can do you three of them nectarines for a quid," he offered. "Best I can do."

"Um," Jenna said, her eyes wandering to the darkness beneath his tables. "No, thank you."

She scuttled away.

"All right then, four!" the greengrocer called after her.

"Tempting, but no," Jenna called back without turning around. She skirted around the Fox and Grapes. Sure enough, as the Bogwitch had said, there was a double-door lying on a slant on the ground. Probably locked, Jenna muttered. Oh well, I tried...

The doors burst open and a rush of air struck Jenna from below. Down in the depths, the Bogwitch's green eyes glowed.

Down you come! the Bogwitch urged.

Jenna hesitated. Every instinct – or perhaps it was every recollection of every horror film she'd ever seen – was screaming, Don't go into the cellar! Don't go into the cellar!

But, like all those unwitting heroines (soon to be victims) she did. There was a steep slope leading to the cellar floor, intended for barrels to roll their way in. The slope was bisected by a narrow set of steps in the centre, barely wide enough even for Jenna's dainty trotters.

Hurry!

Must be hungry, thought Jenna. And what the bloody hell am I doing?

I ain't going to eat you, the Bogwitch cackled, startling Jenna into believing her mind was being read. Jenna glanced around. The last thing she needed right now was for someone to come along and catch her sneaking into the pub. She was underage, for one thing. She crept down into the darkness and almost tumbled into a heap, but the Bogwitch was there to steady her.

"Get off me!" Jenna sprang back from the Bogwitch's damp and musty touch. Repulsed, Jenna couldn't determine whether the mildewed whiff was from the Bogwitch or the cellar.

Presently, her eyes adjusted to the gloom. Metal kegs flanked the whitewashed walls. Stacks of crates reached to the low curve of the vaulted ceiling. Cobwebs spanned the arches overhead. A sudden whirr elicited a yelp from the Bogwitch.

"Somebody's just bought a pint," Jenna explained. "That's the beer pumps."

The Bogwitch fidgeted, edging away from the source of the noise. A second pump buzzed into life.

"Must be getting a round in," Jenna diagnosed. With the Bogwitch so skittish, she felt a little bolder. "Now, say what you have to say and we can both get out of here."

She folded her arms to show she meant business, but she was careful to keep herself between the Bogwitch and the way out.

Yes, the Bogwitch agreed. *You may wish to be seated, mistress.*

"No, ta," Jenna said. "And hurry the fuck up."

***

As you are young now, so was I back then, many, many moons ago.

99

I'm talking centuries! I don't know if your young blood has yet felt the stirrings of first love, if your heart has ached and your soul has pined, but mine most certainly did.

I was out at first light to gather fungi while the dew was still beaded upon them. The bog is rich with mushrooms and toadstools of such power. You really have to know what you are looking for, so my attention was focussed on the task at hand and not on my wider surroundings. I heard a cry, a short, sharp bark of a man in pain. At once, I responded. I dropped my trug, shedding the precious spore heads I had gathered, and bounded over the tuffeted ground until I reached the wellspring of that cry. I kept my gathering-knife at the ready, for you can never be too careful out on the bog.

The man was on the ground, his fine clothes spattered with brackish water. I saw the trouble at once: he had stepped into a rabbit hole and gone over on his ankle. His eyes widened at my approach, luminous pools of white within his mud-splashed features, and he tried to scramble away.

"Be not afeared!" I tried to calm him. I made sure he could see me tuck my knife into my belt, and then I crouched beside him. "I mean not to harm thee," I told him, in the manner of speaking of the times. I could see his ankle was swole. It was merely a sprain and I told him so. Then my gaze moved up his leg and over his chest until it was arrested by his blue eyes. It was like being gawped at by a brace of cornflowers, and I found I could not look away.

"What be ye?" he asked, and his voice was breathy as if he had just run a mile or two.

"Have you not heard?" I laughed. "I am the witch of the bog!"

Laughter shook his whole frame until the pain of his twisted ankle made him wince.

"Come," I helped him to stand. "I have a poultice at home will assuage your agony."

I put my arm around him and took his weight against me. Together we hopped and hobbled, hobbled and hopped, back to my grandmother's shack, a ramshackle thing of peat and thatch, and I was ashamed it would appear as nothing more than a hovel to a man of such finery, but my new companion's eyes were screwed shut from the pain as he trusted me not to lead him into a ditch and cut his lovely throat.

I got him inside and laid him on the coarse pillows my grandmother made from rushes. As I looked for the poultice, I could sense those blue eyes on me, watching by our single candle's meagre glow.

I knelt at his side. "Your boot must come off," I warned him.

He lay back, supported on his elbows as I eased the boot off as gently as I could. He winced and grimaced and bit his lip. The flesh was already discoloured, and I knew I must act fast. When a bone is dislocated, it can cut off the flow of the blood and so the foot may die. Without asking his say-so, I raised his foot and gave it a sharp twist. The man screamed from horror and then passed out from the pain.

For hours he slept; three times I had to replace the candle and, while he was dead to the world, I prepared a fortifying broth. He stirred and started, forgetting where he was. I patted his shining forehead with a damp cloth and redoubled reassurances that no harm would befall him. I spoon-fed him the broth, having first to take some myself to prove it was not poisoned. He grew stronger by the minute and grateful for my ministrations. Before long, he was able to sit up, and we talked and talked another candle through.

His name was Robert, he told me, and he lived up at the manor house. He had been out for a constitutional, he said, a moment of peace and solitude, to be alone with his thoughts. I understand entirely, I replied. Sometimes you need space to get your thoughts in order. Precisely, he agreed. And sometimes, I continued, you need not to think at all. When I am out on the bog, gathering plants and mushrooms, I find I often think of nothing at all, and I feel all the better for it.

And I was aware that he was staring at me, and the colour rushed to my cheeks. You truly are a witch, he said softly, for you have truly enchanted me.

And I did not know what to say. All my words eluded me and I leaned closer to him, and he to me –

"What is the meaning of this?" My grandmother chose that moment to make her presence known. She crashed into the hut and tore me away from Robert's side. "This is how you comport yourself

while I am gone!"

"Grandmother, no!" I cried in shame and mortification. "He was hurt. I gave him broth."

"I wager you would have given him something else had I not interrupted!"

"No!"

She snatched up the blanket I had draped over Robert's lap. "Young man, if you are fit to walk, I shall accompany you back to the Hall. As you have learnt for yourself, the bog can be treacherous for those who know it not."

"Grandmother, I can take him," I offered, with panic rising within me. Robert was to quit my sight, perhaps forever. Grandmother fixed me with a steady glare.

"Oh, no, you won't!" she snapped. "You may tidy this place up while I am gone."

With that, she gathered her shawls around her and steered poor Robert through the door. He gave me one last lingering look – What was that in his eyes? Was it longing? – before a final shove from Grandmother forced him out.

I fell to my knees and sobbed, certain I had been struck by the most powerful enchantment known to mankind. I had fallen deeply and irrevocably in love.

The weeks that followed were torment to me. Grandmother kept me close at hand, under her watchful eye, and I sank into a wordless gloom. I would not, could not eat, nor sleep, nor concentrate on the simplest of tasks. Eventually, when Grandmother lost patience with my long face and weary sighs – and, most probably because she was fed up of me ruining her recipes with my distracted additions of incorrect ingredients – she turfed me out of the hut. Fresh air was prescribed. All I felt like doing was filling my pockets with stones and hurling myself into Potlar's Pond.

Instead, I continued to potter around the bog, filling my trug with specimens. I did not plan it, this I swear, but I found that, day after day, my meanderings took me ever closer to Fladgett Hall. The terrain is firmer there and so you find an entirely different crop of mushrooms. Grandmother was a purist; she was adamant that a bog witch should only make use of what is to be found in the bog, but I thought some stinkhorn might come in useful. Something about their shape attracted me although the stench of them is not for the faint of nose.

As the woodland thinned and the ground became more culti-vated, I looked for him, for signs of him at least, hoping that he might simply stroll up to greet me. Could he stroll? Was his leg sufficiently mended to allow him a stroll? I would not have minded had he hob-bled up, had he crawled on hands and knees! I only wanted to see him again.

Days passed, as days do. Weeks. In my burgeoning boldness, I ventured ever closer to the house, my hope blended with despair as I watched the windows for the chance of seeing that handsome face, that flopping hair. And there were so many windows! But which of them looked in on his room, I had no way of knowing.

And then, one day, there was a flicker, a movement of drapery. A door opened and a man emerged, flanked by a brace of brutish hounds. He levelled a finger at me and I was grateful that a remnant of timidity within me had not shortened the distance between myself and the house, for it was the distance, I believe, that saved my life. The man whistled, piercing the air like a scream, and his dogs sprang into action, sprinting along the driveway like balls from a musket. I lost a few seconds, frozen in terror, before I could get my feet to move. I turned and ran, hurtling for the boundary and dropping my trug in my wake. Panting, I darted for the trees, convinced that powerful jaws would snap around my ankles at any second, certain I could hear the heavy breathing of the hounds, feel the spray of their slobber, smell their hides. My heart was jostled and jounced within me as I blundered wildly on. At last, I regained familiar terrain. I splashed through stagnant pools to throw my canine chasers off my scent. I swung from low-hanging branches to break my trail. I doubled back and back again but such lengths proved unnecessary. The dogs did not pursue me into the bog. Something deterred them, something un-seen, like an invisible wall or an eerie disturbance that kept them at bay.

Exhausted, I staggered to the hut and flopped inside, glad to be alive and gladder that Grandmother was not at home. I cursed my *own foolhardiness and scolded myself for the loss of my basket, for which Grandmother would kill me, to be sure!*

I fell into a slump from which no restorative broth could rouse me. I lost interest in all things, and Grandmother despaired. Her exhortations to 'snap out of it' were in vain, and, to tell the truth, I did not care. I was enjoying the delicious melancholy of it all, the hopelessness, the pining for my inaccessible love.

And then, one afternoon, while Grandmother was out cutting peat or whatever, I stirred from my torpor, called back to the present by a sharp knocking on the door. I froze. Had I imagined it? But no; there it came again. Or had I imagined it a second time? I was in quite a tizzy, no longer being able to distinguish what existed in the world and what in my thoughts only.

And then, there he was, in the doorway, a vision! Had I conjured him into existence with my heat-oppressed brain?

He took a halting step toward me and then another, with trepidation trembling in his lip.

"Forgive the intrusion," he stammered sweetly but did not release my eyes from his, "But I believe this belongs to you and you might have need of it."

His heart?

Mine leapt in my breast and it was a while before I truly beheld the object he was holding out.

My trug!

He explained how he had found it at the boundary of the estate. He had recognised it at once. I took it from him and examined it from every angle. It was indeed mine, as solid and familiar and tangible as it ever was. If the trug were real, might not my visitor be so too? I held out my hand and he took it, wrapping it with both of his and pulling me into an embrace. His eager mouth sought mine as though he would smother me with kisses.

Oh, rapture unexpected!

Let me tell you, you can keep your bittersweet melancholy. Give me the heat, give me the fire within, of lovers reunited!

Following that exquisite afternoon, we embarked on a series of trysts, unbeknown to anyone else. I took to sporting my grand-

mother's shabby habiliments so if anyone were to intercept me, I would be mistaken for her, a shambling, old healing-woman, whom the son of the squire was consulting over some trivial affliction.

Yes, my Robert was the son of the squire and heir to Fladgett Hall – another reason to keep our liaisons clandestine.

For months we lived in secret bliss, stealing happy hours together, our passion and devotion redoubling at every meeting. But even the most beautiful flower may not bloom for long. Eventually, we were discovered and – well – watch out! WATCH OUT!!

Jenna flung herself into the roadside ditch as the lime-green camper van sped through the space she vacated and then came to a screeching stop.

"Fuckin'ell," Jenna said. Her words were echoed by Cassandra when she got out of the van and slammed the door.

"Are you all right, love?" Cassandra scanned the girl's face when they were both safely seat-belted in. "You look like you've seen a ghost."

"I have," Jenna said. "Sort of. And I've been listening to one as well."

***

"Seems to me," Iphigenia took a sip of tea, heavily laced with whisky, "You have two courses of action you can take."

She paused to reach across the table for a second chocolate hobnob. Jenna and Cassandra waited in paroxysms of suspense and impatience while the old woman snapped the biscuit in two and dunked half of it in her tea.

"Well?" Jenna prompted.

Her grandmother put the half-biscuit in her mouth and sucked at the melted chocolate coating, savouring every delicious crumb.

"Gran!" Jenna cried, shrugging off Cassandra's calming hand.

"Well..." the old woman's eyes twinkled, "Step One: you need to go to the rozzers. Tell that Dimwoodie about this Philby fellow. Ten to one it's him what's had that kiddie."

"And?"

"And what?"

"The other step?"

"Oh! Well, Step B: seems to me you need to find out what's behind that door up at Fladgett Hall. Find out what turned poor Philby around the bloomin' twist in the first place."

She set her cup on its saucer and sat back, rather pleased with herself. Jenna and Cassandra exchanged glances.

"What do you reckon?" Jenna asked from the corner of her mouth.

Cassandra pursed her lips. "I don't know... I mean, I was thinking along the same lines. The police..."

Jenna was surprised. "I would have thought you'd be more concerned about what's behind that door."

Cassandra's painted eyebrows shot up. "Oh? Why's that?"

"Because of what happened to whatsisname – Philby."

Cassandra waved a dismissive hand. "Oh. Well, he wasn't prepared for it, was he? Besides which –"

"Besides which," Iphigenia interjected, "You ain't some feeble-minded bloke, are you?"

"Quite!" Cassandra raised her teacup in salute. "Well, the first step will be easier to accomplish, although I have reservations about getting the police involved. They haven't exactly clasped me to their collective bosom since my arrival."

"Bah!" Iphigenia scoffed. "You don't have to show your face. You could do it – whatsit – annonny-onny-mously."

"Anonymously," Jenna clarified. "How much tea is in your whisky?"

The old woman winked and tapped the side of her nose.

"Ooh..." Cassandra considered this new option. "I like that..."

"Turn up in disguise, do you mean?" Jenna asked.

"What? No! Just write it down and –"

"Wrap it around a brick and chuck it through the window!" Iphigenia cackled and clapped her hands.

"I don't think vandalism will be called for," Cassandra said, a little alarmed. "I'll write down what that receptionist told me, and I'll add a few print-outs from web pages about Philby's escape. I'll stay up all night if I have to."

She gave a determined nod.

"And the other?" Jenna looked from her friend to her grandmother and back again, "What are we going to do about – you know?"

Cassandra sighed. "That, my dear, will prove a more difficult nut to crack. We need a whatsit –"

"Nutcracker!" Iphigenia shouted, as though she was watching one of her quizzes.

"A *plan*," Cassandra continued. "Let me think about it. But if either of you come up with any bright ideas, please don't keep them to yourself."

***

Jenna lay awake with all the lights on. Her wardrobe doors were flung wide with two desk lamps shining on the contents. Torches lay on the floor, banishing the darkness from under the bed, banishing, too, the Bogwitch. Sleep, under these conditions, proved elusive. It was like trying to kip in a TV studio.

Now, wait a minute...

Jenna sat bolt upright as an idea took form. She thought about it and thought about it until she was certain it was the way forward.

After that, it was only a matter of time until the others (and the sun) got up and she could tell them all about it – but not the sun, because that would be a bit daft, wouldn't it? You're rambling, Jenna. This is what sleep deprivation does to you.

She was aware her eyes had closed for longer than the average time it took to blink. She rubbed her eyelids with finger and thumb and was startled by a brief glimpse of the Bogwitch's shaggy and bedraggled shape. With a gasp, Jenna sprang from the bed and paced around the room. She could not trust herself to sleep. The Bogwitch would be there in her dreams and there would be no escape.

Is this, Jenna wondered, what going out of your mind feels like? Is this how it is for that man Philby? Or do you have no inkling that the wheels are coming off your wagon? Do you just unwittingly wander out of your wits?

She dipped her fingertips in the bedside glass of water and sprinkled reviving drops on her face.

It was worse than Christmas Eve. Morning could not come too soon.

***

"Well, I can't go, can I?" Cassandra said, politely ignoring the carbon-blackened remains of the slice of bread Jenna placed before her. Jenna had come down at first light to prepare breakfast – anything to keep busy. Three mugs of strong coffee had taken the worst of her drowsiness, but she was still not quite with it.

"Why?" she blinked from across Mug Number Four.

"Because," Cassandra spoke slowly, as if to a dull-witted infant from a foreign country, "They know me there. They've seen me."

"Hmm…" Jenna mulled it over. "You could dress up. Put on a disguise."

"I think you're overestimating my acting abilities, my dear."

The back door crashed open and Jenna's grandmother stomped in, fresh (if that's the word) from a visit to the outside privy.

"Cassie's right," she decreed, kicking off her muddy boots. "Too risky."

The air seemed to escape from Jenna, like a lilo with a slow puncture. She had been certain her idea was a good one. "Well, what then?"

"Well, chicken," Iphigenia pinched her granddaughter's cheek, "you want someone to go up there and pretend to be a television presenter."

"Yes…"

"Why pretend? Why pretend when there's Wendy

Whatsherface knocking around?"

A look darted between Jenna and Cassandra.

"And..." Iphigenia continued, somewhat smugly, "She's got all the paraphernalia, hasn't she? I'm sure she'd jump at the chance if she thinks there's a story in it."

Jenna frowned as she tried to articulate muddled thoughts. "But there is a story in it!"

"Yes!" Iphigenia cried. "But you don't have to tell her that, do you? Stick with the plan. You're doing a psychic wossname – investigation – and you want a professional to host it."

Jenna took this on board. "Well, Cassandra can't be the investigator and I'm too young to have the wossname – gravitas – so..." She sat back, flummoxed.

"Blimey," Iphigenia tutted. "Shall we just sit here and wait for a blind man on a galloping horse to come along and point out the obvious? Me! I'll do it! I'll be the psychic whojimmyflop and you can be my acolyte, my trainee. Having Wendy Whatsherface on side will give us more credibility."

Jenna's jaw dropped.

"And I'll be in the van," Cassandra enthused. "Technical backup." She clapped her tiny hands. "We'll have monitors and earpieces and it'll be just like the FBI."

"Right," Iphigenia said. "That's settled. Now, love, did you write that letter for the policeman?"

"I did," Cassandra beamed, producing an envelope thick with several pages. "Was up half the night. Writer's Cramp set in at three." She flexed her fingers.

"Should have typed it, you silly moo," sniffed Iphigenia. She took the envelope and assessed the weight of it. She seemed impressed.

"Will it do any good?" Jenna peered at the impressively weighty packet.

"We can only hope," Cassandra said. "The police are desperate to find that kiddie. I'm sure they'll follow it up. There'll be a manhunt for Philby – which will keep Dimwoodie occupied and, best case scenario, that little boy will turn up."

"Leaving the coast clear for us to go to Fladgett Hall and stage our little charade." Iphigenia's eyes shone with excitement. "It's going to be such fun, isn't it, Jen?"

But Jenna's head had lolled backwards. She was fast asleep.

***

The trio was intercepted on the cottage doorstep by none other than Constable Dimwoodie himself. His unexpected arrival threw the plotters somewhat; Cassandra was the first to master her composure.

"Good morning, Constable!" she beamed. The thick envelope in her coat pocket took on the weight of a millstone.

"Morning, ladies," the constable touched the peak of his hat. "So glad I caught you in."

Better than catching us out, thought Cassandra.

"Ah, we ain't in," piped up Iphigenia. "We're out."

"Technically, we are on our way out," Cassandra clarified, "Finding us, as you do, on the threshold."

"The threshold of an adventure!" Iphigenia added, as though trailing a movie. Jenna nudged the old woman to shut the fuck up.

"What can we do for you, Constable?" Cassandra's smile was considerably thinner. She was keen to get this interview over and done with as soon as possible – preferably two minutes ago.

"Just conducting enquiries," Dimwoodie took off his hat and looked inside it. "About a missing person."

Each of the three women gave their rendition of the surprised look.

"Not another poor kiddie!" Jenna's Gran clutched at her shawls.

"What?" Dimwoodie said, momentarily thrown.

"Turned up missing," Cassandra said. "How awful!"

"Is there?" frowned the constable.

"Is there what?" Cassandra blinked.

"Another kiddie gone missing?"

"You tell us!" Cassandra said. "You're the copper."

"No, no, we've got our crosses wired a bit, I think. I'm not here about another kiddie – God forbid – I'm here about a grown-up adult person. A woman."

"Who?" squeaked Jenna, with a sinking feeling in her lower intestine.

Constable Dimwoodie reached inside his high-vis jacket and took out a photograph, torn from the local newspaper. As he showed it to the women, he scanned their faces for reactions.

"You recognise her!" he grinned in triumph.

"Well, of course we do," Cassandra scoffed. "It's her off the telly."

Dimwoodie was a little crestfallen.

"But," he persisted, "have you seen her?"

"I usually turn over," Iphigenia sniffed. "Put *The Simpsons* on."

"No, I mean, have you seen her for real? In the flesh? Anywhere around here?"

Furtive looks were exchanged between the trio. Dimwoodie picked up on them.

"Tell me," he pressed.

"Well..." Cassandra sounded pained.

"She was here!" Jenna blurted, much to the others' dismay. "The other night."

"Go on."

Cassandra looked to the skies with an expression of defeat. "She was here, yes. Sort of. She was spying on us through the window."

Sensing the confusion that was clouding the policeman's brow, she clarified. "We were inside the house. She was out here."

"Then she ran off," Iphigenia enthused. "She knew we were on to her, so she legged it. Must have got lost on the bog. Serves her right. Bloody spying."

Jenna opened her mouth and shut it again. If the other two were neglecting to mention the séance part of the story, so would she.

Just like she was neglecting to mention her discourses with the Bogwitch.

Just in case they had never really taken place.

Dimwoodie looked down the lane and the hedge that ran along its perimeter, a barrier between the inhabited land and the eerie expanse of Potlar's Bog. He pulled a face.

"I don't fancy her chances out there. I suppose we'll have to search."

Resigned to this prospect, he put his hat back on. "Thank you, ladies. That will be all for now."

He touched the peak again and turned to his bicycle. Behind his back, Cassandra ushered Jenna and her grandmother to the camper van.

"Before you go," she called after the constable. Dimwoodie turned, caught in the act of swapping his police hat for a cycling helmet.

"This is for you," Cassandra smiled, holding out the fat envelope. Dimwoodie did not have a free hand so she tucked it into his jacket and patted it in place. "I think you will find it interesting reading."

Before he could respond, she turned on her heels and trotted nimbly away. Even as her camper van roared into life and pulled away, Dimwoodie was still thinking, Blimey, for a larger lady, she ain't half quick on her feet!

***

Their first port of call was the Fox and Grapes, where Brenda the barmaid greeted their enquiries with a sniff.

"She ain't here," she practically throttled the half-pint glass she was towelling dry. "Ain't nobody not seen her for ages."

Cassandra's lips formed a sympathetic moue. "And did she, by any chance, leave a forwarding address?"

The barmaid was a picture of disdain. "This is a public house not a sorting office."

"I mean, when the booking was made."

Brenda's throat emitted a growl like a bulldog annoyed to be woken up. "The booking come in via the television channel. Besides which, I ain't supposed to divulge no information, because of the whatsit, the GPO."

A look passed between Cassandra, Jenna and Iphigenia like a parcel at a birthday party. The music stopped with Iphigenia. She slapped the counter hard enough to make the fixtures rattle.

"Now, you listen here, Brenda Bailey. This is a matter of life and death. Or *worse*. If you have any idea where we can find that telly woman, you had better spit it out now. It's the info or your teeth. The choice is yours."

The barmaid backed away until her bouffant became tangled with the optics on the shelf behind her.

"Like I said," she struggled to maintain her composure, "That telly woman ain't here. She's gone. Disappeared and never checked out. Left all her fancy equipment here and a change of undercrackers. I'm holding them hostage until her bill is paid."

Cassandra's eyes signalled to the others. The three of them retreated from the counter to confer in a corner. Brenda watched them with a wary arch of her eyebrow and made sure to keep the sturdy expanse of wood between her and mad old Ma Spenser. She strained to hear what they were whispering to each other, but old Jeb was at the bar, hissing and whistling and waving his freshly drained tankard. Brenda snatched the vessel and refilled it from a pump labelled 'Old Scrotum'.

"Damn your eyes, Jeb," she snarled. "What do you think this is?"

Jeb's eyes darted and his face clouded with uncertainty. "A pub?" he ventured.

"Quit your yapping!" Brenda slammed the tankard in front of him, splashing most of its contents onto his sleeves.

The fat one was approaching.

***

A deal was struck. Cassandra paid Wendy Rabbitt's bill in order to gain access to the camera equipment. Brenda observed, with a characteristic sniff, that it was no skin off her nose and she would be glad to get that clutter out from under her feet.

"What if she comes back for it?" Jenna asked, as the camper van, now loaded with sturdy cases, pulled off the pub car park.

"Who?" Cassandra said.

"Wendy off the telly," Jenna clarified. Clarissa shrugged.

"I left my card with that charming hostess. But just think how credible we're going to look, turning up with all this gear! Fladgett Hall here we come!"

Just think, Jenna mused, how more credible we would look if we had Wendy off the telly with us.

***

"Ahem." Councillor Obadiah Smedley said the word itself, seeing how actually clearing his throat didn't seem to be working. The constable behind the front desk was roused from his perusal of a piece of paper as though from a reverie. He blinked and seemed surprised to see the leader of the town council staring at him like a hawk with a grudge.

"Earth to Dimwoodie," the councillor sneered. "I have been standing here for almost three minutes.

Dimwoodie frowned. "Would you like a chair?"

Councillor Smedley slapped the desk, giving the constable a start. "No, I would not like a fucking chair. I would like a fucking progress report."

Dimwoodie bristled. He wasn't sure you could get away with talking to a police officer like that. There must be laws against it. There ought to be. But then again, if you're the leader of the town council, you can probably get away with murder.

"Ah, well, you see," Dimwoodie floundered, "I might be on to something."

The councillor seemed genuinely surprised. "Oh?"

"Yes," the constable was emboldened by this reaction. "A new lead has just come in."

His eyes darted to the sheet of paper on the desk. Smedley's followed.

"Might I see it?" He reached for the letter but Dimwoodie, moving quickly for once, snatched it away.

"Oh, no," the constable pressed the paper to his chest. "I can't let you do that. It's part of an ongoing investigation."

Smedley's cheeks coloured – red, in case you're wondering. He forced his lips into a reasonable facsimile of a smile and spoke through clenched teeth. "Then tell me what it says."

"I can't do that neither."

The councillor looked ready to blow his stack. He could start swearing again or smashing the police station up at any minute.

"Well..." Dimwoodie adopted a placatory tone. "I will say it puts a new suspect in the frame. If this pans out, that little boy could be back home by teatime."

"Oh? Oh, really?" the councillor seemed appeased. "That is good news. And you can't give me the teensiest hint? Perhaps I could help you search for him. Or her. The suspect."

Dimwoodie seemed to think about it.

"I'm awaiting instruction from the chief constable. But don't you worry, Councillor. We'll nick the bastard before too long."

"Hmm."

Smedley gave a sharp nod but stopped short of clicking his heels together. What a dimwit that constable is, he grumbled as he made his way to his car. So stupid he didn't realise he was holding the blank side of the paper to his chest and I was able to read the whole damn thing while he was prattling on.

Philby, eh?

Smedley had vague memories of the case. Well, if that's who the esteemed constable and his anonymous sources believe is responsible, who am I to argue?

***

Iphigenia rode up front with Cassandra. Jenna was squashed in the back of the van with the camera equipment. Cassandra's eyes flitted to the rear-view mirror.

"Jenna, love, be a peach and pass me my lip balm, would you?"

"Um?" Jenna said, who was expending all her mental energy on keeping her balance and not, most definitely not, thinking about the Bogwitch, oh no.

"In my bag," Cassandra smiled. "Which should be back there with you somewhere."

"Right."

Jenna scanned around. There wasn't much room for man-oeuvre with all the equipment and all of Cassandra's things. Perhaps she lives in her van all the time, Jenna wondered as a clothes rail swung garments shrouded in polythene bags at her face.

"Have you got it, love? Only my lips are as dry as a lizard's arsehole."

"Just a minute!" Jenna called back. Her eyes fell upon the capacious, almost shapeless object that served as Cassandra's handbag. Jenna heaved it from the floor and onto her lap. But she stopped herself, her fingers an inch from the clasp. She knew, with a cold trickle of dread down her spine, what she would see when she opened the bag. The green eyes. The reedy hair.

"Having trouble, Jenna love?" Cassandra smiled at the mirror. "I could have sworn it was in there."

"No, no, I've got it," Jenna's voice was as cracked as Cassandra's lips. She closed her eyes and undid the clasp. She plunged her hand into the bag, not daring to look into its stygian depths. Her fingers rummaged, sifting through a compact, a pair of scissors, a couple of crumpled tissues (ugh, by the way), some loose change and then – Eureka! She seized on the tiny tube and pulled it from the bag.

"Here you go," she leaned forward. Cassandra took a hand off the steering wheel and tried to reach over her shoulder. The van lurched to the right.

"Bloody hell," Iphigenia said. "Watch it!"

Cassandra righted the van. Jenna handed the lip balm to her grandmother.

"I don't want none of that muck on my gob."

"Not on you!" Cassandra cried. "On me!"

"I suppose." Iphigenia unscrewed the cap. Keeping her hands on the wheel and her eyes on the road, Cassandra puckered up.

Jenna tried to shut the bag but something was causing an obstruction. She gave it a shake to shift the contents but still the clasp would not close. She opened the bag wide.

Hello, dearie! The Bogwitch's green eyes twinkled.

Jenna gasped. She screwed her eyes shut. "Not there, not there, not there!" she repeated.

"Not yet, "Cassandra responded, causing Iphigenia to apply balm to her cheek and chin. "Couple more miles yet."

"Sit still, woman!" Iphigenia scolded.

It's not there, Jenna told herself – somewhat lacking in conviction. It's only my imagination. And the worry and the stress of that kiddie going missing, and I haven't been sleeping properly, and perhaps I need to go back on the medication, and I can't tell anybody because they'll think I've lost the plot again and –

A clammy hand like a bunch of wet twigs seized Jenna by the wrist. She bit back the urge to scream and tried to reclaim her hand from the Bogwitch-who-wasn't-there. A vision of being pulled into the bag and never being seen again, rose in Jenna's mind. Fuck that! With an enormous grunt, she pulled her hand free. The bag dropped to the floor, shedding its contents everywhere.

"Sorry!" Jenna called out, rubbing her wrist, a wrist which now smelled of stagnant water. She groped her way to the front of the van and held onto the headrest of her grandmother's seat.

"Oh, you haven't upset my bag, have you?" Cassandra turned

to give her a scowl.

"Sorry," Jenna said. Although it was more a case of your bag upsetting me...

Iphigenia patted her granddaughter's hand. "What's the matter, love? You look like you've seen a –"

"BOGWITCH!" Jenna screamed, pointing at the road ahead.

The tyres squealed as Cassandra brought the van to a swerving, skidding stop. They stopped, breathless and panting, staring at the empty lane ahead, which was framed like a cinematic vista by the windscreen.

All three of them had seen it before it ambled into the hedgerow. A hunched, bedraggled creature of moss and peat and reeds.

A bog witch.

***

Cassandra pulled the van into a layby. Leaving Iphigenia behind, ostensibly to guard the camera equipment, Cassandra and Jenna got out and tried to track the apparition.

"Did we really see it?" Jenna kept close; Cassandra would make a substantial human shield should the need for one arise.

"Yes, we did," Cassandra confirmed. "Emphasis on the 'we'. If it had just been one of us, we could dismiss it as an hallucination or a trick of the light."

"Ah." Jenna chewed her lip. That would explain the Bog-witch in the bag. An hallucination. Perhaps a return to the happy pills would clear that up.

"Also," Cassandra came to a sudden standstill; Jenna just about managed not to collide with her back. Cassandra pointed at the tarmac ahead. "Hallucinations tend not to leave muddy footprints."

Jenna didn't know whether to be cheered or chilled by this observation. If what they were tracking was real and palpable, it could actually harm them. Was that better or worse than something made out of thin air?

"Here, do you see?" Cassandra pointed through a gap in the hedgerow. "See how the foliage is all bent, all pushed aside? She came through here all right."

"She?"

"Of course, my dear! You can't have a bloke as a bog witch. It goes against everything we believe in. It goes against nature itself."

***

The primary school was on lockdown. Constable Dimwoodie had to circle the single storey building in his quest for a way in. The school had called him; you would think there would be someone to greet him. The reception was shuttered but a fire door around the back yielded results. A few knocks with his truncheon did the trick. The door was opened by a ruddy-faced woman in a tabard and a hairnet. She gave the police officer a quick flick of an appraisal and beckoned him in. Dimwoodie stepped into the school kitchen where the air was humid and clammy and stank of old cooking oil.

"They're all in the gym," the woman barked. "Safety in numbers, I suppose you'd call it."

With that, she returned to her labours, which seemed to consist of dropping frozen vegetables into huge pans of boiling water.

Dimwoodie waited for a moment or two in case anything further would be forthcoming but the woman seemed to presume he would know the way to the aforementioned gym.

"Thanks..." Dimwoodie said, eventually. "I'll just..."

He gave the dinner lady a quick salute and headed for a door he guessed would take him deeper into the building. He found himself in the school hall, with its faded wooden floor and its little stage framed by tired curtains. In Dimwoodie's day, such a room would have doubled as a sports hall for days when it was raining too much for even the most sadistic of P.E. teachers. But now, schools have the lot, don't they? Specialised annexes for sports. I.T. suites, and 'learning hubs', whatever *they* were.

He crossed the floor and stepped through to a corridor. The noticeboards that lined the walls between classroom doors were crammed with artwork, most of which seemed to have been fashioned from various types of dried pasta and cut-out handprints, like a serial killer's trophies. The place was eerily quiet and dark, with all the blinds drawn and the doors locked. Dimwoodie padded along, feeling like a trespasser.

He turned a corner. Here were posters demonstrating a range of physical exercises, stressing the importance of hydration and getting your five a day. Double doors at the end of the corridor bore the words, SPORTS GYM in Comic Sans. Dimwoodie brought his truncheon to bear and was answered by the screams of three hundred children on the other side. He took a step back as a crack appeared between the doors and the sharp nose and ornate spectacles of the headteacher peered out. Her magnified eyes widened when she saw him.

"You took your time!" she snapped. She opened the door barely wide enough to insinuate herself through it. "I've got three hundred terrified kiddies in there," she closed the door behind her, "And you come bashing away like a dawn raid on a crack den. As if things weren't bad enough with that poor little boy being snatched, now we have to put up with this – this *thing* prowling the playground."

Dimwoodie's forehead furrowed. "What thing?"

The headteacher's eyes rolled. "The bloody Bogwitch, man!"

She pulled him away from the door and lowered her voice for good measure. "I saw it myself, lumbering along like Bigfoot on YouTube. This is all the fault of that lunatic, you realise. If she hadn't sabotaged the ceremony, the Bogwitch would have stayed banished. Don't talk to me about political correctness."

"I wouldn't dream of it," Dimwoodie muttered. The headteacher was clearly batshit bonkers, but he had a job to do and supposed he had better do it. "Tell me what happened."

"It came from the staff car park and made for the soft play

area. Well, it was only five minutes before playtime; I couldn't risk sending the children outdoors. So I sounded the alarm and went out to confront the creature."

"And did you?"

"Well, yes. I just said so, didn't I?"

"You confronted the – intruder?"

"Well, not exactly. There was no sign. Well, apart from the muddy footprints and the odd clump of moss and so on. I came back in so we could initiate our lockdown procedure. Quite exciting, really. The safeguarding of our customers is paramount."

"Your what?" Dimwoodie looked up from his notebook, his pencil paused.

"The children."

"But you just called them your customers."

"Which is, in a very real sense, what they are." She blinked, challenging him to contradict her. "I had just got them all settled – you should see how berserk they get when there's so much as a dog in the playground – when you come along and terrify them with your truncheon."

"I'm sorry. Are you able to give me a description?"

"Of your truncheon?"

"Of the – intruder."

"Well, I suppose so. What are you going to do about it, Constable?"

"I need to know what I'm looking for, first. Now," he licked the point of his pencil because he'd seen somebody doing it on the telly, "how tall would you say they were?"

***

Jenna followed Cassandra into the bog. "Shouldn't we be like, armed, or something?"

Cassandra's tiny hand waved the question away. "Hush! We don't want her to hear us coming."

Jenna scowled. She looked around for a stray stick or a stone she could use if she needed to defend herself. If the Bogwitch she had been seeing was now showing itself to others, did that make it more or less dangerous? Does it make me more or less crazy?

It's not me

The voice came from a nearby rabbit hole.

It's an imposter

Jenna stopped walking. She crouched over the hole. Sure enough, the emerald glint of the Bogwitch's eyes was there in the darkness.

"Well, who is it, then?" she whispered, mindful that Cassandra might overhear.

I don't know. I thought that's where you were going. To find out. I can't have people swanning around pretending to be me.

"Yes, because you've got such a good reputation to protect!"

A shadow fell over Jenna.

"Who are you talking to?" Cassandra said. "The White Rabbit?"

Jenna straightened but she could not look Cassandra in the eye. "I thought I saw –" She didn't bother trying to finish the sentence.

"Are you OK, love?" Cassandra's hand brushed the sleeve of Jenna's hoodie. "Anything I should know about?"

"No!"

"Anything you'd like to tell me about? I won't even charge."

"No!"

"If you say so. Now, come on; you can visit Wonderland some other time. Our quarry went this-a-way, I believe."

She set off, expecting Jenna to follow. Jenna cast one last glance at the shining green eyes, shrugged and hurried to catch up to her friend.

***

Constable Dimwoodie was happy to leave the primary school shrinking in his bicycle mirror. They didn't need a bloody bog witch skulking around when they already had that scary head-teacher. He had made all the usual noises about following it up and organising a patrol and anything else he could think of to stop the woman from bloody staring at him. He told her he doubted the prowler would be back, neglecting to add that she'd probably scared him off. You wouldn't want to meet the headteacher on Potlar's Bog after sunset. Or at any other time. Or at any other place.

Dimwoodie shook his head to clear his thoughts. Best to put that woman out of his mind or he'd be having nightmares about her later on.

Of the alleged intruder he had found no sign and secretly he wrote off the sighting as hysteria. With all this talk of the Bogwitch in the air, folk were jumping at shadows and keeping their kiddies close. Dimwoodie assumed he'd be getting more call-outs like this one. All because the town hadn't had its annual festivities. They hadn't banished the Bogwitch, and so, in their minds, she was still very much with them.

And snatching the children.

That was the terrible, sickening aspect of the entire business that made things seem all too real. A real little boy had really been taken, although Dimwoodie doubted something out of a legend was responsible.

It was time for real police work.

He stood motionless for a while, at a loss. Then he hooked his leg over his bicycle and rode back to town.

***

"Steady, now." Cassandra Clune tiptoed through the grass, surprising Jenna with her gracefulness. Uncharitably, Jenna was reminded of a cartoon she had seen about a hippopotamus performing ballet. She quashed the memory as quickly as it had arisen. Cassandra turned and mistook Jenna's guilty expression for determination.

"We must be very quiet." Cassandra demonstrated one method of achieving this aim by pressing a finger to our lips. "We don't want to alert our quarry."

To Jenna, a quarry was a big hole in the landscape often seen in low-budget science fiction. Did peat-cutting sites count, she wondered?

Cassandra came to one of her sudden standstills. She gestured to Jenna without turning around, a confusing signal: Jenna was either to squat down, pat a dog, or attempt to fly with one wing. Given the context, Jenna chose the first option.

Cassandra's dainty finger extended, pointing out a hedge that looked like it had been scrunched up and discarded on one of Mother Nature's off days. She nodded. Jenna nodded back, struggling to keep her balance in an ungainly crouch. Cassandra made another gesture, which could have meant 'stay where you are' or 'sort your hair out'. Jenna did both. She watched Cassandra sweep around the hedge – the ballet, again – until the hedge was between the two of them. She held Jenna's gaze and made snapping movements with both hands. Either they were to close in on the hedge in a pincer movement, or she was trying to warn Jenna there was a giant robotic crab sneaking up behind her. Jenna glanced over her shoulder, just in case.

Cassandra's fingers counted down, three, two, one. They both sprang at the hedge. Cassandra let out a war cry that Jenna decided not to emulate. Out of the hedge rose a bog witch – not THE Bogwitch, Jenna noticed. This bog witch's head jerked, taking in her surroundings and her surrounders.

"Oh, thank fuck!" she wailed. "I've been so alone."

She staggered from the hedge and collapsed against Cassandra's chest.

"There, there," Cassandra cooed, plucking grass and thistles from Wendy Rabbitt's hair. "I've got you."

**

They took her back to Iphigenia's cottage so she could clean herself up. While Wendy bathed, Jenna's gran warmed up some bread rolls and broth. The reporter could not express her gratitude to her own satisfaction, so she opted for constant repetition.

"Yes, you've thanked us," Iphigenia said. "Now we want answers!" She pushed the plate of bread rolls closer to the reporter, but kept her hand on it, implying that she could snatch the goodies away at any second.

Wendy Rabbitt, pink-faced from scrubbing the bog away, swaddled in Cassandra's voluminous bathrobe said thanks, and reached for another roll. She tore it in two and wiped the bowl clean.

"I thought I would lose my mind," she said. "How long was I out there?"

"About a week," Cassandra pulled a face. "Give or take."

The news hit Wendy like a shovel to the face. "A week. A whole fucking week? And nobody thought to look for me?"

"What do you think we were doing today, young lady?" Iphigenia said.

"But a week..."

"Potlar's Bog ain't that big," Iphigenia sniffed. "Walk in a straight line, you'll come to one of its edges sooner or later. You're never that far from what passes for civilisation around here."

Wendy shook her head, distress showing in her features. Cassandra patted her forearm.

"Time can be wobbly out on the bog," Cassandra explained. "I've felt it myself. You can be out there, taking a stroll, or gathering specimens, and you sort of get yourself all turned around. And you walk in circles. Or the landscape seems fluid, and landmarks you buttonhole for future reference, don't seem to be where you left them."

Wendy nodded in enthusiastic agreement. "You're right. I didn't know where I was. I would set off, keeping the sun behind me, or a particular tree on my left, and then without me noticing, the tree would be on my right, or not there at all."

Jenna was aghast. "You poor thing."

"Bollocks," Iphigenia said. "You were probably off your head – what did you eat while you were out there? Did you eat any mushrooms, by any chance?"

"Well, yes.." Wendy was puzzled. "Anything I could get my hands on. Mushrooms, berries, anything at all."

Iphigenia smiled as if to say, 'case closed'.

"Well," Cassandra conceded, "perhaps that had something to do with it. But what were you doing out on the bog in the first place, dear?"

Wendy dropped her spoon, her appetite vanished. "It was dark," she began. "I didn't mean to – I wasn't planning on spending a week roaming around the fucking bog."

Iphigenia tutted at the language. Cassandra pouted encouragement.

"It was night," Wendy resumed. "I – I –"

"You were spying on us!" Iphigenia slapped the table and got to her feet. An accusatory finger waggled at the reporter. "Deny it! I dare you!"

Wendy was flustered. "I - I wasn't spying on you, exactly. I had followed your guest. That poor woman. Tina Whatsit. I didn't know she was going to end up here, did I? And then you all sat around the table, and I thought this is a bit weird, so I waited around to see what would happen. I couldn't hear what was going on. You must have excellent double glazing."

Iphigenia dismissed this attempt at a compliment with a grunt of disdain.

"I don't know – you might think I'm daft, but it looked a bit like you were doing a séance, to me. I mean, it was probably just a support group, wasn't it? For distressed women? You see them on the telly. They sit in a circle and take turns to tell their stories, don't they? That was what was going on, wasn't it?"

"Well..." Iphigenia smirked. Cassandra sent her a warning pout.

"Something like that," she smiled.

"Well, I don't like to be blunt," Wendy said, ironically, "but I have to say your counselling or support skills or whatever leave a lot to be desired. That Tina woman couldn't get away fast enough, could she? She nearly trampled me to death when she burst out of here. And I could see she was upset, so I went after her. To see if she needed anything..."

"Out of the goodness of your heart," Iphigenia said, also ironically.

"Gran..." Jenna warned.

"Go on, love," Cassandra prompted.

"Well, it shows what you get for trying to be nice," Wendy laughed bitterly. "I went after her, was going to offer her a lift back to town, and she turned on me! Except it wasn't her. I mean it was her. And it wasn't. She had sort of *changed*, you know? It wasn't Tina whoozit anymore. It was a man – I mean, he still had her clothes on, could have been funny in other circumstances – only it wasn't merely a man, it was – there was – there was something *evil* about him. And before you say anything, I hadn't had a single mushroom that day, so you can't blame my lunch. I pegged it away from there as fast as my shoes would let me, and I didn't know where I was going, and I've been stuck in that bog ever since. Terrified he would come after me. Terrified I was going to starve or die of exposure or hypothermia or tetanus or any number of things. You do believe me, don't you? I'm not around the twist, am I?"

Iphigenia looked away, significantly.

Cassandra patted Wendy's arm.

Jenna said, "Yes."

All eyes turned to the young woman. Jenna could not meet their gaze. If there was a perfect time to tell the others about her experiences with the Bogwitch, this was it. But Jenna could do nothing but squirm under their scrutiny. She had seen the way her grandmother and Cassandra had looked at Wendy Rabbitt. They didn't believe her about Tina Thornbush. They would not believe me about the Bogwitch.

"What is it, love?" Iphigenia smiled kindly.

"Um, nothing," Jenna said, knowing full well her grandmother would see through the lie.

"Out with it!" Iphigenia urged and, realising it had sounded harsher than intended, she added feebly, "I haven't said that since my wedding night."

No one laughed.

"You've seen her, haven't you?" Wendy Rabbitt probed, her reporter's instincts roused.

"Who?" Jenna frowned.

"Tina Thornbush!"

Phew, thought Jenna.

"You have!" Wendy Rabbitt laughed in triumph. "And she scared you too, didn't she? I can see by your face."

"Is this true, dear?" Cassandra pouted in Jenna's direction.

"Well..."

"When was this?" Iphigenia squinted at her granddaughter, as though it was written all over her face but in the tiny print that catches you out on insurance policies.

"Um," Jenna shifted on her seat. When did it get so hot in here? "The other day. I went – I went to see if she was all right."

"And clearly, she wasn't," Cassandra said. "Did she hurt you?"

"No. I mean, she didn't get the chance. But, like Miss Rabbitt said, it was as though she wasn't herself."

Wendy Rabbitt was nodding emphatically, vindication shining in her eyes.

"Go on, Jen," Iphigenia reached across the table and grasped Jenna's hand. "Tell us what happened."

Jenna realised there was no escape. She described her visit to Tina Thornbush's house and the attack in the kitchen, the apparent transformation into something more manly, more diabolical. But she neglected to mention the Bogwitch, the Bogwitch who had saved her and who had been chatting with her ever since.

Cassandra pursed her lips, deep in thought. All eyes turned to her, as though she was the one with the answers.

"Oh, dear," she said eventually. "I think we are responsible for poor Tina's... condition. The séance –" She turned to Wendy Rabbitt. "We held a séance, you see, or tried to. We were trying to put that poor woman's mind at ease. Give her some peace, at least. And I am afraid we did exactly the opposite. We must have tapped into something else, and that something else got a hold of Tina – mentally, she was the weakest of us all, given what she was going through. And now, I fear, she is possessed."

Wendy Rabbitt was aghast. "Well, that would explain it," she shook her head. "If you're complete fucking nutcases. Come off it. She's on steroids or something. She's taking hormones. She's transitioning!"

She trailed off. She couldn't even convince herself.

"So, what next?" her head turned to them each in turn. The weird girl, the crackpot old woman and the giant, economy-sized charlatan.

Cassandra forced her lips into a taut smile. "I am glad you asked."

***

Feeling flustered, Kerry Simmonds shoved the pushchair out of the supermarket doors and into the sunshine. The chair was laden with carrier bags – (Why do I always leave the reusable ones at home, she wailed internally? They give you such dirty looks when you buy plastic bags, as if I'm destroying the planet single-handed) – and, fortunately, the child within it was asleep. Kerry's other hand held the hand of her elder child, five-year-old Leo. Leo's other hand was conducting nasal excavations.

"Oi," Kerry snapped, "Don't do that. People can see you. Where's your tissue?"

Exasperated, Kerry reached for her handbag. Honestly, perhaps I am to blame for the deforestation of South America, the amount of tissues we get through... But her handbag wasn't there. Seized by panic, Kerry searched the pushchair. The handbag wasn't with the shopping. It wasn't underneath the seat or hanging from a handlebar. It wasn't under Sophie's blanket, even though Kerry checked it twice.

She realised she had left it inside at the checkout. With a bit of luck, it was still there. Or perhaps the shop assistant would have tucked it away for safekeeping.

Kerry dithered. Getting the pushchair and all the shopping back indoors was more than she could face. Besides, the checkout was right inside the door, a few feet away. It would only take a few seconds.

"Leo, listen to me," she stooped to her son's level. "You're a big boy now. I want you to stay right here and keep an eye on your sister, while Mummy pops back inside to get her bag. Silly Mummy! You can do that for me, can't you?"

"Can I have a lollipop?" Leo said.

"Oh, all right then. Mummy will get you a lollipop. You just stand right there, OK?"

She tousled his hair. Her hand came away sticky. It always did. Leo had a talent for it.

Biting her lower lip, Kerry went back into the supermarket.

Leo wiped his finger on one of the carrier bags. He put a proprietorial hand on a handlebar. It was what a big brother would do, he felt. He had to show he was earning his lollipop.

A shadow fell over him and the pushchair.

In the supermarket, reunited with her handbag, Kerry looked over her shoulder and screamed. She ran from the shop and used her handbag as a weapon against the man who was towering over her children.

"Get the fuck away from my kids!" She punctuated the words with swats of her handbag. The man held up his arms in self-defence, cowering from the blows. Other shoppers and a couple of members of staff poured from the supermarket, eager to see a spectacle. The man ran away. Within seconds, he had disappeared around the corner.

People flocked around the angry mother and her children. All three were now crying from fear.

"The bastard!" someone observed, succinctly.

"Kids ain't safe," opined someone else.

"Can't leave them for a second," said another, with a meaningful look that did not escape Kerry's attention.

Not everyone was judgmental. A check-out cashier approached and asked if Kerry was all right, if she wanted to come inside for a sit down and a cup of tea.

Kerry shrugged away all advances. She shoved the pushchair into motion, dragging Leo along behind her.

"You should go to the police!" someone called after her.

"I am doing!" Kerry called back. "Thank you!"

Muttering swearwords under her breath, Kerry made her way to the police station, trying to fix the man's description in her mind. Tears coursed down her face. Snot poured from her nose unheeded. How close it had been! How close she had come to losing her children! And all because she'd left her handbag in the fucking shop!

Blaming herself, Kerry struggled to get the pushchair through the front door of the police station. A couple of carrier bags dropped off but she didn't care. Sophie was screaming. Leo was griping for his lollipop.

"Not now, Leo!" she roared, stunning the boy into silence.

Constable Dimwoodie jumped up from his seat at the front desk.

"Hello, hello," he played to stereotype. "What's all this, then?"

*⁎⁎

"So," Wendy Rabbitt ranted, "You got all my gear from the pub but you didn't think to get my clothes as well?"

"Why would we?" Jenna countered.

"For me to wear!" Wendy wailed. "I can't go anywhere like this, can I?" Her gesture swept over the dressing gown Cassandra had provided. "People will think I'm camping out."

"None taken," Cassandra said, through her teeth.

"Jenna'll find you something to wear," Iphigenia tried a soothing tone and still managed to sound like a parrot sliding down a chalk board. "Or I could fix you up with a couple of cardigans and a shawl."

Wendy didn't bother to suppress her shudders. She turned to the girl. "You'll have to do, I suppose. Only no boy band T-shirts or things with rips in them."

"As if!" Jenna said. She stomped off upstairs to root through her wardrobe.

"Any danger of another cuppa?" Wendy held out her empty mug. Iphigenia snatched it away and did the honours with the teapot.

Cassandra, her smile eyelash-thin, asked if Wendy needed to go through the plan one more time.

"I'm all right," the reporter said. "I'm a journalist. I'm used to thinking on my feet. I've been in more dangerous situations then I can shake my fanny at."

Cassandra winced at the turn of phrase but kept the smile going. "I'm sure covering the Greater Fladgett Beetle Drive every September requires untold bravery."

"You're not kidding," Wendy agreed. She grinned, "You've seen me, then! I didn't know I was talking to a fan. Is there anything you'd like me to sign? Only I don't do bare flesh. That's weird. People getting tattoos of your autograph."

"I shall try to live with the disappointment," Cassandra affected a sigh. "I'll go and see if Iphigenia needs any help with that tea."

She tottered into the kitchen, leaving Wendy Rabbitt with a frown on her almost-famous face.

"Who?"

***

Up in her bedroom, Jenna stood before her wardrobe, its doors flung open wide. Nothing seemed appropriate for a television reporter and Jenna found herself hating all her clothing, every garment, every stitch. *When did I get so many hoodies? And plaid shirts? And pedal pushers – Christ, I know, I know, it was a different time. You could get away with that shit then.*

Hello, dearie!

Jenna jumped at the Bogwitch's greeting. She spun around, trying to locate the source. Perhaps the thing was under the bed; that was the darkest spot.

Over here!

The Bogwitch waved from the dressing table mirror. Jenna resisted the impulse to wave back.

"Go away!" she grumbled. "Even if you're not really here. Go away!"

No! said the Bogwitch. *How do you like that?*

"Hang about," Jenna took a tentative step toward the mirror. "How can this be happening? I thought you could only appear in dark places."

The Bogwitch waggled straggly fingers. *Wooo! Like your mind...*

"Not funny," Jenna scowled.

I think it's because your belief in me is growing stronger. So, for that, I thank you. I can now manifest myself almost anywhere.

"Ugh," Jenna grimaced. "Just don't make a mess on the carpet."

I have told you before. If you don't like my company, all you have to do is clear my name and I'll evaporate like the morning dew off a cowpat.

"Nice," Jenna said. "If you'd leave me alone for five minutes, I might be able to get on with it. Clearing your name. What is your name, anyway?"

The Bogwitch's eyes twinkled. *That's part of it. To clear my name, you must also discover what it is. What it was.*

"Oh, for f-- Let me guess: Rumple-fuckin-stiltskin."

Not even close laughed the Bogwitch.

"Jenna love?" Iphigenia called from the foot of the stairs. "Pull your finger out. Time's a ticking."

Jenna let out an exasperated sigh, plunged her hands into the wardrobe and pulled out a not-bad sweater, a cleanish pair of leggings and a pair of patent shoes that hadn't seen the light of day since the day of her college interview.

"Beggars can't be..." she told the mirror, but she was talking to herself.

***

Constable Dimwoodie sat back and looked at what he had drawn. Not for the first time, he wished for a greater proficiency at art and wished he had taken those evening classes before the college was closed down. Little Fladgett police station did not run to a sketch artist; indeed, he had been lucky to find a biro and a scrap of paper, but, following the description furnished by the witness, Ms Kerry Simmonds of Short Street, he had done his best.

The witness went up on her toes, trying to see the drawing. Dimwoodie pressed it protectively to his chest, as though to prevent cheating in an exam.

"His arm was more up, like this," Kerry Simmonds demonstrated.

"I think that's because you were walloping him with your handbag."

"Possibly... It all happened so fast."

With a sigh, Dimwoodie balled up the paper and flung it in the general direction of the bin. Kerry Simmonds was aghast.

"I'll circulate the description," Dimwoodie said, neglecting to elaborate that the people doing the circulating were few in number. Basically, there was him and a traffic warden. "Let's go over it again, one more time. You say he was grey-haired."

"Almost white. And so was his beard. And between five and six feet tall. It was hard to tell."

"Because he was hunched over while you were hitting him."

"Yes."

"Eyes?"

"Yes. Two, I think."

"Colour?"

"Probably."

Kerry Simmonds's own eyes widened and for a second, Dimwoodie believed she was doing an impersonation of the assailant she had assaulted. She let out a squeal of excitement, startling the child in the pushchair awake and into letting out squeals of its own.

"That's him, that's him!" she jumped up and down. Dimwoodie followed the line of her pointing finger. It led his gaze to the papers on his desk: the letter and press clippings that mad medium had given him. On top of the pile was a photograph. A photograph of Philip Philby.

He picked it up. "Are you sure?"

"Yes!" There was a light in Ms Simmonds's eyes that suggested she thought she was in line for a prize. She unstrapped the child from the chair and propped it over her denim-clad shoulder.

Dimwoodie squinted at the mug shot, lifted from medical files. Perhaps his drawing hadn't been far off the mark. Perhaps there were classes in Greater Fladgett he could get to when he wasn't working the evening shift...

"Hello? Hello, hello?" Kerry Simmonds stole his line. He realised she was clicking her fingers in front of his face.

"Yes, I'll get this copied and circulated. Now we know who we're looking for, an arrest can't be far off."

Kerry Simmonds grinned. The grin rounded to form an O. "Is it him? The child snatcher?"

Dimwoodie took a sharp inhalation over his teeth.

"To think, he nearly had it away with my Leo! Or my Sophie! Or both of them!" She marvelled at what might have been. "Mind you," she chuckled, "Half an hour with these two and he'd be bringing them back sharpish." Her eyes darted, seeking her first-born. They found him, emptying a leaflet rack. The floor was covered. "Leo Simmonds! Don't do that! How are people going to know how to lock their bikes up?"

She dragged Leo away by the arm and, with Sophie on her shoulder, shoved the pushchair to the door, leaving churned-up crime prevention leaflets in her wake.

"Sorry," she grimaced. "He's a bugger if you're not watching him."

"Um, that's all right," Dimwoodie said, distracted by the

135

photograph. Philip Philby's eyes, although the photo was in black and white, seemed to glow red. It was like staring into the pits of Hell and having them stare right back. "Thank you!"

Before his witness disappeared, Dimwoodie heard the boy ask if he could have a lollipop now.

"No," the mother said. "You can have two. There's my good boy."

***

Against her will, Iphigenia was left at the cottage. She took some persuading; Jenna expressed concerns about her gran's safety and stamina – concerns that were dismissed with scowls and obscenities; Cassandra opined that someone was needed to stay behind to tell the story in case 'something' happened to the others; Wendy Rabbitt promised to interview the old woman on television on any topic of her choice. It was probably this that clinched it. Iphigenia withdrew to the kitchen table to draw up a list of subjects she could expound upon for the discerning viewer.

The others got into the camper van. Cassandra at the wheel, of course, Wendy riding shotgun, and Jenna in the back among the equipment and other stuff pertinent to Cassandra's occupation.

They were only a few hundred yards from home when Wendy asked Cassandra what she had meant by 'something' happening. Cassandra smirked. Wendy's eyes widened

"You know something! You do! You've had a whatsit, haven't you? A premonition!"

"I don't really do that, you know," Cassandra said. "I don't know where people get the idea."

"You do bloody séances and shit," Wendy countered. "I've seen it, remember."

"That was a one-off," Cassandra said. "And it didn't exactly go to plan, did it?"

"But you profess to be a bog witch."

Jenna leaned forward. "Oh, it's more waving sticks at muddy

ground," she said. "Making potions out of peat and stagnant water."

"Potions!" Cassandra laughed. "You'll be giving me a pointy hat next!"

"Ooh, I like that!" Wendy enthused. "Great visual." She put her hands together to form a frame through which to view Cassandra.

"It's a cliché. And inappropriate," Cassandra said, keeping her eyes on the road. "And more than a little offensive."

Wendy rolled her eyes. "All right. Don't hex me."

Cassandra pressed her lips together. It would not do to tell Wendy what she thought of her – at least not until after all this was over. The reporter, unfortunately, was a vital part of the plan to gain access to the mystery room at Fladgett Hall. Once in, she had better mind her ps and qs or I might try pronouncing a curse upon her just for shits and giggles.

In the back, Jenna was growing anxious. The Bogwitch was quiet but she was there. Jenna could sense her presence, could almost smell the mildew.

"Can we have some music on?" she asked hopefully.

"Sorry, love," Cassandra said, pressing a switch. The radio scratched into life. Country music blared out. "Sorry!" Cassandra stabbed at the controls.

"No! It's all right!" Jenna cried. "Anything is fine."

"My dog ran off with my boyfriend," sang the radio, "And they were hit by a truck on the highway..."

"Fucking hell," said Wendy Rabbitt.

***

The police station at Little Fladgett was ill-equipped when it came to reprographic equipment. Constable Dimwoodie stood dumbfounded for a few minutes, holding the photograph of Philip Philby and not quite knowing what to do about it. The man's image, with its white hair and staring eyes, was freaking him out a little and he could hardly bring himself to look at it for any length of time. The face of the child abductor! It was enough to make your blood run cold. But Kerry Simmonds's witness statement was a big step forward, a giant leap in the case. Dimwoodie knew fairy steps were required. Softly softly catchee child abductor.

The image must be circulated, along with a hotline number (namely, Dimwoodie's mobile). Somebody somewhere would see this monster. The net would close in. Dimwoodie would be made a saint – or at least, a sergeant. Not that this is what it was about, his own advancement. It was about getting that little boy back. It was about safeguarding the other kids of Little Fladgett and the surrounding area.

Dimwoodie forced his feet to move, out of the cop shop and toward the printer's studio around the corner. Parkin's Print Services was usually occupied with the printing of wedding invitations and the occasional newsletter for those local clubs who remained resistant to the concept of email and websites. Dimwoodie would demand they put all other work aside and prioritise the posters he needed.

He pushed the door. Overhead, a bell rang. The shop was empty. Enlargements of family photos adorned the walls, photo albums were stacked in fans on shelves. Examples of novelty items you could order were on display. You could get a newspaper front page, done up to look faded and foxed with age, announcing the occasion of your birth to a grateful nation.
Dimwoodie approached the counter and, in the absence of a bell to ring or button to press, made a noisy business of clearing his throat.

Eventually, a man in a brown overall emerged from a back room. "You want to get that looked at," he gestured at the constable's chest.

"What?" Dimwoodie was thrown by this unconventional greeting.

"That cough."

"Oh, it isn't – I wasn't – I suppose I have been spending more time than usual on the bog."

"You want to get that looked at and all."

"No, Potlar's Bog. Doing search parties and what-not."

The printer nodded. It was a signal to move on rather than one of comprehending. "Now, that what can I do you for, Officer." He raised his hands in mock surrender. "I'll come quietly, if that helps."

"Um, that won't be necessary, I don't think. Unless..."

"I'm just pulling your truncheon! Blimey, where's everybody's sense of humour these days, eh? I like to offer the personal touch, you see. You don't get banter like this with one of those online companies. You might get two thousand business cards by next day delivery, but so what? Here you'll get a laugh and a smile, and a full personal service."

"Um," Dimwoodie. "Here."

He handed over the photograph of Philby. Parkin's eyes widened.

"Blimey," he said. "Wouldn't like to meet him down a well-illuminated alley, never mind a dark one."

"I want a thousand copies," Dimwoodie said.

"Suit yourself."

"And I want you to add this number," he pushed a scrap of paper across the counter. "And I want a headline to say, IF YOU SEE THIS MAN, CALL – and then the number."

Parkin pursed his lips, making internal calculations. "How many did you say?"

"A thousand."

"What size are we talking?"

"Um.. A4?"

Parkin sucked air in through his teeth. "Be cheaper to have two thousand."

"Would it?"

"In the long run."

"I only want one thousand. And this is official police business."

"Is it?"

"Yes! That face there is the face of the child abductor. He's got his hands on one little boy already."

Parkin gave the mugshot a fresh appraisal. "I see. I thought it was a prank. You know. For somebody's stag do or something. Mind you, who'd want to get hitched to that?"

"Can you do it?"

Parkin expelled air this time. "Next Tuesday good enough?"

Dimwoodie blenched. "I was hoping for today. As in right now."

"I don't know. I've got calendars to get out for the dogs' home. Lovely spaniel on the cover. And you should see the poodle for October. Why do they do that to them, eh? Make them look like they've lost a fight with a candy floss machine."

"Can you do it?"

"Well... Seeing as how it's for the kiddies."

"So..."

"I could have a late lunch, I suppose."

"Excellent! Thank you." Dimwoodie turned to go.

"Hold up!" Parkin called him back. "I need a deposit."

Dimwoodie's hand moved to his truncheon.

Parkin backed off. "If you put it like that..."

The bell rang, heralding the constable's departure. Parkin looked at the photo again. The staring eyes. The grim line of the mouth.

"Blimey," he repeated.

***

For the second time in recent memory, Cassandra parked the camper van in the grounds of Fladgett Hall.

"Here we are," she announced redundantly. "Do we need to go over it again before we go in?"

Wendy shook her head.

"Um," Jenna said. "They do know we're coming?"

"Well," Cassandra said. "They know someone's coming. Not us, exactly. They're expecting Wendy Rabbitt and her production assistant. Who is you."

Wendy unclipped her seatbelt and climbed out of the van. She stretched, rolling her head from side to side. Cassandra got out and opened the side door. Jenna sprang out, relieved to be liberated and yet nervous about what was to come. Wendy flipped into professional mode. Cassandra was happy to let the reporter take over this part of their mission.

"Right, this will be your main monitor," Wendy set up a cube on the passenger seat. "Everything Jenna sees on camera will be relayed back here to you. Here's your headset, so you can communicate with Jenna – Jenna, here's yours. I'll just be on the mic, so anything you need to say to me, Cassie, you'll have to relay through Jenna."

Cassandra winced, but decided against objecting to the shortening of her name just this once. She stretched the headband over her hair and twisted the mic arm toward her mouth. "Clean up on Aisle Two," she giggled.

Wendy shot her a look. Cassandra composed herself at once. Wendy popped the catches on the largest case and lifted the lid.

"This piece of kit is for you," she told Jenna, who peered into the case as though paying her last respects to a deceased relative.

"It's a camera," she breathed.

"Well, I can see it's in expert hands," Wendy said. "It's a bit bulky, a bit unwieldy. Try not to drop it."

"Um..."

Wendy pulled the camera from the case, setting it on Jenna's narrow shoulder like a rocket launcher.

"Eye-piece, here. Basically, you just point. To start recording, press this. Then you press it again to stop."

"That's it."

"That's it?" Jenna was incredulous. Surely there had to be more to making telly than this.

"I'll sort out the focus and white balance and sound levels when we set up."

Jenna was already faltering beneath the weight of the camera. "Um, isn't there like a tripod or something?"

"Well, there is," Wendy pulled a face. "But it's even heavier than the camera. Besides, I think we're going to keep on the move, don't you? Can't hang about messing with tripods – in case we have to make a sharp exit."

Jenna's jaw dropped, but Cassandra asked the question. "Why would you have to make a sharp exit?"

Wendy shrugged. "Oh, you know. If we're going to places we're not supposed to. We might get chased off."

"Ah," Cassandra said.

"Oh," Jenna said.

Wendy clapped her hands together and rubbed them. "No point hanging around, is there? Come on, Jen. Cassie, you're directing but I'm calling the shots, OK?"

Cassandra looked as though she had been slapped.

"It's Cassandra," she said coldly. "And you're the pro."

"Exactly," Wendy beamed. "Come on, Jen. Leave the talking to me. I think that's best. And no dawdling. The batteries won't last forever."

"Um," Cassandra raised a finger. "How long will they last? The batteries."

Wendy pulled a face. "An hour if we're lucky. And we've got no way of charging the spares. So let's get a wriggle on, shall we, ladies?"

She set off toward the house, leaving Jenna to wobble and stagger beneath the bulky camera.

"Good luck, love!" Cassandra called after her.

Jenna, unable to swing around to make a response, offered a grunt instead.

Cassandra got back into the van. She turned the monitor around so she could see it. She didn't like relinquishing control to that awful woman but the mission required it.

Hark at me! Mission!

Give me knee-deep stagnant puddles any day!

***

When Constable Dimwoodie got back to the police station, he found an agitated Councillor Smedley waiting at the door. The councillor harrumphed and stamped as though he were preparing to charge while Dimwoodie fumbled a key into the front door. He pushed it open and ushered the councillor inside.

"Closed?" Smedley seethed. "Closed and locked?"

"I had to go out," Dimwoodie replied. "Official business."

"But you locked the door?"

"Basic crime prevention." Dimwoodie skirted around the front desk, glad to have a barrier between him and the powder keg of an angry customer.

"It's a police station!" Smedley gestured at everything in one violent sweep of his arms. "People need to come here for help."

"And they can. I wasn't gone for more than five minutes. If I leave it open, they come in and they nick things. Like pens. I can never find a pen. Or they come in and try to sleep on the chairs. Once the tramps get in, there's no shifting them."

"You could arrest them." It seemed simple to Smedley.

"And what, give them room and board? No, thank you. When is the council going to do something about rough sleeping?"

Smedley pursed his lips and changed the subject. "Out on official business, were you? Anything to do with our kiddie snatcher?"

"I'm not at liberty to discuss –"

Smedley thumped the desk. "This is not about your fucking liberty, sunshine. This is about the safety of the town."

Dimwoodie, proud of himself for not flinching, looked the councillor in the eye. "There has been a development, if you must know."

"Oh? Go on."

"An eyewitness has come forward from a foiled kidnapping attempt earlier this morning. We have a description and a photograph."

At last, the steam seemed to escape from Smedley's ears,

and his face returned to a less fluorescent shade of pink. "Oh, really?" he sounded surprised. "When was this?"

"Couple of hours ago, outside CostBusters."

"And you have a photograph, you say?"

"Well, what do you call them?"

"I mean can I see it?"

"Oh, everybody will see it. It's at the printer's. Which is where I was. See, if the town council could see its way to stumping up for a photocopier..."

Smedley silenced him with a raised hand. "Description?"

"Big, bulky white thing with a keypad and a light that goes from side to side..." Dimwoodie demonstrated with his hand and a humming sound.

Smedley's blood began to boil anew. "Of. The. Kidnapper." He could barely spit the words out.

Dimwoodie, enjoying himself now, picked up a piece of paper with a flourish. He cleared his throat and read out the description of Number One Suspect, Philip Philby. Smedley listened attentively, his mood ameliorating with every detail.

"Good, good," he actually smiled. "And you'll be circulating this?"

"Along with the photograph, yes. Together with a hotline number people can call if they spot him."

"Hotline! Sounds...expensive."

"It's just my mobile, really," Dimwoodie winced apologetically. "Hotline just sounds a bit more professional."

"I suppose," Smedley conceded. "Good work, Constable. Good work!"

He headed for the door.

"Is that what you came for?" Dimwoodie called after him.

"What? Oh, yes! Just an update. Thank you."

Councillor Smedley left the building. Dimwoodie's breathing relaxed. Smedley always had a chest-tightening effect on the constable. Dimwoodie could only hope the councillor would not be back later. He would find the police station closed and locked again, because its only officer would be out and about distributing photographs. It felt good to have positive action to take.

***

The duty manager at Fladgett Hall (the badge on her lanyard disclosed her name was Deborah Fletcher) took some persuading. She made noises about everything being a bit last minute, to which Wendy Rabbitt replied that that was often the nature with news items. She said she had not been informed, nor even contacted, about the filming, for which Wendy Rabbitt apologised, gave her assistant director a stern look and the promise of a dressing-down when they got back to the office. She warned that His Lordship would object to filming taking place in his absence, to which Wendy Rabbitt replied it was practically a free advertisement for the splendid old pile – followed up by a quick aside to Jenna that she was referring to the building and not to His Lordship.

Eventually, Deborah Fletcher capitulated and decided to be helpful. "What can I do to facilitate?" she gave her most professional smile.

"Coffee would be nice, Deb," Wendy patted the sleeve of Deborah Fletcher's blazer.

"It's Deborah," said Deborah. "Flat white?"

"I don't care what ethnicity it is as long as it gives me a jolt," Wendy laughed. "Listen, we'll keep out of your way as much as possible. We want to get some establishing shots, the exterior, the park, the grand staircase and so on. But we also want to give our viewers a glimpse behind the scenes, you know? Tantalise them with a peek at what they don't see on the guided tour. Remind them that this is still someone's home. His Lordship is not in, you said?"

"Yes, I did. No, he isn't. He's out. I'm not sure I can have you traipsing around his private apartment."

Wendy dismissed the concerns with a wave. "We're not going to be rifling through his drawers, or anything like that.

There is nothing I respect more than the privacy of others."

Jenna choked down a laugh, and fought to compose herself, unable to meet Deborah Fletcher's steely gaze.

"We shall be more tantalising than that," Wendy Rabbitt pulled focus back to her. "Just showing the door to his quarters will get the viewers hooked. What's behind there, they'll wonder? Oooohh!"

Deborah Fletcher didn't appear convinced. But, she supposed, the quicker they got on with it, the sooner they would leave. She wondered if she should give His Lordship a call, then quickly dismissed the notion. She had learned in her years at the Hall that it was better to present His Lordship with a fait accompli rather than consulting him on a potential project.

"I'll get your coffee." She stalked away on noisy heels. Wendy Rabbitt held up her hand, silencing and freezing Jenna in one economic gesture, waiting for the tap-tapping to recede to silence.

"Right," she whispered loudly, "Come on!"

She headed for a door marked 'Private'.

"Um," Jenna dithered. "Don't you want to get a wossname – establishing shot of the staircase?"

"Jenna, you sweet girl, we're not really here to film a report, remember? Now, come on!"

"Oh," Jenna said, hitching the equipment bags onto her shoulders. "Oh, right."

She followed Wendy through the door.

***

Wendy and Jenna (moving considerably more slowly) stole along an old service corridor. It was dingy and showing signs of neglect. The paintwork was grubby. Cobwebs spanned the corners and the ancient floorboards had not been swept since Methuselah was in nappies. Jenna wrinkled her nose, powerless against any arachnid that might drop into her hair. Wendy, ever the intrepid reporter, strode on, counting the doors they passed and naming them. "Ballroom. Library. Drawing Room. Solar –

What the fuck is a solar?" She stopped abruptly.

A door, as nondescript as all the others, was before her. "This is our baby," she announced in a stage whisper. Jenna caught up and sloughed off the equipment bags. She rubbed and rotated her aching shoulders.

"This is the door to the private wing." There was a light in the reporter's eyes, like a predator finding the scent of some juicy prey. Wendy dropped to a crouch and unzipped the bags. She took out the camera, fitted the battery pack like a soldier slapping a magazine of ammo into a gun. She put a hand on Jenna's forearm and looked her in the eye. "Are you sure you can handle this? This is not your smartphone. This is not for duckpout selfies."

Jenna was offended. She took the camera and held it to her eye.

"You're looking in the lens," Wendy said flatly. "Perhaps I should do this. You can stand watch or something."

"No!" Jenna held the camera to her, a child in danger of being snatched away. "I was only messing. I can do this." She stared for a few seconds. "Give her a chance."

"Give who a chance?"

"No, I'm just repeating what Cassandra's just said in my earpiece. I think she means give me a chance. Yeah! Give me a chance. I can do it."

Wendy Rabbitt chewed her lip, uncertain. She rose from her crouch and put her cheek to the door. She listened. "It's quiet."

"That's – good, isn't it?" Jenna said. She righted the camera. Wendy appeared in the viewfinder. She scowled over her shoulder.

"Don't waste the battery!" She gave the door a trial shove. It moved slightly. "And stay close. But not too close. My roots need doing."

She pushed the door again. And stepped out into a grander corridor. Jenna followed, wobbling a little; she couldn't see where she was treading, but at least this new corridor was much cleaner and, she trusted, devoid of spiders.

The corridor was richly carpeted. Portraits in gilded frames lined the walls; faces suspended in brown puddles, like bread rolls in onion soup. Jenna zoomed in on a few of them. They all had the same heavy brows, the same glowering expression. It was only their headwear that gave any indication of gender, but, Jenna was 'woke' enough to know, you shouldn't assume a person's gender, even if they have been dead for centuries and they invariably conformed to expectations back then. Jenna realised she was looking forward to her sociology course. There you could be as judgmental as you liked.

Wendy was padding along, like a burglar in a cartoon, toward the ornate double doors at the corridor's end. Jenna plodded after. She was getting the hang of this camera lark. Perhaps she could switch to Media Studies.

Wendy stopped short of the doors that led to Lord Fladgett's private apartment. She consulted the diagram Cassandra had sketched out, based on the account of the employee whose palm she had read. "This is His Lordship's gaff," she jerked her thumb at the double doors, so this..." She patted the wall to the left with the flat of her hands. Something clicked. "This is the hidden, secret door."

She pushed and a section of the wall gave way, opening inward, rather than outward like all the other service doors. Jenna gasped. In her earpiece, Cassandra squealed and clapped her hands. The door was so carefully camouflaged you'd never know it was there. And that was the point.

Wendy, gleeful with anticipation, loomed large in the viewfinder as she attached a light to the top of the camera. "You'll need this," she predicted. She took out a rubber-coated flashlight of her own and beckoned, with a jerk of her head, for Jenna to follow her into the darkness. Jenna's heart was racing but she could hear Cassandra in her camper van, holding her breath.

***

Cassandra realised she had been holding her breath ever since Jenna and that Rabbitt woman emerged from the service corridor. She exhaled, misting up the camper van's windscreen. I could totally have been a deep-sea diver or a marine biologist or whomever spends a lot of time underwater, she mused. Inspiration struck: bog-snorkelling! Is that still a thing? And what is it, by the way?

I must be light-headed from lack of breath! She drew her attention back to the same screen nestled on the passenger seat. Jenna's wobbly camerawork showed the back of Wendy Rabbitt's head, entering the 'secret room' and going down a flight of stairs. Her roots need doing, Cassandra observed absently.

"Jenna, love? Can you show me the walls a bit, please?"

"I'll break my bloody neck," Jenna replied in Cassandra's headset.

"What?" Wendy Rabbitt said.

"Just stand still a mo," Cassandra advised. "And pan up or across or whatever the terminology is. Let me see what's there."

"OK," Jenna said.

"What?" Wendy Rabbitt said.

Jenna stood still, halfway down the staircase, which was made of red brick – and cobwebs too, she noticed with a sinking feeling. She swept the camera from side to side. Cassandra's screen showed a dizzying blur.

"Slow down!" she urged. "You'll make me sick."

Jenna performed the sweep again, much slower this time. The light from the camera threw the wall into stark relief. The wall was not brick. It was fashioned by round stones, their shadows stretching long and waving in the wake of the camera lens.

"Hold up," Cassandra instructed. "Stop there a minute, love."

Jenna held the camera as still as she could. She saw what Cassandra saw at the same time.

"Oh, shit!" Jenna said.

"Oh, no!" Cassandra cried, looking away.

"What?" Wendy said, coming back up the stairs.

The wall was not made of round stones. They were skulls.

Human skulls. The skulls of human children.

Wendy withdrew the hand she had run over the bumpy surface.

"Eww," was her eloquent assessment.

"Fucking hell," Jenna said, leaning back, so the light spread further up the wall. The skulls were stacked to the ceiling. "There's hundreds of them. Cassandra, are you seeing this shit?"

"I am, love," Cassandra said, weakly. "Although I wish I wasn't."

Wendy peered closer. "They all look pretty old. I mean, I'm no bone-ologist, or whatever you call them. But I don't think these are a recent installation."

"It's horrible," Jenna said, in case they hadn't worked that out for themselves.

"All those poor kiddies," Cassandra put a hand to her mouth. "No wonder the people in this town are so antsy about child abduction."

"Antsy?" Jenna said. "I think people in every town are pretty much against child abduction."

"That's not what I mean," Cassandra said. "That's enough of the wall, thank you. Those eye sockets. They look right into you, don't they?"

"What's she saying?" Wendy leant an ear towards Jenna's headphones.

"She says we should look at something else," Jenna said.

"She's not wrong," Wendy said. She faced directly into the lens. "You're right. Come on, Jen."

She continued down the stairs with Jenna not far behind. After about thirty steps they came to a dirt floor, uneven but dry. Jenna did a slow pan around the cellar. There were no more skulls, thank goodness, but there were arcane symbols etched into the walls. Triangles and stars in circles, ringed by unfamiliar letters and glyphs.

"My God..." Wendy Rabbitt breathed. "Do you know what this means?"

"No," Jenna said. "I took French."

"Not the symbols, as such," Wendy said. "The whole set-up." She turned to the camera. "Cassie? Any ideas?"

Cassandra bit back the correction of her name. "It could be satanic," she did her best to sound like an expert on the *Antiques Roadshow*. "Given the nature of the symbols. And the runes."

Jenna relayed these words to the reporter.

"The runes!" laughed Wendy. "I know what you mean. I nearly shit myself as well."

"Get some still photos as well," Cassandra advised. "We might be able to translate them later on. Only be careful in there, love. Both of you. Remember, something in that room knocked poor Philip Philby off his rocker."

"Thanks for reminding me," Jenna muttered.

"What?" Wendy said. Jenna told her.

While Wendy took photographs on Jenna's smartphone, Jenna continued to peer around the room. The flash from the camera app showed something glinting green.

The Bogwitch was in a corner, jiggling excitedly. Jenna pointed the camera at the floor.

Do you see? Do you see? It wasn't me who took the kiddies! It wasn't me!

"Then who was it?" Jenna said.

"What?" Wendy said and Cassandra in unison.

***

Constable Dimwoodie was pleased with the results. He took the topmost flyer from the box and admired it – as much as the glowering stare of Public Enemy Number One, Philip Philby could be admired. Parkin had done a bang-up job and Dimwoodie had told him so, before asking him to forward his invoice to the police station.

Now, it was a matter of distribution. A brainwave took Dimwoodie to the newsagent. A flyer was to be inserted into every copy of the evening paper. The boys and girls who delivered that fine organ around the area would do most of Dimwoodie's dissemination for him.

While in the shop, Dimwoodie acquired a couple of rolls of Sellotape. By the time he got back to the police station, he had affixed dozens of flyers to lampposts all along the High Street. Feeling pretty pleased with his progress, he fished in his pocket for the key to the door.

On the doorstep was Tina Thornbush. No doubt she wants an update, Dimwoodie surmised. And, for once, he was happy to supply one. Well, not 'happy' as such, no. 'Prepared' was a better word for it. He could show her the flyer, for one thing. And tell her the name of the bastard who had taken her son. That had to count for something.

The poor woman's eyes, red-rimmed and watery, were brimming with sorrow. Her neck was bent and her shoulders were slumped beneath the weight of her worry and grief. It broke Dimwoodie's heart to see her.

"Hello, Tina," he turned the key in the lock. He refrained from asking how she was doing because he could see that for himself. "Come in. We'll have a cuppa and a chat."

***

"Something's not right," Wendy Rabbitt gazed around the cellar, drumming her fingers on her chin.

"No shit," Jenna agreed.

"No, it's not just the wall of skulls and the satanic scribbling," Wendy continued. "Don't you think it's all a bit – you know, obvious?"

"Uh?"

"It's all a bit too easy. We found the door with no problems. We got in here with no problems. It's almost as though someone wanted us to find this place."

She's good, the Bogwitch approved.

"Ssh!" Jenna said.

"Excuse me?" Wendy rounded on the camera.

"Not you," Jenna said. She gestured feebly at her headset.

I never said a word, thought Cassandra.

"Think about it," the light was in Wendy's eyes again. "Why wasn't the door locked? Why has no one come looking for us?"

Jenna thought about it. "We're not in danger, are we?"

"Pphh!" Wendy scoffed. "I've been in stickier spots than this, I can tell you."

Huh, thought Cassandra. A bust-up at a church fete is hardly Early Closing Day in Beirut, love.

"There's something we're missing," Wendy turned on the spot. "Something we haven't noticed..."

"Oh, I don't know, Miss Rabbitt," said a male voice from the top of the stairs. "I think you've seen the bare bones of it."

***

Once Tina Thornbush was installed on a chair, Constable Dimwoodie put the kettle on. The poor woman hadn't uttered a word, not even to confirm whether she wanted milk and sugar. Dimwoodie thought it best to keep these embellishments on the side. If she wanted them, she could add them herself. It's not rocket science, he thought. It's not even forensic science.

He breezed from the back room bearing two steaming mugs in his hands, and a carton of milk that didn't smell too iffy and a crumpled bag of sugar under his arm.

"Here we go," he smiled. He may as well have been addressing the leaflet rack.

He set the tea things down and took a seat facing Tina.

"I've got something to show you," he hoped his words didn't sound too playful, too teasing. This was the most serious case he'd ever handled, after all, and this woman was the mother of the abductee.

He presented a flyer. Tina Thornbush didn't reach out to accept it, so Dimwoodie held it up where she could not fail to see it. Tina Thornbush's eyes were open but didn't seem to be seeing anything.

"This is our suspect," Dimwoodie explained. "We are extremely interested in having a conversation with this man."

Tina Thornbush didn't even blink.

"I've distributed this image all around the town," the constable continued. "As you can observe, there's a telephone hotline. I expect the phone to be ringing off the hook any minute now, as people see the photograph and then have sightings of the suspect – Oh, shit! No!"

He turned the flyer around to get a closer look. His eyes raced over the paper, his despair growing with every rapid perusal.

"Oh, no! No, no! That bloody idiot."

But it was true. And would be true for every flyer he had posted, for every flyer that was still lying in the box with Philby's eyes staring up at him.

The phone number was wrong. A seven and an eight had been transposed.

That idiot Parkin had fucked it up, good and proper. Dimwoodie's heart sank to his standard-issue boots. The phone would not be ringing at all. Shit. Well, let him send his invoice! Fat chance of that ever getting paid!

He tried to maintain a professional demeanour. There was no point upsetting the poor woman any further. Not that she was taking any of it in. Poor cow. No wonder she was out of it. Probably the best place to be, considering.

He looked up from the fucked-up flyer with a view to offering the poor cow a sympathetic smile and was alarmed to find himself almost nose-to-nose with her. The red, staring eyes were inches from his baby blues. Dimwoodie leant back, trying to increase the distance between them. The woman's nostrils were flaring, and her face seemed to have elongated to the extent that she no longer looked like Tina Thornbush. This countenance, with its malevolent leer, was more masculine, more... diabolical.

Dimwoodie slipped down in his seat, preparing to make a break for it. A laugh arose from deep within the woman who was no longer a woman – deeper than that: from the bowels of Hell itself.

"You fool!" The voice was deep enough to vibrate the floor beneath the soles of Dimwoodie's boots. "You – *mortal!*"

Dimwoodie shook with fear. The word had been made to sound like the most contemptible thing the demonic creature could call him.

"Um..." Dimwoodie shrank further. If he was fast enough, he could duck down and hurl himself at the front door. Perhaps he could topple the leaflet rack in his wake to buy himself precious seconds in which to flee...

It was a good plan except a hand was cupped around his lower jaw. Heat from the hand seared through Dimwoodie's head, but that was nothing compared to the blistering glare from the creature's eyes.

"Stop them," the voice intoned, reverberating through Dimwoodie's skeleton. "Stop them or perish."

Dimwoodie's overheated brain struggled to form the question. "Stop who?" he forced the words out in a strangulated squeak.

He swooned.

"Here," said Tina Thornbush, holding out a mug of tea. "Get this down you. You must have fainted for a minute there."

"Aargh!" Dimwoodie yelped in terror.

"Poor love," cooed Tina Thornbush. "Must be under a lot of stress." She put the mug down and sat back with a flyer. She looked at Philip Philby's photograph. "So this is the bastard, is it? This is the fucking bastard who's got my Tommy? You can see it, can't you? In his eyes. They stare right into you, don't they? Talk about face of evil."

Let's not, Dimwoodie squirmed, his entire body slick with sweat.

What the hell had happened?

***

"It's not quite finished," Lord Fladgett smiled from the top of the cellar stairs. He slapped a light switch and the cellar was flooded with light from overhead fluorescent tubes. Jenna and Wendy blinked from the sudden intake of harsh illumination. Lord Fladgett, in plus fours and Harris tweed, ambled down to join them. "But what do you think of it so far?"

"You what?" Jenna said.

"You monster!" Wendy growled. "You won't get away with this. We've got it all on tape."

"Oh?" Lord Fladgett looked directly into the lens. "I should sincerely hope so." He waggled his fingers in a greeting. "Is that Miss Clune in her van outside? Good day, Miss Clune. Why don't you come and join us?"

In her camper van, Cassandra flushed red. She gabbled something to Jenna.

"She says she's going to call the cops," Jenna relayed the message. "And don't think she won't."

Lord Fladgett laughed. "Go right ahead. You can even use my phone. If you're hell bent on making bigger fools of yourselves."

Wendy's reporter instincts were flaring up. She gave the room a fresh appraisal. Lord Fladgett watched her inspect everything in the harsh lighting. A smile twitched his handlebar moustache.

"Well?" he asked.

"It's fake," Wendy concluded. "All of it."

"Well, of course, it is!" Lord Fladgett laughed. "But it had you going for a few minutes, and don't you deny it! Your faces, honestly."

He pointed at the gleaming domes of security cameras nestled high in corners. "I've been watching you since you arrived in the car park. I'm surprised you didn't tumble it sooner. Don't you think I made it easy for you?"

"I don't get it," Jenna admitted. "What's he going on about?"

"We've been had," Wendy said. "We've been stitched up like kippers."

Lord Fladgett addressed the camera a second time. "Well, Miss Clune? Are you coming in? Please say you will. I would hate to have to explain everything twice."

You did not need to be fitted with a headset to make out Cassandra's reply, but Jenna translated the string of invective for the others' benefit.

"She's coming," she said.

"Capital!" His Lordship clapped his hands together and then reached inside his jacket for a metallic flask. "Little tipple while we wait?" he offered. "Take the edge off those jangled nerves of yours."

Jenna declined but Wendy was quick to snatch the flask and gulp a large swig. Lord Fladgett smiled benevolently. What's the word, thought Jenna? Carbuncular? No... There was something *avuncular* about him. He was like a dotty old uncle, keen to share a secret with his favourite nieces.

Jenna swept the camera once more around the room, getting the clearest shots so far of the satanic markings and the wall of skulls.

What the hell is going on?

***

"If you're sure you're OK..." Tina Thornbush was a picture of concern. The colour had returned to the constable's cheeks and his breathing had returned to normal – as far as she could tell.

"I'm – fine," Dimwoodie's voice cracked mid-utterance.

"I'll be off then."

Dimwoodie sprang to his feet. "Are you sure I can't walk you back? See you home."

"That's all right," Tina Thornbush squeezed his hand. "You need a lie-down and a drink of something stronger. Perhaps give the doctor a call. You look like you've seen a ghost."

"If only!"

"Promise me you'll take better care of yourself. You've got a kidnapper to catch. Promise me you'll get him for me." Her eyes sought his, but there was nothing demonic about them now. The imploring sadness in Tina Thornbush's penetrating gaze was all too human.

"I'll do my best," Dimwoodie offered, feebly. He even raised his hand in a fumbled version of the boy scouts' salute.

Tina Thornbush patted his arm and left. Dimwoodie sat down again.

Stop them! That's what Tina had said when she wasn't Tina.

But stop who from doing what? That's what I'd like to know...

His gaze fell on the flyer. Philip Philby's eyes bore into him, mocking, foreboding, relentless.

"What are you staring at?" Dimwoodie whimpered.

***

When Cassandra appeared in the doorway, Lord Fladgett bounded up the brick staircase to intercept her. He offered to take her hand but she waved him away. Gingerly, she made her way down, unable to see where she was putting her feet, and making great efforts not to look at the wall of skulls as she went past. At least if I fall, I'll bowl right into this bastard, she consoled herself.

The women stood together, mindful of keeping themselves between His Lordship and the stairs to the exit.

"Now," Wendy Rabbitt crossed her arms. "What the bloody blue fuck is going on?"

Lord Fladgett laughed, indulging the reporter's foul-mouthed outburst. He spread his arms expansively.

"Welcome, ladies," he beamed. "Welcome to the latest attraction at Fladgett Hall!"

"Attraction?" Cassandra frowned. "Not the word I'd use."

"If I may continue?" His Lordship raised his eyebrows. Cassandra nodded. Jenna was filming it all, so if the worst happened, perhaps someone would find the footage and see what had happened to them. It would be like one of those low-budget films.

"It's not quite finished. There are things I've got on order but they haven't turned up yet. You know, the sort of thing. An iron maiden here, a rack over there. It's going to be marvellous."

"You mentioned an attraction?" Wendy Rabbitt prompted.

"Why, yes! This kind of thing is all the rage nowadays and here at Fladgett Hall, we like to keep up with the times."

"What kind of thing?"

"Why, an escape room, of course! I thought you were a little brighter than this."

The three women exchanged puzzled looks.

"But the skulls?" Jenna said. "All those poor kiddies."

Lord Fladgett laughed, horrifying them all. He skipped over to the gruesome feature and rapped his knuckles on a couple of the nearest specimens. They emitted sickening, hollow notes.

"Fibreglass, the whole lot," he explained. "Had to be commissioned especially, of course. And this kind of thing doesn't come cheap."

"And this lot?" Wendy moved to the wall with the occult symbols and scrawlings.

Lord Fladgett laughed. "Load of gobbledegook, of course. Until..." he raised a finger, "You find the key. You know the sort of thing, I'm sure. You solve a few smaller puzzles which yield clues to the larger puzzle, which is on that very wall. That's how you find your way out. That's how you escape."

The women were nonplussed.

"I did mention it is an escape room."

Wendy beat her fingertips against her forehead as though stimulating thoughts. "Let me see if I've got this straight. You're installing an escape room under the house, and it's based on the most horrific aspects of local history?"

"Bingo!" Lord Fladgett cheered. "Actually, in point of fact, we tried having bingo nights last year. Never caught on. But I'm sure this one will turn the tide for us."

Cassandra was struggling to form a sentence. Eventually, she managed. "So, what the hell are we doing here? Clearly, you've lured us down here for some reason."

"Quite so," His Lordship smiled. "If I'd told you what was

going on, would you have had the same reaction, the same experience? Would you have been as frightened as you so obviously were?"

They thought about this and concluded that perhaps they wouldn't.

"Best way to test run the thing," Lord Fladgett went on. "You see, not only do you have to find your way out of the escape room, you have to find your way into it too. That part of the experience still needs a bit of work, the staff need a little more training and so forth."

"So what are we doing here?" Cassandra had found her voice now. She drew herself up to her most imposing stature. "Us in particular, I mean."

"Too good a chance to pass up," Lord Fladgett was not fazed in the slightest. "You were snooping around the other day. My staff are a loyal bunch. They tell me everything, don't you know? I knew you'd be back. I just wish everything had been in place. But please, you must return for the grand opening. You can be my special guests. There'll be champagne."

"No, thank you," Cassandra sniffed, more than a little miffed that she had been taken in. "Come on, girls. Let us get out of this tawdry sideshow."

She headed for the stairs.

"Hold up," Jenna said. "There's something I want to know."

"And what's that, my dear?" Lord Fladgett smiled indulgently.

"What was here before?"

"What?"

"What was down here, before you put all this shit in?"

"My dear girl, I don't know what you're getting at. This was just a cellar, an unassuming place of storage. A waste of space, in fact."

"I don't think so," Jenna shook her head, and the camera with it. "Something was down here. Something horrible."

Cassandra cottoned on. "Yes, she's right! There was something horrible down here. Why else would Philip Philby's hair turn white in an instant? What made him lose his marbles?"

Lord Fladgett's moustache twitched as his smile faltered. "I don't –"

Wendy Rabbitt rounded on him. "You know who we mean," she accused. "So you might as well tell us everything."

Lord Fladgett looked from face to face to camera. He let out a sigh that just about fell short of theatrical.

"Poor Philip. He was a good worker. But as for what he saw – or thought he saw – on that terrible stormy night – well, you'll have to ask him, I'm afraid. If you look here, you can just about make out the watermark. That's how flooded this cellar was."

He gestured vaguely at a tidemark halfway up the stairs.

"Now, I must get on. Chase up that iron maiden. You will be sure to make a report, won't you?" he addressed Wendy Rabbitt. "We need the publicity, don't you know. Nothing too detailed, of course. A sort of Coming Attractions kind of thing. I'm sure you know the sort."

Wendy's blood boiled. She had been conned. Tricked! Duped! Fooled into filming a free advertisement for this tasteless tourist attraction.

Cassandra sensed trouble was brewing. She curled her hand around the reporter's biceps and drew her to the stairs.

"Come on, Wendy," she said in soothing tones. "Let's regroup in the van. Jen."

Jen skirted around His Lordship. The three of them headed up the stairs and out. The duty manager was waiting for them in the corridor.

"I'll show you the quickest way out," she smirked. "We do hope you enjoyed your visit to Fladgett Hall."

"Don't expect a five-star review," Jenna jeered.

Chastened and downhearted, the trio trudged back to the camper van.

"That could have gone better," Cassandra concluded. "You all right, Jen?"

"Hmm," Jenna said, gazing back at the house. "It is plausible, I suppose."

"But…" Wendy prompted.

"There's still something else," Jenna shook her head.

"Blimey," Cassandra said. "Words out of my mouth. We'll make a bog witch out of you yet!"

She got into the van and started the engine while the others loaded the equipment in the back.

No, thanks, thought Jenna.

The Bogwitch herself was notably absent. And Jenna was grateful for that.

***

The drive back to the cottage was filled with disgruntled silence. Each in their turn thought of something to say but stopped themselves. They were equally embarrassed and frustrated by the way the tables had been turned on their undercover ruse. They were coming away with nothing. Meanwhile, that little boy was still missing and the kidnapper was still at large.

Cassandra slowed as they travelled along the High Street. Dimwoodie's flyers fluttered and flapped from every lamppost. The evil eyes of Philip Philby glowered at them from both sides. It made Cassandra long for the days of the cabbage leaf bunting.

"Philby," Wendy declared. "We need to have a chat with Philby."

Jenna shuddered. "I don't fancy that," she said from the back of the van.

"He's the culprit," Wendy set her jaw. "Any money."

"We're crossing Lord Whatsit off the list then, are we?" Cassandra countered.

"Dead herring," Wendy's shoulder jerked half a shrug.

"Red," Cassandra corrected. What did they teach them at journalism college?

"Dead red, then," Wendy amended her statement and made it worse.

"It looks like the police are after him," Jenna observed.

"Who, love?

"Philby," Jenna said. "Why else would they put out all these pictures?"

"Well, we did tip them off," Cassandra said. "Glad to see he's pulled his finger out."

"Who, Philby?"

"Constable Whatsit. Takes the 'plod' part of his job too seriously."

"That's a bit harsh," Jenna said, suddenly feeling sorry for Constable Dimwoodie.

"Well," Cassandra said. "It's hardly *Starsky and Hutch* around here, is it?"

"Who?" Jenna said.

"Ask your gran," Cassandra sighed.

***

Constable Dimwoodie, in contradiction of Cassandra's words, was not so much plodding through town as powerwalking. Where he was going, he was not entirely sure. But he was striding with purpose. Although he wasn't sure what his purpose was, either. He had vague recollections about finding the man with staring eyes, but where that man might be found remained a mystery. So, no change there.

The supermarket!

The thought seemed to come out of the blue, but now that it had occurred to him, it made perfect sense. There would be other witnesses who had seen Philby there earlier. All right, so the customers would be long gone, but the staff would still be there. Unless they were part-timers, as a lot of retail workers are, Dimwoodie knew. Stuff it; it was worth a try. It was not like his head was brimming with alternatives.

He strode past CostBusters and had to backtrack in a reasonable facsimile of a moonwalk.

Where had all this energy come from? Why did it feel that he was no longer in charge of his own limbs?

Perhaps the milk he had had in his tea had been off after all, and was responsible for this hallucinatory state.

He entered the store and was assailed by the aroma of freshly baked bread and the soothing tones of *The Girl From Ipanema* played on a marimba. A meet-and-greeter offered him a wire basket.

"Enjoy your shopping experience with us today," she smiled.

Dimwoodie looked her up and down, with predatory interest. The woman's smile didn't falter but her eyes darted, seeking backup.

"Officer?" she sounded nervous.

Dimwoodie's nostrils flared. "No," he said and walked away. *Too old...*

He took off his peaked cap and gave his head a wobble. Where had those words come from? And what did they mean, 'too old'?

Not feeling well, Dimwoodie moved through the verdant aisles of fresh fruit and vegetables, heading for the in-store pharmacy at the rear of the store.

What is wrong with me? he wondered, not for the first time. Why don't my thoughts feel like my own? Why don't my limbs feel like I'm driving them?

"Welcome to our pharmacy," smiled a meet-and-greeter in a white coat.

"Help...me..." Dimwoodie sank to one knee, holding out an imploring hand toward the counter. "I'm looking for a man."

The pharmacy assistant's smile wavered. "I see..." she lied. "Damon's on his break. But I can assure you, we are all trained to deal with issues of every kind. There is no need to be embarrassed. We have heard it all before, believe me!"

"No," Dimwoodie shook his head. He was sinking lower, his hands on the floor.

"We can offer complete privacy for your consultation," the assistant leaned over the counter. "And complete and total confidentiality, of course – it literally goes without saying."

She watched the policeman fumble in his pocket for a piece of paper. Bless, she thought; he's probably written down the name of some medication he doesn't want to say out loud. Poor love. A little blue pill for the boy in blue!

She stretched out to take the paper and was surprised it wasn't an ad for an erectile dysfunction remedy. Moreover, she was startled to meet the gaze of the man in the picture. Those eyes, they bored right into your brain.

Meanwhile, Dimwoodie was clinging to the counter as he attempted to climb back onto his feet. "Has he – been in?"

The assistant pursed her lips as she took another look at the staring man. "No..."

Dimwoodie panted out a sigh.

"But he was outside earlier on," the assistant's words perked him up a little. "Yeah, that's right. There was some altercation with a woman and a pushchair. She didn't half wallop him."

"Go on," Dimwoodie felt encouraged, and the encouragement made him feel a little stronger. "Did you see where he went?"

"No... If you ask me, she shouldn't have left her kiddies out there unattended. Especially not with, you know..." She trailed off, her sentence hanging ominously unfinished.

Dimwoodie, almost vertical now, snatched the flyer away. "Thanks," he snarled. "I'll ask around."

"Fine," the assistant said. "Is there anything else I could help you with today, sir?"

Dimwoodie bought some painkillers for his headache, even though he wasn't certain it was a headache. He thanked the assistant again and a floorwalker escorted him around all the staff who were still on duty and might be able to help him with his enquiries.

The shop staff were happy to help. They liked having a policeman in the store. It gave the shoplifters something to think about. In terms of actual, useful information, they could not offer much. There was a consensus about the direction the man with the staring eyes had taken after the woman had beaten him up with her handbag.

Dimwoodie made notes, underlined them and ringed them.

He thanked the staff for their help.

Stop them!

Dimwoodie staggered against a display of baked bean cans. The last time he had heard those words they had come from Tina Thornbush. Or had he dreamt that?

He dismissed the concerned grimaces of the shop staff and several assorted customers, claiming he just needed fresh air. He tottered from the supermarket, pausing only briefly to observe the site of the Great Handbag Walloping. He lingered long enough to dry-swallow a couple of paracetamols and then flung himself around the corner, hoping to be able to retrace Philby's steps.

Oh, why couldn't it have been snowing, he wailed inwardly! Then I might have stood a fighting chance.

Damn it, police work is hard!

"Watch where you're going!" said the man Dimwoodie collided with around the corner.

"I'm terribly sorry, I –" Dimwoodie's words failed him. He pulled out a flyer and looked from the picture to the face of the man before him and then back to the picture again.

Two sets of eyes pierced him with the same stare.

"Philip Philby?" Dimwoodie pulled himself together. "I've been looking for you."

Damn it, police work is easy!

***

Wendy Rabbitt connected the camera to Iphigenia's antiquated television so they could review the footage Jenna had shot at Fladgett Hall. Throughout the screening, Jenna, sitting on the floor so the grown-ups could have the sofa, cringed and blushed, hugging her knees and hiding her face.

"Sorry it's so wobbly," she cringed.

"It's not too bad, love," Cassandra said, dunking a sponge finger in her cup of tea.

"It's practically *avant garde*," Wendy Rabbitt said. "I knew I should have done the filming."

"You never said," Cassandra said. "You wanted to be on-screen. In the limelight."

"We don't have limelight in telly," Wendy sneered.

"Figuratively, you do," Cassandra countered.

They watched the camera zip across the wall of skulls and then take a second, slower pass. Iphigenia made sounds of disgust and said she was glad they'd told her beforehand that it was all fakery and humbug. The screen filled with the supposedly satanic markings. Closer inspection revealed them to be scrawled in gloss paint, rather than fresh blood – human or otherwise.

"Wonder what it says," Iphigenia said. "Any ideas, Cassandra?"

Cassandra waved the hand that wasn't holding her cup and saucer. "Oh, they've tried to make it look authentic, but it's all nonsense. Reading that lot out won't summon anything nasty. It'd probably hurt your throat a bit, that's all. His Lordship said it was a code, with the final clue of how to get out of the cellar, but you need to solve other clues before you get the key to this one."

Iphigenia understood but was far from impressed. "The things people get up to these days. Why can't they all just go down the pub and talk to each other?"

"When was the last time you went to the pub?" was Jenna's cynical question.

Her grandmother smiled her crooked smile. "Ah, I don't need to, do I, my sweetness? Because I have you here to talk to, don't I?"

Jenna rolled her eyes.

Amused, Iphigenia returned her attention to the screen. "Isn't that the way out, there?"

"Where?" Wendy Rabbitt said.

"There! Pause it again, will you, chicken?"

Wendy obliged.

There was a door near the stairs, painted to look like the brickwork, but a tiny plaque was visible. It read, PRIVATE.

"That's probably where the staff sit, monitoring the action," Wendy said.

"I don't think so," Jenna said. "Remember, Lord Whatsit said he'd been watching us from his apartment."

"Well done, love!" Cassandra beamed.

"Well, then, it's probably a broom cupboard or something," Wendy said. "I doubt very much it's the way out of the escape room. You'd be out of there in two minutes flat."

"Hmm," Cassandra took a pensive bite of her biscuit. "It's a shame you didn't find that door while you were down there."

"You were down there too!"

"I mean before His Lordship came and collared you."

"Wait!" Iphigenia cried, startling everybody. "What was that?"

She pointed at the screen, which was almost completely black at this point.

"What was what?" Jenna said, looking up from her knees.

"That's what I'm asking," Iphigenia said. "Can you make it go backwards?"

"I'll do it," Wendy rose from the sofa and knelt by the camera. On screen, the image showed white lines over the blackness.

"There!" Iphigenia cried again. "Stop it there!"

They peered at the frozen screen. In the darkness of a corner of the cellar twinkled two green glints. Jenna gasped.

"Hold up," Wendy said. She fiddled with some controls on the television, adjusting brightness and contrast.

"Lighten our darkness!" Iphigenia marvelled.

Around the two green glints, a figure emerged from the gloom, a ragged, hunched figure that Jenna found all too familiar.

"The Bogwitch..." Cassandra breathed.

"The what?" Wendy said.

"She was right there!" Cassandra leaned closer to the television. "She was with us all along."

"Pphh," Wendy scoffed. "I don't think so. It was probably

one of Lord Whatsit's little tricks. A dummy, a mannequin, stashed in the corner. He's probably going to rig it so it wags its finger at you. Whoooh!"

Cassandra was deflated. She sat back. "I suppose you're right. Wishful thinking, I suppose. We see what we want to see."

"No," Jenna said.

"No?" Cassandra said.

"No," Jenna confirmed. "It was the Bogwitch. The actual Bogwitch. She was there. She's been with me for ages, following me around, talking to me. She's real. I'm telling you. The Bogwitch is really real."

Iphigenia bit her lower lip in concern. "Jenna, love, have you been overdoing it? You know you're not supposed to get over-stimulated."

"It's not that, Gran," Jenna protested. "I'm fine. Well, as fine as I can be, considering. But the Bogwitch is real. She really is. You have to believe me."

Wendy turned away, preferring to tinker with technology, but Cassandra's interest was piqued.

"Is she with us right now, chicken?" she whispered. "Is she talking to you right this minute?"

"No," Jenna said.

"Oh," Cassandra looked put out.

"That's because she's sitting on the sofa beside you, watching the television."

Cassandra, startled, looked at the space only a few moments earlier Wendy had vacated.

The Bogwitch smiled at Jenna and waved fingers like tendrils.

Hello!

Jenna gave a slow wave back.

Everyone else stared at the empty seat.

"Hello?" they said.

***

Dimwoodie backed Philip Philby into a doorway. Somehow,

close up and in person, the staring eyes were nowhere near as intense as the mugshot would lead you to believe. In fact, the man could not meet the policeman's gaze at all. Philip Philby, in stained hospital clothes, his face and hands filthy from weeks of living rough, a dirty beard sprouting in all directions like an exploded Pekingese, looked more wretched than anything Dimwoodie had ever seen.

"We meet at last," Dimwoodie said, because it sounded appropriate. Philby shuddered and shrank away, his arms up in self-defence. "I think you and me had better have a little chat."

Philby whimpered. Dimwoodie reached for his wrist to apply handcuffs but Philby was quicker than the copper anticipated. He ducked and dodged, blindsiding Dimwoodie and shoving him against the wall. Philby was off, around the corner, towards the main shopping area. Winded, Dimwoodie gave chase. He tried to blow his whistle, but only feeble peeps came out.

Philby plunged into the shoppers on the High Street, leaving angry, shouting people in his wake. These same people were further disturbed by the intrusion of Constable Dimwoodie into their midst.

"Stop him!" Dimwoodie urged. The shoppers got out of the way; that was as far as their assistance went.

Dimwoodie's standard-issue boots pounded the pavement. Every step jolted his heart against his ribcage. He remembered to breathe – it was a key part of exercise, he recalled from his training. Philby was slowing. The wretched man could not have much in the way of energy reserves. Unless –

Unless –

The thought knocked the wind out of Dimwoodie and brought him to a sickening standstill. He doubled over and tried to spit out the image that had seared across his mind.

Unless the sick bastard has been eating human flesh!

Dimwoodie forced himself to resume pursuit, despite the stitch that was threatening his left side. He pressed a hand against it and carried on.

They were clear of the main streets now. The shops gave way to terraced houses and the odd business premises. Funeral directors. Building suppliers. A scrapyard.

It was here, Dimwoodie saw a flash of grey among the stacked remains of smashed-up vehicles. Philby was picking his way through this metallic landscape. Perhaps he was hoping to hide in a battered chassis or to crawl underneath a written-off van...

Dimwoodie slowed to a walk. Oh, if only he could call for backup. But the forces of Greater Fladgett and Praxton were too far away to do him any good.

Stop them!

Dimwoodie spun around on the spot, although he knew the voice had come from inside his own head.

I am! He's right there! I'm going to arrest him and get him to tell me where he's hidden that little boy.

This last part sounded less than convincing. Dimwoodie would work out how to get Philby to talk later on, when he was securely in police custody. For now, he would focus on apprehending the suspect and getting him back to the station.

He hoped that would appease the intrusive voice. It seemed to have gone quiet for now.

And what the bloody hell was going on with that anyway?

Perhaps I'm over-stressed. It's been a trying time ever since that poor kiddie went missing. I've been overdoing it.

But it would soon be over. The culprit was within his grasp. He wouldn't let Philby take him by surprise again.

With cuffs in one hand and his truncheon in the other, Dimwoodie prowled through the scrapyard, trying to make as little noise as possible. He thought about demanding that Philby give himself up but discarded that idea. He wanted to retain the element of surprise. If he could just sneak up on him...

There was a creak like a rusty hinge in a giant's castle. It tore through the air and Dimwoodie's ears as he spun around, trying to locate the source. A shadow fell over him, a forerunner of the tower of car corpses that was about to topple and crush him to death.

***

For the second time in its history, Spenser Cottage was to host a séance. Cassandra had resisted the idea initially, reminding them of how it had gone for Tina Thornbush the first time they had tried it.

"All the more reason to talk to this Bogwitch then," Iphigenia had insisted. "The more we know, the more power we have."

Wendy Rabbitt wondered if she should record the whole thing but everyone else was quick to pour cold water on the idea, threatening to do the same to her precious camera equipment if she went ahead. According to the rules (that Cassandra had found on the internet) no electronic devices of any kind were permitted at a séance. Wendy held up her hands in surrender.

"All right, all right!" She made a show of packing the camera in its case. "No filming here. Not a sausage."

"I can empathise," Iphigenia patted her hand. "I've been a widow for donkeys'."

"Shouldn't Tina Thornbush be here as well?" Jenna asked. "Perhaps we can help her. Perhaps the Bogwitch can help her?"

She looked at the Bogwitch, who was still loafing on the sofa and generally making herself at home. The Bogwitch shrugged and carried on watching a quiz show on the television.

"I suspect time is of the essence," Iphigenia said, setting up the table. "We can sort old Tina Thingybob out some other time."

"Well, why can't I just tell you what the Bogwitch is saying?" Jenna cried. She was met with concerned looks from her grandmother and her friend.

"Well..." Cassandra pouted.

"Because it's too much of a strain on you, love," Iphigenia patted Jenna's hand.

"No, it isn't!" Jenna snapped. "We've been talking for ages.

She's not dangerous – well, not to me, at any rate. Not so far. She even saved me from whatever it is that's got into Tina Thornbush."

The Bogwitch nodded confirmation but only Jenna could see it.

"Listen, love," Cassandra took her seat at the head of the table. "If the Bogwitch is there, this is the best way to talk to her."

"What do you mean, 'if'?" Jenna roared. "I'm telling you, she's right there. Gran, tell her! I'm not making it up."

"Of course not, dear," Iphigenia said, taking her seat at the table. Wendy Rabbitt sat opposite Cassandra.

Cassandra offered a hand. "We need a fourth," she said.

Jenna shook her head. "You don't believe me, do you? You think I've lost my grip again, don't you?" There was pain in her voice and accusation in her eyes. Iphigenia felt terrible; the poor girl had been through so much in her young life.

"Give it a go, dear," Gran smiled sadly.

"Don't you think we should ask the guest of honour first?" Jenna snarled. She stomped over to stand between the Bogwitch and the television. The Bogwitch, with an annoyed expression, tried to see past her to find out who would win the bonus round.

"Will you speak to us? To all of us?"

The Bogwitch, exasperated, looked Jenna in the eye.

I suppose so. Can't watch anything in this madhouse.

"Good!" Jenna said. She sat at the table. The Bogwitch was dismayed to see she had missed the question that led to the star prize. People were clapping. Glittering strips were falling from on high.

With a sigh, the Bogwitch rose from the sofa and approached the table.

Where do you want me?

***

"Hey! Hey, hey!" Malcolm Mackenzie, proprietor of the scrap-yard, came hobbling from the shed that served as his office. His dogs, Fang and Frobisher, ran ahead, barking nastily. Fortunately for Constable Dimwoodie, they couldn't get to him. The policeman stood in a ring of fallen cars, unscathed but surrounded. "Gotcha!" Malcolm Mackenzie roared in triumph.

"Um, hello?" Dimwoodie tried to call through broken windows. "Who's that?"

"I'll ask the questions," Malcolm Mackenzie snarled. "Fucking cheek of it. Who are you?"

"I'm the police," Dimwoodie said. "I was in pursuit of a suspected child abductor."

"Oh," Malcolm Mackenzie blinked in surprise. "Came in here, did he?"

"Who?"

"Your child abductor."

"Yes! I gave chase and the next thing I know, he's pushing a pile of cars on top of me."

"I see. Are you hurt?"

"No. Not a scratch."

"Right. Then you can piss off out of it then, can you?"

"Have you seen him?"

"Who?"

"The child abductor?"

"I wouldn't know him from Adam. And I'll be wanting reparations for all this. Going to cost me to get all this lot shifted. I'll have to rent a crane and all sorts."

"Perhaps you'll store them more securely next time."

"What's that supposed to mean?"

"I could report you for Health and Safety violations..." Dimwoodie let the threat hang in the air.

Malcolm Mackenzie frowned. He couldn't do that, could he? He looked at his dogs. Neither Fang nor Frobisher seemed prepared to give an answer. They were snarling at the policeman, their hackles bristling. Mackenzie whistled to call them off.

They ignored him.

"We better get you out of there," he called over the top of a Ford Fiesta.

"That would be nice," Dimwoodie agreed.

"But I reckon your man's long gone."

"You're probably right."

"Fang! Frobisher! Heel!"

The dogs promptly sat on their haunches.

Close enough, thought Malcolm Mackenzie.

***

"How is this going to work?" Jenna opened one eye. Across the table, Cassandra opened both of hers.

"I don't know, do I?" she spoke in a stage whisper. "I've never done this before, remember? Well, not properly."

I can hear her. Does she know that? The Bogwitch's presence made Jenna's elbow itch.

"Speak when you're spoken to!" Jenna snapped.

"Is she there?" Cassandra urged.

"Of course she's there!" Jenna cried. "Otherwise, what would be the bloody point of this charade? Look, why don't you ask me your questions and I'll relay the answers."

Iphigenia frowned. "Now, where's the fun in that?"

"I'm not doing this for fun!" Cassandra was aghast. "Now can we talk to the fucking Bogwitch or what?"

She composed herself. She reached her hands across the table to take one of Iphigenia's and one of Jenna's in hers. "We must be united. We must be open."

Jenna and her grandmother rolled their eyes at each other and joined their free hands to Wendy's to complete the rather squarish circle.

Aww, cooed the Bogwitch. *But where do I fit in?*

"Anywhere you want," Jenna said, through the side of her mouth.

Cassandra cleared her throat even though she didn't need to.

"Let us begin!" she intoned. Iphigenia tried not to laugh.

"Bogwitch..." Cassandra's head rolled. "If you are with us here and now, give us a sign."

Is she serious?

"Just do as she says," Jenna whispered.

Very well.

There was the sound of breaking glass as the Bogwitch knocked something over.

"My vase!" Iphigenia jumped up. Cassandra pulled her down again.

"Speak to us, Bogwitch! Give us your message!"

I don't know... the Bogwitch seemed hesitant. *I'm not very comfortable with these things. I always get flustered.*

"It's not an answering machine," Jenna said. "Just imagine you're talking to me. You never seem to have trouble doing that."

No. I have a better idea. Follow me!

A rush of air circled the table, displacing the women's hair. The lights flickered on and off and then the television switched itself on – or rather, the Bogwitch turned it on. Her voice, previously only heard by Jenna, crackled from the speaker.

Hello, ladies! Gather round and make yourselves comfortable. I have something to show you.

Around the table, four pairs of eyes opened and blinked.

"Did you hear that?" Jenna gasped. "Tell me you heard that."

"It came from the telly," Iphigenia said.

"Probably just coincidence," Cassandra said. "Let's refocus." She held out her hands.

"It did come from the television," Wendy confirmed, standing up. "And the television is not even plugged in."

Four heads turned. On screen, an image resolved itself. Murky and monochromatic, as though seen through a prism of stagnant water, the face of the Bogwitch – what could be seen beneath the reedy tendrils of her hair – peered at them.

Make yourselves comfy, she advised. *I have a story to tell.*

Iphigenia was the first to leave the table, practically bounding toward her armchair. Wendy followed, wondering how such an apparition was technically possible. Jenna and Cassandra exchanged looks. A now-do-you-believe-me look, which was answered by a this-is-unorthodox-but-I'll-go-along-with-it look. They adjourned to the sofa. When they were all sitting comfortably, the Bogwitch began.

Pictures swam on the screen, like objects floating on the surface of a pond. Everything was in shades of green, and the images lacked definition. Figures were little more than silhouettes, backgrounds were hazy, but it was the voice of the Bogwitch that drew them in.

***

Constable Dimwoodie picked his way out of the circle of toppled car carcasses. Malcolm Mackenzie shook his head, as if this was exactly the kind of thing he expected from the police force today. He was about to give the constable a piece of his mind, when Fang and Frobisher drew his attention to a nearby ruin of an ambulance, its front flattened in by some high-speed collision during a mercy mission, no doubt. The dogs closed in on the vehicle, growling deeply and moving with stealth.

"Friend of yours?" Malcolm Mackenzie chuckled. He motioned for the policeman to stay put and then, whistling through his fingers like a shepherd, literally called off the dogs. Fang trotted instantly to heel, but Frobisher lingered at the ambulance's backdoor. "What you got there, Frobe? Good boy!"

He approached the dog and scratched it between the ears. Frobisher's tail swished enthusiastically. Malcolm Mackenzie slowly lifted a hand toward the door release.

"Don't!" Dimwoodie warned, but Fang was between him and the ambulance.

Malcolm Mackenzie's hand closed around the handle. "I know what I'm do—"

Philip Philby leapt from the roof of the ambulance, knocking Malcolm Mackenzie to the ground. Instantly, the dogs were upon him, their jaws clamping onto his shirt collar and trouser leg. Malcolm Mackenzie writhed beneath the wild-eyed man, unable to issue any whistling commands to his dogs.

Nevertheless, a piercing shriek rent the air. At first, Malcolm Mackenzie thought it was the policeman, screaming like a little girl. True, the sound had emitted from Dimwoodie, but from his police-issue whistle, rather than his vocal cords.

Fang and Frobisher came bounding toward Dimwoodie, but rather than rip him to shreds, as was their usual modus operandi, they sat either side of him, tails thumping the ground and tongues lolling. Malcolm Mackenzie had never seen anything like it. He shoved his way free of the madman. Philip Philby, given this new opportunity to flee, stayed where he was, face down on the dirty ground, weeping his heart out. Fang and Frobisher set to howling in sympathy. Dusting himself off, Malcolm Mackenzie whistled a coded message that sent the dogs sloping back to their kennels.

"He's all yours," the scrapyard owner jerked his thumb toward the crying man. "Get him out of here. The dogs'll be expecting their dinner soon. They seemed to take a shine to you, though. Got dogs yourself, have you? I expect so. Whopping great Alsatians in your line of work."

Dimwoodie didn't respond. He approached the sorry-looking figure of Philip Philby with trepidation slowing his gait. But Philby offered no resistance to the handcuffs and allowed the constable to help him to his feet. Dimwoodie guided him to the exit. It was a long walk back to the station. Oh, for a squad car! Or even a tandem.

Malcolm Mackenzie watched them go. "I'll send you a bill," he called after the constable. "You know, for the crane."

Dimwoodie waved without turning back.

This was turning out to be the most expensive investigation of his career.

***

We lived simply, my grandmother and I, in our cottage in the bog. She taught me her skills, her knowledge, the lore of the bog, but she would never let me provide a remedy for any of the people who sought her out. People with agues, mysterious rashes in embarrassing places, people who could not get with child, people who were with child but did not want to be. They came from far and wide, and they paid what they could. My grandmother preferred a plump chicken or a bunch of carrots to any number of coins, but these she would accept if the client had nothing else. She never spent a crown; she kept the money in a locked box under her bed. It was for a rainy day, she said, but I knew that the day would come when she would turf me out to make my own way in the world, a prospect that was as frightening as it was tantalising.

I had no desire, in those early years, to step beyond the boundaries of the bog, until I met Robert.

Robert changed everything.

We had to sneak around. My grandmother did not approve of our association and neither did Robert's father, the Squire of Fladgett Hall. It would not do for one of noble birth to mingle with the lowliest of the lower orders; the grandchild of a bog witch is surely beneath the belly of the most wretched slug to crawl the bog. I was unworthy of him, except to him. He filled my head with ideas and my heart with excitement. O, we could run away! But whither could we run? There was no place, nowhere on this good earth to shelter us. His father would track us down, Robert was sure of it. And, cut off from his fortune, how were we to fend for ourselves?

In those tender moments, when we lay, spent, in each other's arms, I would suggest that I could provide. I knew enough of my grandmother's trade to be able to sell cures and amulets. There are people in difficulty wherever you find people, but Robert was too proud. He insisted that he should be the one to furnish our table with bread – and then I would point out that we would not even have a table, and we would laugh, and resume our lovemaking.

We were living in a fool's paradise.

Nothing lasts forever, especially nothing good. We were discovered. Of course we were. One dark day, our luck ran out, and we were interrupted in the cellars under Fladgett Hall. The Squire and three of his men came down, with firearms and cudgels. They pulled

Robert away, silencing him with a blow to his jaw. They kicked and they beat me, and they threatened to blast my brains from my head if I ever came near my beloved again. They chased me through the priest's hole and along the underground passage that had been such a boon to our clandestine encounters. In the woodland, they lost me. I ran and I ran, and I hid in a hollow.

Morning came, as mornings come, and I wended my world-weary way back to my grandmother's cottage. A ring of ash lay where the building had stood. A cold fist clenched my guts. My grandmother was hanging from a nearby tree. The Squire's men had destroyed her because they had been unable to find me.

I cut her down and buried her deep beneath the peat. I vowed vengeance on the beasts who had done this. I vowed to bring down the Squire, to burn down the Hall, to do anything and everything I could to tame the savage beating of my heart.

And then I thought of Robert, my sweet Robert, and I fell to the ground and wept for our cancelled love.

And then a dark spark ignited within me. There was still a way for us to be together. I knew enough of my grandmother's trade to be able to kill a man. I could concoct a potion and devise a way to introduce it into the Squire's food – there was the sticking place, for I did not wish for my sweet Robert to be a confederate in my crime.

Deep within the ruins of the cottage, Grandmother's strongbox was scorched but intact. Unfortunately, so was the lock that kept its contents so secure. I bashed away at the infernal thing with stones. I tried to prise it off with sharpened sticks.

And then I remembered where the key was.

It hung from a chain around my grandmother's neck. Oh, not for all the money in the world would I have committed such an atrocity! But the coins were not for me, they were for the plan, the plan to bring down the Squire of Fladgett Hall and avenge my grandmother's murder.

Believe me, I did not want to do it. Had there been any other way, I would have done it, no matter what the cost. But there was no other way. I had no other recourse.

Grandmother forgive me, and you ladies, understand. I violated my grandmother's final resting place to retrieve that key. I sobbed with every handful of peat I clawed away with my bare hands, begging for forgiveness.

She looked serene, so peaceful in her slumber, and fresh and hale. The restorative properties of peat working their magic! Believe me, she appeared to be quick and about to roll over or wake up at any second. I feared I might rouse her so with exquisite delicacy, I reached in her garments to find the key, expecting at any moment for those eyes to open, for her bony hand to seize my wrist, for her jaws to stretch open with an eldritch screech...

My hand closed around cold metal and I pulled the chain free. Repeating apology upon apology, I scrambled to shove the peat back over her. It was the worst thing I had done, and I was sickened to my stomach. I vomited more than once, but I would not leave until I had finished the reburial.

Unthinking, unfeeling, I stumbled to Potlar's Pond, walking ever onward until the water folded over me. Perhaps I was trying to wash the sin away, the sin of desecration, the sin of robbing the dead. For a long time, I considered staying immersed in the water. If I were to drown, who would care? What difference would it make in this wicked world? My grandmother would still be dead and would remain unavenged.

And so I left the bog and walked all the way to Praxton. I used some of my grandmother's coins to purchase clothes, fine dresses, hats and wigs. No one knew me there – no one knew me anywhere, but it was far enough from the Hall for any of the Squire's people to recognise me.

Thus began my plan to bring him down.

At the same time, the child murders began.

***

Councillor Smedley was all smiles. He even thumped Constable Dimwoodie's upper arm in his delight.

"Oops!" he laughed. "I hope that doesn't count as assaulting a police officer."

"I'll let you off," muttered Dimwoodie. "Just this once, mind."

Smedley laughed again. "So, can I see him?"

"See who?"

"The bastard. The kiddie-snatcher."

"No."

"Oh, go on. Haven't you got one of those mirrors that's a window on the other side?"

"No. We can't afford anything like that."

"Ah. Well, just you remember who fixes your budget, and there's a council meeting looming..."

"So not only have you assaulted me, you're now trying to bribe me?"

Smedley gaped. He was not sure if Dimwoodie was joking. He decided he must be and continued his pleas. "Oh, go on; just a peek. I want to see what one looks like."

"They don't all look the same, you know. Besides, you've seen the poster."

"Yes, well, it's not the same, is it?"

"I suppose not." Dimwoodie stood his ground.

"I've always liked you, Tim..." Smedley idled around the room, running his finger casually over the desk.

"It's Daniel," Dimwoodie said. "Constable Dimwoodie to you. Councillor."

"And I think you're doing a bang-up job here, I really do. But think how much better, how much more efficient you would be with, say, I don't know, some administrative support. A squad car, perhaps. I'm sure we could stretch to a new whistle."

Dimwoodie shook his head. "You could show me all the kingdoms of the Earth. You're still not getting a peek at the prisoner."

Smedley's smile thinned. "Now, listen to me, you jumped-up little toy soldier. I could close this branch down like that –" he clicked his fingers "—but I won't, because I don't want the good people of this town to have to suffer, because you're digging your heels in, like a mule's teenage daughter."

"What?"

"You're being stubborn is what I'm trying to convey. Stand aside. Give me five minutes with that bastard. It's all I'm asking. I'm not going to lay a finger on him. I just want to see what kind of sick fuck has had this town living in fear."

"Five minutes? A moment ago, it was a peek."

"You can come in with me if you like. Actually, that's a good idea. You can be a deterrent in case he tries anything."

"You're not a kiddie. You'll be safe."

"So, I can go in?"

Dimwoodie groaned. He consulted the clock on the wall and then the watch on his wrist, as though guidance could be found on those implacable faces. "Two minutes," he conceded.

"I've always liked you, Tim," Smedley grinned. "You'll go far."

"I wish you bloody would," Dimwoodie muttered.

"What was that?"

"Nothing." Dimwoodie pulled out his keys. "Step this way, Councillor."

***

The Squire knew I was still out there, you see. The child murders were part of his campaign to turn the people against me. Oh, I didn't know he was responsible, not right away. All I knew was there were rumblings around the towns and villages. The Bogwitch – previously known as my grandmother – was back from the dead and taking their little ones and subjecting them to unspeakable acts. In my disguise, I was privy to all the gossip, all the rumours; I heard all the things they would never dare to say to my face. Apparently, my grandmother had been in league with the Devil all along. He had granted her eternal life and all she had to do in return was supply him with innocent souls as sacrificial offerings. The more I heard, the more I had to fight to control myself. This is nonsense, I wanted to scream. You all knew my grandmother. You knew she was not like that. She fixed your swollen knees. She cured your goat of the gout. She taught you how to charm an egg from a chicken. She gave you all so many things and this is how you besmirch her memory!

But I could say none of this. I had to hold my tongue and bide my time and stick to the plan.

***

Philip Philby, handcuffed and docile, sat at the table in the interview room – well, at the moment it was an interview room. More often than not, it served as the space where Dimwoodie ate his sandwiches and solved word searches. Councillor Smedley pulled out the chair opposite and sat. Constable Dimwoodie stood a little way off, like an umpire at a lazy table-tennis match.

"So," Smedley began with a conjunction, "This is what evil looks like."

Dimwoodie bristled. "You can't talk to him like that. He hasn't even been charged."

"Then why is he wearing bracelets?"

"For your safety."

Smedley paled and sat back. Across the table, Philby seemed preoccupied and would not meet his visitor's gaze. Smedley turned to the constable. "Has he said anything?"

Dimwoodie shook his head. "Quiet as the – quiet as a mouse."

"Has he got legal representation?"

Dimwoodie puffed out his cheeks. "Not yet. Not as far as I know."

"Which doesn't seem to be very far. Honestly, it's like you've never arrested anyone before."

Dimwoodie reddened. He made a show of checking his watch. "You have one more minute."

Smedley got to his feet. "I'll sort it. The lawyer, I mean. Clearly, the fellow's not entirely present. I want things handled correctly. To the letter. I don't want this one slipping the net on a technicality because someone didn't do his job properly. I say, what's that ringing sound?"

Dimwoodie listened. "A bell? Oh, it's the bell on the front desk."

"It sounds pretty urgent..."

Dimwoodie dithered.

"Go!"

Dimwoodie darted away. Smedley sat down again.

"Now, Philip – or may I call you Phil? Let's make a deal, just between us."

***

I found employment at Fladgett Hall, assisting the cook. My duties included a lot of washing of pots and chopping of vegetables, but once a week I would be sent out to forage for mushrooms and berries, herbs and all the bounty that nature provides. The cook could see I had an eye for these ingredients and trusted me to bring back only the finest specimens. Unable to live on the bog, I was glad of the accommodation: a small room at the very top of the house, with a sloping ceiling and the tiniest of windows, but I visited the bog as often as I could. There, I dressed as my grandmother. It lessened the pain of her loss a little and it certainly kept the locals at bay. Unfortunately, it added credence to the stories that the old woman was haunting the place and, even worse, was sacrificing children to her satanic master.

At the Hall, I kept below stairs as best as I could. The Squire I never saw at all, although I would often hear him railing at the footmen because his tea was too cold or his newspaper too wrinkled. As for my Robert, I sometimes glimpsed him taking a walk through the grounds and it was all I could do to remain in the kitchen. Once, the cook despatched me on an errand to the gardener, but I dithered and dawdled so much, she gave up and went to see him herself. I could not risk, despite my skills at disguise and deception, my Robert recognising me. At all costs, he must be kept out of the picture. He must not be aware of my plan lest he be implicated in its fruition.

If you have not guessed it, my plan was to kill the Squire.

It sounds so simple, phrased like that, but I knew I must take the utmost care and bide my time. I could not just rush in with the carv-

ing knife, much as I might have enjoyed it.   I kept my head down, did my chores and learned the lie of the land.

One day, Benjamin, the youngest of the footmen, came down to the kitchen, cursing under his breath and generally stamping his feet and crashing around. The cook rolled her eyes and ignored this display, but I sidled over, offering a cup of rosehip tea.

Benjamin, in his agitated state, was glad of the opportunity to vent his grievances. The Squire, he ranted, had got it in for him. There was nothing he could do to that tyrant's satisfaction. Today, it had been the newspaper. There was a crease on the front page Benjamin had neglected to iron out. The Squire had flown immediately into a rage and had hurled the fire irons at the young footman's head.

I cooed and pulled faces as sympathetically as I could.

"It's not as though the paper stays wrinkle-free for two minutes," Benjamin went on, "He folds it over, he screws it up, and sometimes he turns the page so swiftly it tears. And he smudges the ink, rendering it illegible. It is quite disgusting to behold, the way he licks his fingers to turn the pages. And yet, I am at fault if the paper falls short of pristine."

"A tyrant indeed," I dared to pat Benjamin's hand. He did not pull away. I leant closer so the cook would not hear. "Let me iron the newspapers from now on. Then you may bear it up to him on a tray. You will not have to touch it yourself."

Benjamin's eyes widened. "You would do that for me? But you have so many duties of your own –"

I laughed. "It's the fire irons I'm thinking about. Those things are expensive. We can't have you breaking them with your head."

He laughed too, his eyes twinkling. I had won a heart, it seemed. All is fair in love and war and murderous plans.

The next morning, I had the flat iron heated and ready when Benjamin appeared, bright-eyed with the day's paper. He stood to watch me pass the iron carefully over every inch but I dismissed him, saying he should use the time to polish his weskit buttons or comb his periwig lest the Squire find fault in his attire. He scooted away, pleased to do my bidding, and I set my plan into motion.

***

At the front desk, hammering the bell as though sending an S.O.S. stood Samantha Smedley, wife to the councillor. Dimwoodie appeared, with a guilty expression and a 'good afternoon'.

"I was told my husband would be here," she intoned, looking down her nose as though sighting him with her rifle.

"Who told you?"

"My husband. Is he here?"

"Yes, he's – I'll just get him."

"Please."

Dimwoodie froze for a second and then sprang into action. He dashed back to the lunchroom – the *interview* room.

In his brief absence, Councillor Smedley had laid out a proposition to Philip Philby. The two men sat smiling at each other. Dimwoodie was more disturbed by this than if they had been at each other's throats.

"It's your Mrs," he said.

"She can wait," the councillor sneered. "Our friend Philip here has something he wants to say."

"Oh?" Dimwoodie drew nearer. "What's that then?"

Philip Philby turned his head slowly and met the constable's gaze for the first time since his incarceration.

"I want to confess," his lips curled into a smile. "I took that kid."

Back at the front desk, Samantha Smedley resumed her impatient bell ringing. The noise filled Dimwoodie's head.

***

For a fortnight, Benjamin reported no abuse from the Squire. He practically skipped into the laundry each morning, keen for me to iron the newspaper, and he would watch intently, each pass of the flat iron across each page. Before delivery, he would stand to attention so I could check him for loose buttons or hanging threads or any little defect for which the Squire might berate him. During these inspections, I would be aware of Benjamin's eyes upon me, drinking me in like a parched man in a wine cellar. I would have to be careful there. I did not want to upset my little footman in case he started ironing his own newspapers.

The rest of my days were spent either on domestic tasks in the kitchen – I was becoming quite the scrubber, I can tell you! – or out in the herb garden, or farther afield, gathering plants and fungi. The cook eyed me with suspicion most of the time until the day came when she hurt her hand with boiling water. I applied a salve of my grandmother's invention to cool and heal the scalded skin. The cook marvelled at the efficacy of the remedy.

"You're a strange one, Cornelia Crowe," she informed me. "Full of secrets, to be sure, but you are not without your uses."

I blushed, turning as red as her injured hand. Cornelia Crowe was the name I went by because, of course, no one must guess my true identity.

It was all going to plan. The Squire was ailing. His habit of licking his fingers before turning the pages of his daily paper was to be his undoing. Every morning, you see, I coated the flat iron with a mist of my own devising, a distillation of the deadliest toadstools that grow on Potlar's Bog. Slowly, inexorably, the poison was building in his hateful body. He took to his bed, barking and coughing his orders from there – Benjamin kept me apprised of his master's deteriorating condition. Doctors were summoned and subsequently dismissed when they could do no more than scratch their heads and profess their ignorance. And gradually, the Squire worsened, kindling the dark flame of vengeance deep within my heart.

And then, an insect in the ointment of my schemes! I should have foreseen it. I should have made allowances, contingencies, but I did not.

One morning, Benjamin reported his master had grown so enfeebled he could no longer hold his own newspaper. It had to be held up before him and, more often than not, read out loud while the Squire lolled on his pillows. My heart shrank like a clenched fist.

"Tell me it is not you who performs this duty!" I implored him. I

was quite fond of my little accomplice.

"Oh, no!" he blushed, delighted by the signs of my concern. "Not I! I cannot read."

"Some other servant, then? Another footman? A butler?"

"No, no!" Benjamin shook his head, enjoying knowing something I did not. "He has his own son come to him every morning and sit beside the bed and read him the newspaper from cover to cover."

My blood congealed within its vessels. Not my Robert! Oh, no, no, no!

"And does he..." I could hardly bring myself to form the question, "Does he – share his father's habit?"

Benjamin's face clouded. "What mean you?"

"Does the son also lick his fingers to turn the page?"

"I – I don't know, I don't know!" Benjamin squirmed. "You're hurting me!"

I had not realised I had gripped his arm and my nails were digging into his flesh. I released him. He backed off, seeing something in my eyes he did not like, something he even feared perhaps.

"Is he up there now?" I shook him by the shoulders. "Tell me!"

"I – I believe so," he stammered.

I shoved him aside and hurried upstairs, heedless of the disapproving glares of all who saw me. This was no time to stand on ceremony. I had to get my Robert away from the newspaper. Perhaps I had done enough. Perhaps his father was already finished and would not evade his lingering death.

I burst into the Squire's apartment. The attendants leapt from my path. I entered the bedchamber. Robert rose from his bedside chair, the newspaper in his hand.

"Miss Crowe!" he gasped.

I snatched the paper from him and cast it into the fireplace. It burned with a green flame.

On his pillows, the Squire appeared shrunken, his head a caricature of his former vigour. A painted walnut or a withered apple had more life in it than he. He reached feebly for his son and gasped out a question. "What is the meaning of this intrusion?"

"Yes, Miss Crowe, I should like to know that too."

But there, at the foot of the monster's bed, with his son looking at me and not seeing who I was, I faltered. I could think up no excuse. No explanation could I offer but the truth.

I raised my hand and pulled off my wig. It was time to bid farewell to Cornelia Crowe.

"You!" Robert gasped. He stepped toward me. but he was stayed by his father's hand. The old man summoned strength enough to sit up. He levelled his gaze at me, his face a contorted mask of contempt and loathing.

"Foul creature," he spat and, wildly, I spared a thought of pity for the servant who would have to launder those sheets. "I see you have your claws in my son and heir still."

"No!" I cried. "That is not the way of it at all."

"I see it now," Robert was aghast. "You use your grandmother's trickery to finagle your way into our house and to murder my father!"

"Robert, please! Listen –"

I stepped toward him and it hurt to see him back away. The old man trained a knotted finger at me, a twisted twig like a rudimentary magic wand.

"With my last breath, I place my curse upon thee," he rasped. "May you forever be reviled and detested, doomed to roam. May you find no rest, no succour. May you be forever damned!"

He fell back, his eyes wide, his heart stopped.

"Robert, I –"

My Robert shook his handsome head. "Go," he said, his voice small but firm.

"Let me explain –"

"Go!" he roared, and I saw his father's venom in his face. "You were a dalliance and nothing more. How could you be? Did you think you could move in here? Did you think we had a future? You, of all people, should be able to see what is to come and know there is no you and me."

"Don't say these things!" I wept. "We are good together. Our love is like no other."

It was Robert's turn to spit at me. "You disgust me. You en-

tranced me with your wicked wiles. That must be it! What a blind fool I was! I am Squire now, and I am to be married. I will produce my own heir. There is no place for you here."

I was almost bent double with grief. How could he speak this way? After every tender thing we had shared!

"Now, leave," he pointed at the door as though to remind me where it stood. "And be thankful I do not have you burned for witchery."

"Robert..." His name caught in my throat, rising like a bubble in the bog water.

"Poor deluded fellow," he said. "Take your unnatural love and let that keep you warm. I am to marry a woman, as the Lord intended. Your spell is broken. Your enchantment has failed."

There was nothing for it. I tried to hold my head as high as I could. I walked out of the house, feeling the stares of all I passed bore into me as they watched me go, the strange young man in the garments of Cornelia Crowe.

***

"Bugger me!" Wendy Rabbitt gasped. "Not for real, though," she added quickly.

"Bravo!" Cassandra clapped her little hands.

Jenna was gobsmacked. She gaped at the Bogwitch who was filling the television screen like a newsreader. "You're a – bloke!"

Last time I checked, the Bogwitch chuckled. *I never said I wasn't.*

"And you – and Robert –"

That's right.

"I can't take it all in," Jenna sat back.

"That's what *he* said," Iphigenia chuckled.

"Let me get this straight – no pun intended," Wendy Rabbitt had her professional interviewer's voice on, "You dressed up as a woman so you and he could – have your liaisons?"

Yes! The Bogwitch nodded encouragement. *As two men, we*

could not risk being seen. But the son of a squire having a dalliance with a local girl – that was acceptable. Expected, even! Sowing of wild oats and all that. And then, I would dress as my murdered grandmother as a means of keeping her memory alive.

"And then what happened?" Wendy pressed on. "After all that, after you left the Hall for the last time?"

The Bogwitch made an expansive gesture that told them nothing.

I lived. On the bog, like a wildling, or a newt with a broken heart. At some point, I expired, I suppose, but that did not stop me wandering the bog.

"And the child murders?"

Coincidentally, they ceased around the time the Squire took to his sick bed. It was Robert who established the ritual, the annual banishing of the Bogwitch. It was a public rejection of everything we had had. It caught on. Every year I am mocked in effigy and told to keep my distance.

"Not this year!" Iphigenia interjected.

"Oops," Cassandra said.

No, no, I thank you for your intervention, Mistress Clune. It has increased belief in me to the extent that I can be here with you today.

"You're welcome!" Cassandra looked pleased with herself.

"So, what happens now?" Wendy Rabbitt addressed the screen. "What's next for the Bogwitch?"

"You can't call her that – him that," Jenna corrected herself. "What's your name?"

The Bogwitch smiled. *Thank you for asking, Jenna Jones. I have neither spoken nor heard my name for many a year.*

"Out with it!" Iphigenia urged. "And I haven't said that –"

"—Since your wedding night," they all chorused.

"Honestly, Gran," Jenna laughed, "You need some new material."

They returned their attention to the television.

My name is Anaxagoras. How strange it feels on my tongue! Anaxagoras Spenser, at your service.

"Spenser?" said Cassandra Clune.

"Oops," said Iphigenia Spenser.

***

Constable Dimwoodie and Councillor Smedley watched officers from the police station in Praxton bundle Philip Philby into the back of their black Maria. Since his confession, Philby had not uttered another word.

"They'll get him to talk," Dimwoodie said grimly. "He'll tell them where that little boy is."

"It makes no odds," Smedley was all smiles. "It's case closed as far as I'm concerned. At last things can get back to normal around here."

"Normal? There's still a child missing. There's no normal for Tina Thornbush. People want answers! That mother wants her little boy back."

Smedley placed a calming hand on the constable's arm. "It's out of your hands now, Tim. You did your best – you did very well, considering. Those Praxton boys will handle it from now on."

"But what am I going to tell Tina Thornbush?"

"Tell them the bastard has been caught. That will be of some comfort to them, I am sure. And you never know, he might reveal where he hid the body."

"Body!"

"Or, he might turn up without a scratch on him. Either way, just let go of it. I'm sure you've got some leaflets about bicycle locks you can distribute."

Councillor Smedley walked away, a little too jauntily for Dimwoodie's liking.

Dimwoodie went back inside the station. The leaflets about bicycle locks offered no succour. He paced the floor for a bit and then snatched up the phone. Just a quick call to Praxton nick. He would offer his assistance, let them know he was at their disposal. He had considerable knowledge of the case and –

Dimwoodie's face fell and his heart skipped a beat.

"What do you mean, it's nothing to do with you?" He listened, barely able to make sense of what he was hearing. "What do you mean, you never sent a van? What do you mean you've never heard of Philip Philby? I called you myself and – No, not from this phone. I used the Councillor's, it was handiest... Councillor Smedley. Obadiah Smedley... Right here in Little Fladgett."

He was on the brink of saying, No, that's all right, I can handle it, but he managed to stop himself. This was not about him, not about his pride. This was about getting that little boy back.

"Yes, please," he said. "Any help you can offer is most welcome. Thank you."

***

"She's not picking up..." Cassandra fretted. The smartphone was hot against her cheek but that was the least of her worries. They had to get to Tina Thornbush or things would never be put to rights.

The Bogwitch – Anaxagoras – had told them their first séance had brought him into touch with Jenna. Unfortunately, the séance had brought another presence to the cottage.

"Well, we kind of guessed that," Cassandra said. "Who is it?"

Anaxagoras didn't know. Something evil, he reckoned. He also reckoned that they had kind of guessed that as well.

"When she chased me into the bog," Wendy was pacing as she thought, "Tina Thornbush, I mean, there was something, I don't know, not human about her. Her face was rather mannish and yet beastly at the same time. Am I making sense?"

"Yes!" cried Jenna. "I saw the same thing in Tina's kitchen. If it hadn't been for –" She addressed the television directly, "Thank you, Anaxagoras."

Anaxagoras nodded. He had doffed most of his Bogwitch guise. Beneath the moss and the reeds, he was a good-looking lad. Jenna imagined, in different circumstances, she could quite fancy him – and then she remembered. Typical, she thought, another wrong tree for me to bark up!

Jenna's grandmother had been uncharacteristically quiet since it became known she and the Bogwitch shared a last name. She kept the tea and biscuits coming and didn't look anyone in the eye.

"Grandmother Spenser!" Anaxagoras called from the television. "A word, if I may?"

Iphigenia muttered something about topping up the custard creams and shuffled into the kitchen.

"Jenna," Anaxagoras beckoned her to him with a jerk of his head. Jenna approached the screen. "Grandmother Spenser. Is she... well?"

Jenna thought about it. Her grandmother was remarkably robust for someone of her age. Always on the go. Still as sharp as a box of tacks. Could spot the potential for innuendo from a mile away. "I guess," Jenna shrugged.

"I am overjoyed and overwhelmed to see her. After all this time. Nothing should surprise me in this wicked world, but there she is, bustling around as she ever did. I swear, even the shawl is the same."

"What are you talking about? You know my gran?"

"She is my grandmother too. It is miraculous, is it not? That she should be here after all this time!"

Jenna was baffled. She backed away from the television. Gran was nowhere to be seen. Cassandra and Wendy were talking animatedly around the table. Jenna went through to the kitchen. Gran wasn't there either. A packet of custard creams lay unopened on the counter.

And the back door was wide open.

"Gran?" Jenna called. What a time to use the outdoor toilet! When they had guests! How embarrassing!

She returned to the living room. Cassandra glanced at her and looked disappointed.

"Somebody said something about custard creams," she sighed.

"My gran was fetching them, but I suppose she was caught

short."

Cassandra wasn't listening. Wendy was.

"Where did she go?" she asked.

"Oh..." Jenna squirmed, "Just outside for a sh – a short while."

Wendy nodded slowly. "What do you think – about your grandmother and our friend the TV star over there having the same name?"

Jenna gave a nervous laugh. "What are you talking about? His name's Anaxagoras and her name's –"

"Iphigenia!" Anaxagoras shouted from the television. "When I was little, I couldn't say it and so I called her Figgy."

"Figgy?!" Jenna was amazed. "But there must be some mistake. They can't possibly be the same grandmother. I thought yours was – you know." She mimed being hanged.

"I thought so too..." Anaxagoras's forehead furrowed.

"You even buried her."

"I did!"

"And you even dug her up again to get the key to her money-box."

"I did that too, didn't I?"

"Gross, by the way. So, you must be mistaken. That Figgy is my Figgy. Your Figgy is gone."

"Possibly..." Anaxagoras pouted. "We must put the question to her. Where is she?"

"She went to the –" Jenna gestured vaguely at the kitchen and beyond.

"She is taking her time."

"Well, you know, old people..."

"I think you should check on her," Anaxagoras advised.

"Do you think she's fallen in?"

"Well, *now* I'm thinking that. Go! Bring her here. Let's see whose grandmother she really is."

Jenna darted out.

"Ladies," Anaxagoras raised his volume. "I know you are occupied with planning the denouement of this particular tale, but there is something you need to hear."

"What's that, love?" Cassandra looked up from her notes.

"When Figgy – Grandmother Spenser returns," Anaxagoras said. "You too, Mistress Rabbitt. Perhaps you might want to have your apparatus ready?"

"My what?"

"He means your camera," Cassandra said.

***

The van trundled along the road across Potlar's Bog with no particular urgency. The hard part of the job had been done: fooling that fool of a copper. Next came the unpleasant bit, namely getting shot of the prisoner. Their instructions were to take him to the centre of the bog, do him in, and conceal the body deep under the peat. The method of doing him in was entirely up to them. It was nice to have leeway in a job. It engendered a sense of ownership.

"Say when?" the driver gestured at the windscreen. On either side, in front and behind them, desolate landscape stretched beneath a lowering sky.

"Anywhere along here is fine," said his confederate in the passenger seat.

"You make me feel like a fucking taxi driver," grumbled the driver.

"Well, the ride's over for this one," laughed a third man from the back. "Time for him to pay his fare."

They laughed.

"Do you think he'll leave a tip?" said the fourth.

"No!" the driver was stern. "There can't be a trace of him to be found. Boss's orders."

The humorous mood evaporated. In the back, on the floor, with the knees of two men pinning him down, Philip Philby had withdrawn into himself. He'd done a lot of that in the secure unit. It was the best place to be, he'd found.

"Watch out!" cried the man in the passenger seat.

"Fuck!" the driver tried to swerve, slamming on the brakes.

The van screamed and screeched and spun around before flipping over and landing on its roof in a ditch with an almighty crunch.

In the road, Iphigenia Spenser straightened her clothing. It had been a close call. She tiptoed to the ditch's edge and peered over.

"Hello?" she called. "Are you all right down there?"

The bodies of four men in police uniforms littered the scene. Two hung from the crumpled chassis, the other two had been thrown across the landscape to land like broken scarecrows.

"Oh, dear," Iphigenia fretted. The sound of movement came from within the wreck. Someone was alive. "Hang on, chicken; I'm coming."

Gingerly, she made her way down the sloping side of the ditch. It took quite a tug, but she managed to wrench open the van's back door.

Lying on the ceiling and blinking against the sudden influx of daylight, Philip Philby was amazed to see the silhouette of his rescuer framed in the doorway.

"Are you – an angel?" he gasped.

Iphigenia smiled. "I have my moments."

***

Calling for her gran, Jenna trod the primrose path to the outside lavvy. She could see the door was wide open before she got there and braced herself for the unseemly sight of her grandmother on the throne. But Gran wasn't there and, now Jenna was right outside, neither was the toilet. Instead, a narrow staircase led underground. Jenna was astounded. Where the hell was Gran?

Presently, she was joined by Cassandra and Wendy, who peered over her shoulders at the scene.

"Blimey," Cassandra said, "I wasn't expecting that."

"Some psychic you are," Wendy scoffed. "No, it's probably an access thing. You know, down to the septic tank or something."

The others stared at her.

"You seem to know a lot about it," Jenna said.

"I know my shit," Wendy said. "Perhaps the old girl has gone to check on it, or something."

"With everything else that's going on?" Jenna said. "I know my gran's a bit off-kilter, shall we say, but she doesn't get distracted."

"Somebody should go down and have a look," Cassandra suggested. "Check she's OK."

"Not me!" Wendy said. "This is a clean blouse."

"Some intrepid reporter you are," Cassandra scoffed.

"I'll go," Jenna volunteered. "She's my gran."

"We'll all go," Cassandra said. "Clean blouses be damned."

"I'll get my camera," Wendy headed back inside.

"What about Anaxagoras?" Jenna called after her.

"I can't carry the bloody telly as well," Wendy called back.

"Tell him we'll be back soon," Cassandra said. She noticed Jenna was staring at her. "What's up, love? Have I got jam on my nose again?"

"No," Jenna said. "Well, a bit. No, I was just thinking, how quickly we've adapted to the weirdness. It turns out there really was a Bogwitch and not just in my head, and it turns out she's a he and now he's in my gran's telly – if she even is my gran. And we're just going along with it like it's nothing."

"It's not nothing, love," Cassandra rubbed her nose with a tissue. "Did I get it? There'll be time to sit back and freak out later. Right now, we're doing whatever we can to get that little boy back. That's what we focus on, right? Right?"

"Right," Jenna said, but her face was clouded with uncertainty.

Wendy, camera on her shoulder, strode up the path to join them. "Ready?"

"Ready!" Cassandra and Jenna confirmed, the former speaking with more conviction than the latter.

They followed the reporter down into the dark.

***

Dimwoodie dithered. He made for the door so many times and stopped himself, anyone might think he was a gif. The phone call to Praxton was preying on his mind. Were they joking? Or was it simply a case of miscommunication? The person he spoke to might not necessarily be in the loop about despatches... Was that likely or even possible? Having been a one-man operation for the entirety of his time in the force, Dimwoodie was not sure how things worked with the Big Boys.

He could not shake the niggling feeling, gnawing away at him, the possibility that he had been tricked. How he wished he had taken note of the van's registration number! Perhaps the councillor might remember it... Dimwoodie performed another gif of reaching for the phone and snatching his hand back again. He couldn't let the irascible Councillor Smedley know he had been duped. The repercussions could be devastating, not just for him personally but for policing in Little Fladgett.

Dimwoodie felt lost and alone. There was no one to whom he could turn for advice or assistance. No one at all.

Unless...

This time there was no gif. He strode right across the floor and was out through the door and into the street before he could change his mind.

That woman in the yellow coat and the green camper van. If she was still around, she might be able to shed some light...

Dimwoodie swapped his police hat for his cycling helmet and unchained his trusty bike from its lamppost.

He had an inkling where she might be and, if she wasn't there, surely Old Ma Spenser or her weirdo granddaughter might know where she could be found.

***

"What on Earth is this place?" Wendy marvelled. The light from her camera stretched along the tunnel before her, showing uneven walls of peat, bolstered by the occasional red brick and strengthened by wooden props.

"What *in* Earth, would be more accurate," Cassandra was at her shoulder. "The countryside is riddled with tunnels like these. They date back to the civil war – earlier, in fact. The whatsname – the Reformation. It was a way for people to escape their persecutors." Realisation made her gape. "We're probably going to end up in the cellar at Fladgett Hall. There was a bolt hole there. Good gods above! That's how the Squire was able to nip out and about to snatch the children!"

"Really?" Jenna was at Cassandra's shoulder. "You think that's what happened? You don't think that prat up at the Hall is following in his ancestor's footsteps? You don't think Lord Fladgett has got Tommy Thornbush?"

"I don't know, maybe, perhaps, no..." Cassandra was non-committal. "Just make sure you're following my footsteps, love. We must be near the end of it now."

"There's light ahead," Wendy Rabbitt announced. "Either we're approaching the exit or there's a train coming."

"Either would be welcome right now," Jenna muttered, darkly.

"Lighten up, love," Cassandra urged. "If this blasted tunnel can do it, so can you."

It wasn't a train, of course, but it wasn't the cellar at Fladgett Hall either. Daylight and blue sky awaited them as the floor beneath their feet rose to an opening in the ground. Wendy exited first, and turned around to film the others emerge, blinking and squinting.

"We're on the bog," Cassandra correctly identified their location.

Jenna turned around on the spot. "We're near the road. Look."

She pointed at the perimeter hedge a little way off. Beyond that was the road that bisected the bog.

"Don't just stand there!" a voice rang out. "Come and give me a hand!"

"What was that?" Wendy Rabbit spun around.

"It came from the other side," Cassandra said flatly.

Wendy paled. "The other side?"

"Of the hedge," Jenna clarified. "It's my gran."

She stomped across the tufted ground. The others followed in silence, letting Jenna take the lead. "Gran?" she repeated. "What the bloody hell are you up to now?"

***

They found Iphigenia in the ditch next to the van. Jenna ran up to join her. Wendy yomped with her camera and even Cassandra quickened her step.

"Gran! Are you OK? What happened?"

Iphigenia blew out her cheeks in a where-do-I-begin expression. "It came out of nowhere, I swear. I'd just come out of the priest's hole – you found it, I see, well done – and this van comes hurtling along, gunning for me, it felt like. Well, I wasn't standing for that. I knew one of us would end up in the ditch and it wasn't going to be me. Not with these hips."

Jenna's eyes narrowed. "What did you do?"

Her grandmother's shoulder twitched beneath her shawls. "I stood my ground. Stared them down. They – went into the ditch."

Wendy was scanning the scene through her lens. "Are they – were they policemen? Have you been playing a deadly game of Chicken with a bunch of policemen?"

Iphigenia dismissed the notion. "They're not real coppers. Any fool can see that. It's fancy dress."

"So what were they?" Wendy focussed on the old woman. "A stag night?"

"I doubt that," Cassandra arrived, pressing two fingers to her temple. "Iphigenia, where is he?"

"Where's who, dear?"

"The man from the van."

Iphigenia looked sheepish.

"Gran..." Jenna warned. "Don't you dare say 'what, man?'"

Iphigenia gave up, but not before she had awarded Cassandra a hard stare. "He's under that bush. If you must know."

Jenna hurried over. She let out a squeak of astonishment when she saw who it was.

"Philip Philby," Cassandra announced before she even saw him.

"Is he dead?" Wendy zoomed in on Jenna and the man prostrate beneath the bush.

"No," Cassandra and Iphigenia spoke at once. Their eyes met. Iphigenia's crinkled in a smile.

"But he could do with an ambulance, a hospital," Jenna cried. "Somebody call 999."

"No time for that, chicken," her grandmother said sadly. "He's not long for this world."

"We have to try!" Jenna pleaded. "How else are we going to find out what happened?"

Cassandra and Iphigenia shared another look. Jenna clocked it. "What?" she said. "What are you two cooking up now?"

"Are we just going to stand here and watch him die?" Wendy demanded. "Because I'm not into making snuff movies."

"No, we'll get him help..." Cassandra trailed off, vaguely.

"Yes, we will.." Iphigenia adopted the same tone. "Right after we get him to talk."

"What?" Wendy panned quickly from one woman to the other.

"Whatever you're planning," Jenna marched over, "Call the ambulance first. Then do – whatever you're planning – before it gets here. As long as what you're planning isn't going to hurt him."

"Hurt him?" Iphigenia seemed scandalised by the prospect. "No, chicken."

"The very idea!" Cassandra flapped a little hand. "Pphh!" she added for good measure.

"What's going on?" Wendy asked. "Somebody tell the camera."

"Just a little hypnosis," Cassandra took Wendy by the elbow and steered her away.

"It'll be like he's asleep," Iphigenia took the other elbow, "And sleep, as we all know, is nature's great whatsit for hurt minds and all the rest of it."

Together, they frogmarched Wendy away from the ditch. They told her to keep her distance and her eye out for the ambulance. Which she should definitely summon. In ten minutes or so. Both women winked as though to draw Wendy into their conspiracy.

With the reporter installed on the road, Cassandra and Iphigenia returned to the bush. They rolled Philip Philby out from under it and sat him up. His head lolled but he lifted his chin from his chest to utter a groan.

"It's not going to hurt him, is it?" Jenna sought confirmation.

"Your concern for this kiddie snatcher is admirable," Cassandra smiled thinly, "but you should know me well enough by now to know I don't hurt people. Not on purpose, anyway."

"Stand back, chicken," Iphigenia shooed her granddaughter away.

"Shouldn't we – shouldn't we get Wendy to record it? You know, for evidence?"

Cassandra and Iphigenia shared yet another look. There was an understanding between them that required little verbalisation. Iphigenia conceded with an exhalation.

"You're right," Cassandra told Jenna. "Go and get her. But you might want to stay up on the road, love. Look out for the ambulance."

Jenna nodded, but as she scrambled out of the ditch to fetch the reporter, she thought, No fucking way.

**

Constable Dimwoodie dismounted his bicycle and lent it against a tree. He was heartened to see the lime green camper van parked outside Old Ma Spenser's cottage. He unclipped his helmet and put on his police hat. Then he took it off again. Perhaps it would be better to approach in an off duty rather than an official capacity. Just asking for friendly advice. And all the help she could offer.

He approached the front door with his hat tucked under his arm. He raised his fist to knock and realised the door was ajar. He knocked anyway and called hello into the crack. There was no answer, so he called hello again, and again. His stomach flipped. Something was wrong! His police instincts told him so – hah, he reflected bitterly on exactly what his police instincts were worth. He gave the door a cautious push.

"Hello?" he called for a fourth time, breaking with tradition. "Mrs Spenser?"

Still no answer. Dimwoodie stepped inside as though easing himself into a hot bath. "Mrs Spenser, are you there? Miss Clune? Um...Jenna?"

He looked in the front room. It was empty. Tea things, including biscuits, lay abandoned on the table. It was like that ship, he thought. That famous ship. Not the Titanic. The other one.

They had left the television on. The Horror Channel, it looked like. A face was staring out of the screen, not bad looking, but it was all artily done in greens and white. And it was as though the face was staring directly at him, the eyes following him around the room. It was unnerving.

"Hello," the face spoke through the television speaker. Dimwoodie almost jumped out of his boots. He stared at the screen, at the face that seemed to be staring back. And smiling.

He shook his head. It was only a film. A weird, arthouse film. He reached for the off switch.

"No, don't!" the face cried. "Don't switch me off."

Dimwoodie froze. "I was just going to see what's on the other side."

"Oh, you wouldn't like it," the face grinned. "Trust me."

"You're not a film, are you?"

"I'm not, no," the face admitted. "And you're some kind of

soldier?"

"I'm a policeman," Dimwoodie gestured at his uniform. "And I know what you are."

"That's refreshing," the face beamed.

"You're one of those video calls," Dimwoodie decided. "You're one of Jenna's mates from college and she's hooked the internet up to the telly."

"If you say so," the face laughed. "But you're a friend of Jenna's! You should have said. She's not here. They're not here. None of them."

"Where – ah, when will they be back?"

"No idea. But they went out the back, I can tell you that much."

"Thanks. Um –"

"Anaxagoras."

"Blimey. I'm Daniel." He cleared his throat. "Constable Daniel Dimwoodie."

"A pleasure! Do come back and talk to me again, won't you? They've left me on my own. Which is the height of rudeness, if you ask me."

"Um.. Out the back, you said?" Dimwoodie pointed his thumbs at the door to the kitchen. He hurried away.

Anaxagoras called after him, "Lovely to meet you, Daniel!"

Dimwoodie tore through the kitchen. The back door was wide open. It was as though Old Ma Spenser was just asking to be burgled. He would have to drop off some of his crime prevention leaflets.

The back garden was empty too. Of people. There were plenty of flowers and vegetables he could talk to – was that a thing? The ability to talk to plants. He added it to the list of questions he had for Miss Clune. He followed the strip of crazy paving to a ramshackle outhouse at the far end of the garden. He had heard about Old Ma Spenser's primitive plumbing arrangements – he paled. They weren't all in there, were they?

The privy door was open. "Hello?" Dimwoodie approached. "Is there anybody there?"

It occurred to him that that was one of Miss Clune's lines, at one of her whatsits, séances. "Flush once for yes and twice for no."

Still no answer. Holding his breath, Dimwoodie peered over the threshold and almost fell down the staircase. He clung to the door frame, dropping his truncheon into the dark.

Oh.

Well, that settled it then. He would have to go down and get it back. There was no saying the council would stump up the dosh to get him a new one. Not if Smedley had any say in the matter.

**

A roadside ditch. An upturned vehicle. Bodies scattered, broken. The blood.

Jenna screwed her face up, trying to squeeze the images from her head. Not now, traumatic flashback, she urged! But the pictures kept coming. The dizzying spin as her parents' car rolled over and over. Her mother's screams. The sickening smash. The silent darkness. The concerned stranger wrapping her in a blanket. The soft voice, the cooed reassurances. The fire engine. The ambulance. The flashing lights. The busy scene. The fog in head as she tried to remember her name. The stranger with the kind face kept asking for her name. And her age. Finally, the answers, cutting through the fog like a - like a – like a car flung through the air.

"I'm Jenna and I'm five years old!"

Cassandra and Wendy turned to stare at her, little more than a pair of concerned strangers themselves. No, that wasn't fair. They were – what were they? – friends, she supposed. Well, Cassandra more so than the reporter, even though her face was so familiar from the television.

"Are you all right, chicken?" Iphigenia patted her hand. Jenna pulled it away.

"I don't know who you are," she said. Iphigenia was visibly stricken by this rejection.

"I should have thought, love," she held back tears. "Scene of an accident, not the best place for you."

"Get away from me!" Jenna screamed in the old woman's face.

"Is there a problem?" Cassandra called over. She and Wendy had made Philip Philby as comfortable as they could against the side of the ditch. "Only time is of the essence here."

Jenna ran a hand down her face and shook herself out of the memories. "Sorry," she said. "What do you need me to do?"

She walked over to join them, leaving Iphigenia fretting in her wake.

"Work the camera," Wendy instructed in a whisper. "You did a good job last time. I'll take notes."

"Can we just get on with it?" Cassandra urged through clenched teeth. "I can't keep him under forever."

"Under?" Jenna hoisted the camera onto her shoulder.

"I've got him in a hypnotic state," Cassandra explained. "Used my wristwatch as a pendulum."

"Oh," Jenna said. "Where would we be without YouTube?"

"Eh?" Wendy said.

"Never mind," Cassandra said. "Let us begin. Philip Philby, can you hear me? Listen to the sound of my voice and the words I am saying. I want to take you back. It is a dark and stormy night."

"Original," Wendy said. Cassandra shot her a scowl and then resumed her sonorous tone.

"It is a dark and stormy night at Fladgett Hall. You are the duty manager. The flood waters are rising. The cellars are filling with waters. The staff are working hard to protect the valuable furniture and pieces of art. You stride along the corridor toward His Lordship's apartment. You come to a door, a hidden door, but you notice it is slightly ajar. You push it open and you enter..."

Cassandra let her voice trail off. She even waggled her fingers in front of Philby's unseeing eyes for good measure.

"Ham," Wendy muttered. Cassandra glared at her so she pretended to be clearing her throat. "Hem, hem!"

"Philip Philby... What did you see? Tell us now and be free of it forever!"

Philip Philby did not move. Then, slowly, he blinked. When his eyes were open again, they were more alert, seeing a scene the others could not. His mouth twitched. And then he spoke, his voice monotonous and expressionless.

"It was a dark and stormy night..."

***

"...It is a dark and stormy night, and we are working hard to keep things dry. I am on duty and I am supervising. Get them paintings upstairs! All the furniture that can be carried, carry it! Sandbags! We need more sandbags! They are a good team. You don't have to tell them twice. They stay late, past the end of their shifts, to keep things secure. And not just because they fear for their jobs. Because they love the place and everything in it. We all do. Regular hive of activity. Proper teamwork like you wouldn't believe.

"I can see everything's under control so I go to give His Lordship an update. Perhaps advise him to go upstairs, camp out in one of the grand bedrooms for the night. So I make my way toward his apartment. I'm not even sure he's in residence tonight but I think I'd better check. Could do with giving that part of the house the onceover, anyway.

"And then, then I come to a crack in the wall. Only it isn't a crack. It's a door, a door disguised as the wall, so you can't see it. Unless it's open. And it's only open by a – crack, as I say. And I have never noticed it before. I don't remember it from any of the plans. But, duty manager's hat on, I think I'd better check on it, just in case, or else His Lordship'll have my guts for suspenders, if there's anything valuable in there and it gets ruined by water damage. Oh, I know there's insurance up to the hilt, but that's not the same is it. Some of the things in the Hall are irreplaceable. So, I think I'd better check, and I push the door just a little.

"And it swings open, and I can hear it right away. Water rushing, filling the room below – it's a cellar, you see, and it's like the water is climbing the stairs. It's swallowing them step by step. It's about halfway up the staircase by now, so I gauge the water to be about waist deep and I'm thinking if it gets much higher there'll be no stopping it. So I go down the stairs...

"The water's cold and dark and stinks like the bog, that rich peaty smell, like good earth and rotting plants. It reeks of life and death. And I'm up to my shins in it and already regretting it, but I keep going down. Perhaps I can find where it's coming in and block it with something. Then we can pump out the water and dry the place out. But the water's coming in faster and faster.

"It's up past my knees and I've still got a few steps left to go. My feet reach the floor and the water's up to my belt and I'm wishing I'd left my wallet upstairs, I don't want to ruin it. And the water keeps coming and it's swirling around me. It's up to my chest and I'm fighting my way through it. I know I'm going to have to submerge myself to look for the grill or the vent or the hole or whatever it is that's letting the water in, so I begin to take deep breaths, preparing myself for a big one before I go under.

"And then something hits me, bounces off my chest before swirling away. Then something else. And another. I bat them away with my arms and I catch hold of one and hold it up and I look at it and it looks back at me. It's a skull, a human skull, its eye sockets looking right into me, its joyless grin mocking me. Revolted, I throw it away. And I realise it's too small to be a man's skull. It's a kiddie's skull. They all are. And they keep coming. Dozens and dozens of them, whirling around me in a vortex of rushing water. And I cringe every time one of them touches me, which is happening more and more often. I'm becoming overwhelmed, more by the skulls than by the water.

"And as the water roars and swells, it's as though I can hear them. Those children. Screaming at me. They're screaming for me to join them, to be one of them. And the water's up to my chin. I tilt my head back, gasping for air, all thoughts of controlling my breath forgotten. And the skulls are attaching themselves to me, sinking their teeth in, pulling me down. And I scream. And close my eyes as the filthy water surges into my mouth.

"And then it's gone. It's all gone. There's one last gurgle like when you pull the plug out of the bathtub. I open my eyes. I'm standing in the cellar, soaking wet and filthy. The stench of the peat is in the air, in my bones, I think. The floor is mud. The mud is wet and it sucks at my shoes as I try to run out of there, because I know they're still down there, all those kiddies, and they want me to stay with them.

"And I hurl myself up the stairs. My heart is racing. I'm like an animal, a hunted animal. And there's somebody standing there. A woman. She screams when she sees me. But all I can think of is getting away. I get to the main entrance, and lighting cracks the scene. I am startled by my reflection in the grand mirror. I am a man of mud, and my hair is completely white."

**

"What's all this then?"

You did not need to be Cassandra Clune to know who had spoken without turning around. Constable Dimwoodie had emerged from the tunnel under Old Ma Spenser's outdoor privy and had come across the scene of an RTA. He recognised the van at once – how could he not? It – or rather its occupants, now dead – had duped him a mere hour or so ago. With the bogus policemen dead, they were unable to answer his questions. Questions like, Who put you up to this? And, Where were you taking him?

He approached the women, who were grouped around the supine Philip Philby like a Renaissance painting. Philby was very much alive, thank goodness, lying there staring wildly like in his wanted poster.

"Has someone called this in?" Dimwoodie asked, his gesture

indicating the whole scene.

"Ambulance should be here any minute," Cassandra replied, offhandedly.

"Did you call for an ambulance?" Wendy Rabbitt whispered.

"I didn't," Cassandra frowned. "Did you?"

"Why would I when I thought you were going to?"

Their heads turned to Jenna.

"Don't look at me," Jenna protested. "I was a bit distracted..."

Constable Dimwoodie pulled out his phone and made a call to the Emergency Services.

"And these other guys, they're all..."

"Dodo's doornails," Iphigenia shook her head, sadly.

"I beg your pardon?"

"They're dead, love," she clarified. She patted his arm as though he had suffered a personal loss.

"And the suspect?" Dimwoodie addressed the question to Cassandra, who he hoped would provide less enigmatic responses.

"The who?"

He jerked his head at Philby. "How is he?"

"Oh, he's not the suspect," Cassandra laughed.

"He's not?"

"No! Of course not."

"Then, who is?"

"Who is who, love?"

"Who is the suspect?"

"Well, you tell us. You're the one who does the suspecting."

Dimwoodie lifted his hat to scratch his head. "So, this man here did not abduct Tommy Thornbush?"

"Of course not!" Cassandra stood, so she and the policeman were eye to eye. "Bless you. This man isn't capable of abducting candy from a baby. Never mind the actual baby. I mean, look at him."

Dimwoodie looked at him. Philby did seem to be a little spaced out, it was true.

"Oops!" Cassandra giggled. "He's still under. Hang on a minute."

She lowered herself to Philby's side and spoke in a soft and low voice. "I'm going to bring you back," she said. "I will count down from three and when you awake, you will be free of your torment."

Dimwoodie interceded. "You hypnotised him? What's he going to do, cluck like a chicken?"

"Actually," Wendy Rabbitt smiled in triumph, "he sang like a canary."

"We'll fill you in later," Cassandra whispered. "Now, let me get on with it!"

Wendy put a finger to her lips and winked at the constable. Dimwoodie blushed.

"And..." Cassandra held her watch in front of Philby's nose. "Three...two...one..."

Philby's staring eyes blinked and blinked again. He sat up, glancing around. "Where am I?"

"It's all right, love," Cassandra patted his hand. "You're safe now."

Philby noticed the policeman and tensed up. A siren was approaching. Philby scrambled to his feet, ready to bolt. Cassandra pulled him by the arm and sat on him.

"He'll need checking over at the hospital," she explained, "and not just because I'm squashing him. Psychiatrically, I mean. I think he's well on the road to recovery. And soon he will be able to return to society and live as a normal bloke again."

"Get off me, you fat cow!" Philby roared, squirming like a pinned insect.

"Do you see?" Cassandra smiled.

The ambulance pulled up and paramedics poured out. One did a quick recce of the scene and the other headed directly to Dimwoodie.

"I've just arrived myself," Dimwoodie told her. "These witnesses will have to make a statement."

"Oh, we're not witnesses," Wendy Rabbitt said. "It was like

this when we got here."

"Right..." Dimwoodie turned to Old Ma Spenser. "Is this true?"

Iphigenia smiled and patted his cheek. "What else would it be?"

***

The women decided to reconvene at the cottage. Iphigenia took the underground path, claiming she needed to 'pay a visit' en route. The others took the overland way, striding across the bog. A fresh breeze danced across the longer grasses. It tugged at their clothes and brushed their faces.

"Isn't it beautiful out here?" Cassandra beamed, throwing her arms wide.

Wendy nudged Jenna, "If she starts singing the bog is alive with the sound of music, I'm going."

"Oh, she's just happy she's helped someone," Jenna said. "You know, brought Philby back to his senses. It's amazing, really. She always said she was never into things like that."

"How do you mean?"

"Are you asking as a friend or as a reporter?"

Wendy smirked. "Can't I be both?"

"When she first came, Cassandra was more pragmatic. She was all about natural remedies. And reclaiming the image of bog witches. Now, she's hypnotising madmen and summoning the dead."

"And what do you think about that? Has it changed her as a person?"

"No... Not changed. Developed, I think. Yes. She's brilliant."

"But you don't really think she gets it all from internet tutorials."

Jenna stopped walking. "I once tried to learn the guitar from the internet. And I picked up a bit. Couple of chords. How to strum. How to tune. But I knew I'd never be as good as the guy giving the lesson. You can learn all the theory you like, and you can practice all the hours you can, but you have to have something extra, you know? Something inside you that puts it all together and – makes magic."

Wendy took this all in. "That's wisdom, that is."

Jenna laughed. "I have my moments too. Just like my bloody gran…"

She set her jaw. She and her bloody gran would have to have a talk, sooner rather than later. Perhaps she could get Cassandra to hypnotise the old witch. That way, Jenna might get a straight answer.

Old witch…

Just a turn of phrase!

"Are you all right, Jen?" Wendy nudged her again. "You've come over all pensive."

Jenna glanced over the shoulder, back the way they had come. "The accident. It brought back some memories."

"Not pleasant ones, I bet."

"Not exactly!"

"You can talk to me, you know. As a friend!" she added quickly. "See, my camera's not even on."

"Thanks," Jenna said. "There's only one person I need to talk to."

***

"I've been looking for you," Samantha Smedley confronted her husband in their bedroom. "I even went to the police station." She stopped, mid-rant, to ask him what he thought he was doing.

"What does it look like I'm doing?" Councillor Smedley continued to throw shirts into the open suitcase on the bed.

"Oh!" Samantha Smedley clapped her hands. "Are we going somewhere?"

"We?" Smedley froze. He thought about the pronoun and decided he liked it. "Yes, we! We are going somewhere, yes. You'd better get packing."

"It would help if I knew where we were going. Sweaters or bikinis, darling?"

Smedley had a mental image of his wife in a bikini. Perhaps twenty years earlier... he shuddered. "Sweaters, I think. I've always wanted to see the Northern Lights."

"How exciting! I'd better get my hair done."

"There's no time for that. You know, last-minute deal. We have to go. Now!"

"There's so much to do. Cancel the newspapers. How long will we be gone?"

"I don't bloody know. It's open-ended. Where's your sense of adventure, woman? Leave a note. Carol can take care of all of that."

"Hmm," Samantha went through a checklist in her head. "I'll have to ask Carol if she can come in every day. Water the plants. She'll want more money, of course."

"Whatever!" Smedley heaved the suitcase shut, trapping his hand. "Fuck sake!"

"Oh, darling!" Samantha hurried over to kiss it better. "More haste, less speed. Now, I'll have to go and get my winter clothes out of storage. Shan't be a tick."

She pecked his cheek and swanned out of the room. Smedley sank onto the suitcase lid. He checked his watch, then checked it again because he didn't register the time at first. Ten minutes to get to the storage unit... plus ten minutes faffing around...ten minutes to get back...In half an hour, they could be on their way to the airport...

The colour drained from his cheeks.

Storage unit...

He jumped off the suitcase. If he hurried, perhaps he could head her off. Perhaps he could get there before her.

He sat down again, defeated. It was no use. The jig, as they say, was up.

But there was nothing to stop him from leaving without her. He could be miles away, perhaps even on a plane... Somewhere hot. Somewhere no one could reach him. Yes.

He snatched up his passport, an urgent fire in his eyes.

Abandoning the suitcase, he bolted from the house.

***

"Gran?" Jenna went straight through to the kitchen where, predictably, her grandmother was cutting open tea bags and pouring the contents into a pot. "How many times? You don't have to do that! Oh, never mind the damned tea. Can we have a talk?"

"What's that, Jenna chicken?" Iphigenia smiled, upending the steaming kettle and drowning the newly liberated leaves. "Can't it wait. We've still got a lot on."

Jenna put her hands to her face. "There are things I need to know."

"And know them you shall," Iphigenia skirted around her with a tea-tray laden with cups, saucers, and biscuits. "Now, come through. We've still got an evil child snatcher to stop."

"Is there another kind?" Jenna wondered. She followed her grandmother to the living room. Cassandra and Wendy had moved the table closer to the television, so that Anaxagoras could participate. "What's going on?"

"We're going to contact the Squire," Cassandra said. She patted the vacant seat next to hers. "With Anaxagoras pitching in, we should be able to banish him back to wherever."

"Hello, Jenna!" Anaxagoras waved from the screen. Jenna nodded in reciprocation.
She took a seat beside the medium.

"There's a book in this," Wendy Rabbitt enthused. "Forget local news. I could go global." The light of ambition shone in her eyes.

"I wouldn't write about your chickens yet, chicken. Not until they've hatched and been coated in breadcrumbs." Iphigenia set a plate of bourbons before her guest.

"I think I know what you're saying," Wendy frowned.

"Well, that makes one of us," Iphigenia winked, patting the reporter's hand. She took her seat. "But hang on. The Squire won't know where the kiddie is, will he? I mean, he appeared on the scene after the boy was taken."

"You're right," Cassandra conceded. "But he might know something. Either way, we're going to send him back where he came from. We can't have malevolent presences roaming around."

"Suppose not," Iphigenia reached for a biscuit and bit it in half. "Are we ready?"

"I think so," Cassandra glanced around. "Link hands, everyone."

"Oh, dear," Anaxagoras pulled a face.

"Don't worry," Cassandra told him. She took Jenna's hand and placed her free hand on top of the television. She indicated to Wendy to do likewise. "I'm sure it won't be a problem," Cassandra reassured them, but herself mainly. "Now, clear your minds, close your eyes, and focus on our circle. I would like to ask now, for the Squire, if he is present, to come through and communicate with us."

They listened.

They waited.

There was nothing.

Cassandra repeated her entreaty.

They listened.

They waited.

Again, there was nothing.

Cassandra opened one eye. Everything seemed to be in order, as far as she, with her limited knowledge and experience, could tell. Perhaps it was the television. It was a little unorthodox to include electrical appliances within the circle, even if that electrical appliance was possessed by the spirit of a bog witch. What was different? What had changed since the last time they had attempted this?

Well, Wendy was here, taking part this time instead of peering in through the window. And – Cassandra's pulse quickened – Tina Thornbush was here! She had become a conduit for the evil Squire. Oh, what an idiot I am! Fancy trying to do this without the star guest present!

She opened her eyes and broke the circle.

"We need Tina," she announced. "She's got the Squire inside her."

Iphigenia almost choked on her biscuit.

***

Samantha Smedley parked outside the storage facility, an ugly block of corrugated grey. In an attempt to make it more visually appealing, the edges were trimmed in primary colours. Hideous, Samantha Smedley sneered, but it served its purpose as a handy and affordable place to stash all that stuff you had no room for at home. Like her winter outfits, and her skis. She had probably better fish those out. She knew you could always rent them when you got there, but it was never the same as having your own. And hers were top of the range.

She breezed through Reception, where a man in a security guard outfit with his feet up on the desk was solving word searches. "Hello, Darren," she said, without slowing down.

She walked along the narrow corridors. Their unit was at the far end - you paid a premium for the bigger spaces. She reached the door and then had to rummage in her handbag to find the key.

"Come on, you bugger," she said through clenched teeth, trying to balance the bag on her raised thigh.

A noise came from the other side of the door. A rustling sound.

Samantha Smedley froze.

Rats!

Rats had got into the supposedly impenetrable unit!

She would have to go all the way back and get Darren off his fat arse. What the hell were they paying for if rats could get in and she couldn't even find her key?

"Mummy!" the rat called from the other side of the door.

Samantha Smedley squealed and dropped her bag. The contents spilled across the cement floor, among them the key! She squatted to retrieve it then fumbled it into the lock. What had she told her husband? More haste, less speed. Taking a steadying breath, Samantha Smedley unlocked the door to her storage unit, bracing herself for what she might find.

Tommy Thornbush bolted from captivity, bowling Samantha Smedley over, and tearing along the corridor.

Winded, Samantha Smedley tried to call him back. What the hell was going on? She picked herself up, dusted herself down and peered into the unit. A space had been cleared between the boxes of her extraneous clothes, room enough for a cot, a potty and a supply of juice boxes and bars of chocolate.

What was it? That little boy had been squatting in the unit? Was it even a little boy? Perhaps it was a little person! A refugee, no doubt. Come here for a chance at a better life only to end up, camping in a metal box. At least, he wouldn't be short of things to wear, she reflected wildly.

Then her thoughts cleared. She knew the identity of the runaway squatter – how could she not? His little face was plastered all over town.

She gave chase. Surely, not even Darren would let him get by…

Darren was not at his post, but standing, huffing and puffing at the desk, was Councillor Smedley.

"Obadiah!" his wife gasped, one hand clutching at her breastbone. "What are you doing here?"

"Waiting for that oaf to find me a spare key," Smedley grumbled. "I'll just take yours, shall I?"

"Um, well," Samantha couldn't meet his gaze, this man to whom she had been married for twenty-four years and was no longer anyone she recognised. "The door's open…"

"It's what?" Smedley roared, turning a brighter shade of red. He shoved her aside and strode off towards the unit. Samantha calculated she had roughly two minutes to find the boy and get out of there.

Darren emerged from a back room. "Find everything?"

"I found… something," Samantha said, warily. "Did you?"

"Did I…"

"Find… anything?"

"Might have," Darren tapped the side of his nose. He leant in and spoke in a conspiratorial whisper. "He's in the back. Colouring my puzzle magazine. Have you called the police?"

"No. Have you?"

"I think I'd better. Watch out." He slipped back to the back room as Smedley returned, red and panting like a breathless tomato.

"Where is he?" he demanded.

"Who? Darren?"

"Who the fuck is Darren?"

"He works here," Samantha pointed at the vacant chair. "Who do you mean?"

"Never you mind. We'd better get going if we're going to get to the airport in time."

"Oh, we can't take two cars," Samantha shook her head. "You know what they charge for parking."

"I don't give a toss."

"Well, I need to go home and pick up some bits and bobs."

"Go then. Meet me at the airport. Or don't. It's up to you."

"Right, then."

"Right, then."

With tears brimming, Samantha Smedley turned her back on her husband and stalked out to the car park. As she walked, she took out her phone and dialled 999.

"Hello, sir," Darren came out of the backroom. He made a show of tucking his shirt in so that the angry customer would think he'd been taking a shit. "Sorry about the wait."

"I want to see your CCTV," Smedley slapped the counter. "I think something has been taken from my unit."

Darren sucked in air and shook his head. "No can do, mate. Only the police can see that. And they have to submit a formal request. In writing."

"This is outrageous! Don't you know who I am?"

"Oh, yes," Darren nodded. "I know exactly who you are."

"So show me the fucking tape!"

"It's not tapes. It's all digital these days, granddad."

"How dare you!"

The sound of sirens cut the air. Police cars poured onto the car park. Behind her steering wheel, Samantha Smedley watched with keen interest. As the cars pulled up, she saw her husband spring from the building and sprint to his car. She watched him get in and start the engine. Then she watched him get out again and register that all four of his tyres were flat. His shoulders slumped. Police officers converged on the councillor.

The jig was up.

Samantha Smedley grinned as she put away the nail file that had wreaked so much pneumatic havoc.

"Oops," she said.

**

The women were in Cassandra's camper van when the news came though on the radio that little Tommy Thornbush had been found safe and well. They cheered with relief and burst into tears.

"That is good news," Iphigenia said, in case they were in any doubt.

"The best!" Cassandra agreed.

"Typical," Wendy Rabbitt looked disgruntled. "Biggest story to happen on my patch and I'm not the one to break it."

"I thought you were giving up local news to write a book," Jenna said.

"Oh, yeah," Wendy nodded, but she still looked put out. "I thought we were going to save that kiddie too, but someone else has beaten us to it."

"So did I," Cassandra said. "He's been saved, that's the main thing."

"Suppose," Wendy reflected, with a sniff.

"We still have plenty to do," Cassandra continued. "There's that business with the evil squire."

"Oh, no!" Jenna cried.

"What is it, chicken?" Iphigenia turned in her seat.

"If they give little Tommy back to his mum, they'll be handing him over to a child murderer!"

The others thought about this. The idea was a real buzz kill.

"Dimwoodie?" Cassandra suggested.

"Dimwoodie!" the others agreed in unison.

"Hold onto your weaves, ladies!"

She turned the steering wheel sharply, causing the wheels to squeal in protest, and headed to Little Fladgett Police Station, while Wendy Rabbitt tried to get through to the constable on the phone.

***

Tina Thornbush was pacing the floor of the police station. Constable Dimwoodie was anxious for his leaflet spinner, but he said nothing because he knew what a nerve-wracking time it must be for the mother. She hadn't stopped crying since he told her the news. Happy tears had long since given way to tears of anxiety. The pacing was an attempt to dispel the energy. It wasn't working.

"How much longer?" she asked, chewing at a thumbnail.

"They must be on their way," Dimwoodie gave his standard answer. It was becoming as engrained in his psyche as saying Who's there? whenever somebody said Knock knock.

Tommy Thornbush had been taken to Praxton police HQ, to be checked over by the medical examiner. Two women officers had tried to befriend him with stickers and lollipops but all he wanted was his mum. A call had been put through to the boy's local nick in Little Fladgett, wherever that was, and the constable who answered was instructed to send someone to fetch the mother in. Dimwoodie, of course, had no option but to send himself, and now, he and the mother were waiting for the big reunion.

"There's a car or something pulling up!" Tina halted mid-pace. "Should we go out to meet him?"

Dimwoodie rose from his desk. "I don't know... Perhaps it would be better out of the public gaze."

Tina scoffed at that. She headed for the exit and was almost bowled over as four women stormed in, sprinkling her with water and casting arcane gestures in her direction. She backed into the leaflet spinner, sending it crashing to the floor. Leaflets flew everywhere. Tina slipped on some that got underfoot. The women bore down on her.

"Aroint thee!" the fattest one snarled, dipping her fingers into a jar of water and sprinkling the toppled mother. Some got in Tina's mouth. She spat it out.

"Ugh! What is that? Holy water?"

"Better than that!" the oldest of the women grinned. "It's bog water!"

Tina scrambled backwards, propelled mostly by her elbows. "Do something!" she called to Dimwoodie, who with arms raised was trying to calm the intruders. He stepped between them and Tina Thornbush.

"Ladies, ladies! What on Earth are you doing?"

"Stand aside," Wendy Rabbitt commanded. "This is women's work!"

"It looks more like an assault to me. Hasn't this poor woman been through enough? And now, only moments before she gets her little boy back, she gets attacked by you four nutters. Well, not on my watch!"

He drew his truncheon. The women saw it and found it wanting. They laughed.

Cassandra took Dimwoodie's elbow and tried to draw him aside. "Constable. Daniel. A word, if I may. This is not what it looks like."

"It's not?" Dimwoodie shook her off. "Because with all the water sprinkling, the strange gestures and the muttered incantations, it looks to me like an exorcism. So, what is it, then?"

"Well, ah, um, you see," Cassandra was suddenly quiet. "Well, yes, it is an exorcism, actually."

"And why would you think one is necessary? If anything, this woman is a victim."

"Exactly!" Cassandra perked up. "A victim of malevolent intrusion! She is possessed!"

"And yet you're the ones carrying on like there's something wrong with you. Honestly, ladies, this mumbo-jumbo is not welcome in my police station."

"Cassandra!" Jenna called over. "A little help, if you're not too busy."

They had backed Tina Thornbush against the desk. Iphigenia was speaking in tongues, Wendy was making signs of the cross, and Jenna was flicking the filthy water. Cassandra stepped past the constable.

"Any reaction?" she asked.

"Yes!" roared Tina Thornbush. "I'm fucking furious. This top was clean on."

"No pea-green vomit, no 360 degree rotation of the head?"

"Not yet," Iphigenia enthused. "Won't be long now, I reckon." She resumed her guttural utterings.

Wendy Rabbitt looked over her shoulder. "Hey, copper, have you got a Bible?"

"Um..." Dimwoodie was thrown by the question. In his desk there was a book proclaiming itself to be the Paleo Diet Bible, from the days when he was trying anything to keep his waistline at a trim 32. He doubted that would help, unless they wanted to use it as a blunt instrument, in which case they most definitely couldn't have it.

Out in the street, a siren whooped and blue lights played through the windows.

"He's here!" Tina got to her feet, pushing off her assailants.

"Wait!" Cassandra cried.

But Tina was unstoppable. She strode across the floor, the blue light accentuating the colour of her eyes (also blue, by the way). A beatific smile spread across her face, illuminating her from within.

She reached for the front door.

And it slammed shut, shoved by unseen hands.

"No!" Dimwoodie roared, in a voice that was not his own. His face was contorting, the features elongating and shrinking. He was at once vulpine, simian, snakelike and inhuman.

"Bugger me," Iphigenia gasped. "We sprinkled the wrong one."

The constable rose into the air, taller, broader. He floated across the room, his standard-issue boots not touching the floor.

"The child is mine!" A sharp tongue licked sharper teeth.

"Cassandra!" Jenna yelled. "Do something!"

"Um...uh..." Cassandra was frantically typing on her smartphone, but YouTube was inaccessible. "He's interfering with my signal."

The thing that had been Dimwoodie swept his arm. Cassandra flew backwards into the wall.

"Fuck this," Wendy Rabbit hurled herself at the policeman's legs. Dimwoodie glared down at her with malevolent eyes. He kicked and she rebounded off the ceiling. A pile of spilled leaflets failed to cushion her fall. Stunned, Wendy Rabbitt blinked and rubbed her head. It was then she realised she was holding the policeman's trousers. It was a victory of sorts, she supposed.

"Let me at him," Iphigenia pushed up her sleeves. She took off her shawl and waved it around and around above her head, like a lasso.

"Careful, Gran!" Jenna warned.

The old woman lashed at the constable's bare legs. The shawl snaked around them, pulling him down. It crept and climbed, wrapping itself around him, encasing him in a cocoon of old wool and older magic. Before long, Dimwoodie was a writhing slug on the floor. Iphigenia emptied the jar of smelly bog water over his head.

"Bugger off out of that boy!" she commanded.

The shrouded figure stiffened and then lay still. The doors of the police station flew open.

"Mummy?" Tommy Thornbush burst in and threw his arms around a somewhat bewildered Tina Thornbush. In the doorway, two policewomen surveyed the scene. Was that really an officer of the law being unwrapped from some oversize knitwear? And did he really have no trousers on? And what was he doing, rolling around on the floor with all these women? And if this is the way they treat their leaflets out here in the sticks, perhaps they don't deserve to have them.

"Mummy!" Tommy Thornbush laughed with joy. His mother enfolded him tightly in her arms, her tears spilling into his hair, and everyone stopped what they were doing to bear witness to this tender moment of heart-warming love.

***

The women rode back to the cottage, beaming all the way. Laughter kept bursting out of them. They were exhilarated with relief and the satisfaction of a dangerous job well done.

"I can't believe it," Wendy Rabbitt said, looking pained.

"You were bloody well there with the rest of us," Cassandra said. "You'd better believe it,"

"No, I don't mean all the weirdness and possessions and what-not. I mean, it was that bastard councillor who took the kid. Those policewomen said it's going to be all over the news. Reckons it was all to boost the tourist trade in the town, get the Bogwitch ritual reestablished."

"Oops," Cassandra blushed.

"And I can't believe I missed the scoop on the biggest story of my career. Here I was, right in the thick of it, and I didn't get the story. That's it. I'm quitting."

"I thought you were going to write a book," Jenna piped up from the back.

"I am. I will!" Wendy replied. "But it had better be labelled Fiction or no one's going to buy it."

They all laughed again.

The lime-green camper van pulled up outside the cottage for the last time.

***

Anaxagoras was keen to hear what had transpired. Jenna crouched by the television and gave him a garbled version while Cassandra and Wendy cleaned themselves up and Iphigenia fussed about in the kitchen. His eyes widened with every added detail.

"And it was the Squire! Inside the policeman somehow?"

"Yes," Jenna said. "He must have transferred himself from the mother at some point."

"It was all because of me, you know. Me and Robert. The Squire tried to turn the locals against us, by taking the children and stirring up hatred for the bog witch – namely, me. But then he got a taste for it – taking the children. Because he could. Because he could get away with it. Being so powerful is not good for the soul. Look how he turned out. It seems that Heaven did not want him."

"We sent him packing, don't you worry about that."

"And is he all right? The policeman, I mean."

Jenna shrugged. "Seems to be. Once he got his trousers back, he was very much his old self again."

"Tell me that bit again!" Anaxagoras chuckled.

"Later," Jenna stood. "I'm going to help Gran in the kitchen."

At first, Iphigenia was nowhere to be seen. Jenna wondered if she'd nipped out to the privy again, but the back door was shut and bolted. The kettle was boiling away unattended on the hob.

"Gran?"

Iphigenia was on the floor, a packet of biscuits clutched to her chest. Jenna screamed and dropped to knees. Cassandra and Wendy came running.

"She's breathing," Cassandra discovered. "Let's get her up."

Between them, they lifted Iphigenia to the kitchen table. She seemed to weigh nothing at all. Her eyelids fluttered and opened. She placed a hand like damp parchment on her granddaughter's cheek.

"Jenna love," she smiled her crooked smile.

"Don't speak," Cassandra whispered.

"No, you better bloody speak!" Jenna sobbed. "You've got some explaining to do."

Iphigenia laughed, wheezing like punctured bellows. "I can

do better than that. I can show you. Take me through to the telly."

"Gran!" Jenna despaired. "You can go without *Countdown* for once in your life."

They carried her through to the sofa, propping her up with cushions so she could see the screen. Anaxagoras was dismayed. He put the flat of his hand against the glass.

"Can't somebody do something?" he asked. "You, bog witch," he addressed Cassandra. "Help my grandmother."

Cassandra's mouth worked but nothing came out. She felt utterly helpless. There was no internet tutorial for this kind of thing.

"Anaxagoras, quiet!" Iphigenia levelled a stare at the television. "And get out of that television. I need it."

Anaxagoras was nonplussed. "How do I –"

"—Get out?" he said, and then realised he was standing in the room. Still wearing his Bogwitch clothes. "Well, I'll be –"

"Ssh!" Iphigenia's face filled the screen. "Now, sit down, shut up, and watch this."

Anaxagoras lowered himself onto a chair, marvelling at his hands and his restored ability to be able to touch things.

Jenna looked from the television to the sofa. Gran was still there but sleeping or in a coma or a trance or something. Astral projection, probably, right into the television. Well, it wasn't the weirdest thing that had happened recently.

"Are you sitting comfortably?" Iphigenia grinned in full colour and high definition. "Then I'll begin."

***

The road through the bog. A rainy day. A car speeds along. It swerves around an old woman. It flips and bounces, landing on its roof in a ditch. The police arrive. An ambulance. The old woman stands watching. She is holding the hand of a child. A little girl. Jenna Jones.

"My granddaughter and I were just out for a walk, picking wildflowers. We heard the horrible noise. Such a shame. Such a terrible thing to happen to nice people."

The cottage. Iphigenia bringing plate after plate of biscuits to the kitchen table while in her seat, Jenna grows from a five-year-old to her present teenage state, within the passing of a moment.

Iphigenia's voice, soft and warm, tells Jenna it was the only way. Her parents didn't survive the crash. She would have been taken into care, into some institution somewhere.

"And look at you now, my brave, beautiful girl. Ready to take on the world. And you, my boy, my Anaxagoras. I have brought you to a more tolerant age. Go out and find the love that you deserve. I am so sorry you have had to wait all these years but now is your time."

Anaxagoras let out a sob. He knuckled a tear from his cheek and was amazed to feel its wetness. Jenna took his hand and squeezed it.

"My magic is coming to its end," Iphigenia's eyes were wet, but she was smiling. "But don't write me off just yet. I think I'll stay in here for a while. I'll never miss my favourite programmes ever again! But for now, I need to rest. Goodnight, chicken. Goodnight, my friends. Thank you for everything you have done."

The eyelids closed. The screen went blank.

Jenna hurried to the sofa. Iphigenia's clothes, including her shawls, were empty, collapsing in on themselves. "She was the bog witch," Jenna's words caught in her throat, "And I was the child she took…"

***

The next morning, Cassandra loaded up her camper van. She was going to drop Wendy off in town at the car rental place, and Anaxagoras at the shops; he needed to buy some present-day clothes. A pair of Cassandra's wellington boots, a pair of Jenna's jeans that he couldn't quite fasten, and one of her Minnie Mouse T-shirts, would have to do until he could pick something out for himself.

Jenna, eyes red from sitting up all night, staring at the blank television, waved them off from the doorstep.

"You could come with us?" Anaxagoras beckoned. "Help me choose my new outfit."

Jenna glanced over her shoulder at the living room and the silent television. "I –"

Ready to take on the world...

She wasn't sure if the voice was in her head or was coming from the television.

"Wait! Wait just a minute!"

She disappeared inside.

"She's a good kid," Wendy observed. "If I change her name to Jenny in my book, do you think she'll mind?"

"I shouldn't think so," Cassandra turned off the ignition. "Change the names to protect the guilty. What have you got in mind for me?"

"Oh, I don't know. Miranda? Melissa? What do you think?"

Cassandra's nose wrinkled. "I kind of like my real name. Cassandra, you see, was doomed to tell the truth and have no one listen to her. Which is exactly how I felt when I was trying to stop that bloody Bogwitch banishing."

"Well, you did it!" Anaxagoras leaned forward from the back seat. "The Bogwitch has been well and truly banished."

"And yet you're still here!" Wendy teased. They laughed.

Jenna came out of the cottage, a bulging holdall hooked over her shoulder. She locked the front door and hurried to the van. Anaxagoras slid the side door open to let her in. She dropped the keys into his palm.

"You'll need somewhere to live. And Gran will need watching. But if you solve the anagrams before she does, don't you dare shout them out. Who knows what she might do to you?"

"We set?" Cassandra turned the key.

"Yes," Jenna nodded. She turned to watch the cottage shrink away. Would she be back? She didn't know. And she didn't mind not knowing.

***

They dropped Wendy Rabbitt off first. There were hugs and smiles and watery eyes. Telephone numbers and Twitter handles were exchanged. Their sisterhood would continue, even over a long distance, and they were all invited to the book launch, of course.

"Free copies at least!" Cassandra grinned.

"Discount," Wendy conceded.

She gave one last wave and went into the reception of the car rental lot, where she was gratified to be recognised as 'her off the telly' and didn't even have to show her i.d. Off she went, on her way to write the novel that would renew the fortunes of Little Fladgett. Tourists would flock to the little town to walk in the steps of the Bogwitch, taking the tunnel under the bog to the great hall, and marvelling at the beauty and bounty that Nature provides. Lord Fladgett's ghoulish escape room never took off, but the Nature Walk he established in the grounds proved a big hit.

Anaxagoras was next.

"Anywhere here is fine," he gestured vaguely at the High Street.

"Are you sure you'll be OK?" Jenna held his hand. "You're not used to the ways of the modern world."

"I've been around," he laughed. "For a long, long time. Everything is old news to me. Apart from getting used to being in physical form."

They said their goodbyes and Jenna felt a twinge in her heart. He was her only relative, she supposed. Of a sort.

"Take care, love," Cassandra advised as he got out of the van. He came to her window.

"Thank you, Mistress Clune," he said. "Your intervention was the trigger for all of this."

Cassandra batted the words away like gnats in the air, but her cheeks were wet. "Who knew?"

Anaxagoras stood and waved them off. As soon as the van turned the corner, he steeled himself and went into the police station.

Constable Dimwoodie looked up from his desk. A handsome stranger in a Disney T-shirt and a snug-fitting pair of jeans was smiling at him. He seemed familiar... Where have I seen him before, Dimwoodie wondered. Perhaps he's been on the telly.

"Can I help you?"

Anaxagoras's smile broadened. "Yes, Daniel, I think we can help each other."

***

"So, where can I take you?" The van was approaching a roundabout. "You want dropping off somewhere? Praxton College perhaps. I think it's Enrolment Day."

Jenna fretted. "I – I'd - Which way are you going?"

"The West Midlands. Well, somebody's got to go there. The word on the web is that someone has unleashed the Hell Hounds of Halesowen."

"They haven't!" Jenna affected shock. "Well, I suppose I could come with. For the ride. And I've always wanted a dog."

Cassandra laughed and took the exit for the motorway. "I knew you were going to say that."

"No, you didn't!" Jenna laughed.

"No, I didn't," Cassandra agreed.

The lime-green camper van merged with the traffic and took them far away.

THE END

ABOUT THE AUTHOR

William Stafford

 William Stafford is a novelist, playwright and actor, with over two dozen novels to his credit. When he's not writing, you might find him guiding tourists around Stratford upon Avon in the guise of William Shakespeare.

BOOKS BY THIS AUTHOR

Trapping Fog

A killer is slaughtering the prostitutes of Victorian London and Inspector John Kipper is baffled. Meanwhile, Damien Deacus, sidekick to a mysterious doctor, strives to keep himself out of trouble - and fails! Author William Stafford combines humour, horror and steampunk in this historical fantasy of gruesome crime and comic invention.

Printed in Great Britain
by Amazon